# CHAOS DOWN UNDER

Nishant Kaushik is the bestselling author of *Watch Out! We are MBA*, *A Romance with Chaos* and *Conditions Apply*. This book is the second instalment of the Chaos trilogy. He keeps a day job with Infosys Limited and currently lives in Australia. You can find him on Twitter @chaosparticle and can also write to him at nkaushik.23@gmail.com.

# CHAOS DOWN UNDER

## NISHANT KAUSHIK

RUPA

First published by
Rupa Publications India Pvt. Ltd 2014
7/16, Ansari Road, Daryaganj
New Delhi 110002

*Sales Centres:*

Allahabad  Bengaluru  Chennai
Hyderabad  Jaipur  Kathmandu
Kolkata  Mumbai

ISBN: 978-81-291-2430-2

First impression 2014

10 9 8 7 6 5 4 3 2 1

The moral right of the author has been asserted.

Printed by Thomson Press India, Faridabad

# Contents

# Prologue

Calm down. I know it has been over three years since I shared the first installment of my early encounters with an uninspiring job at Bytesphere. And I am sure you have been aching to know what happened after that freak streak of recognition I acquired at a time I was almost certain of idling my way into oblivion. But I strongly believe a sequel is worthy of a narration only once the character's life has evolved a good degree since the last time you heard of his laurels. And my bloody character was taking longer than the Mumbai Monorail has taken to evolve.

From where I last left you—my humble acceptance of the Young Achievers' Award—I spent the next few months under the comfortable illusion that I was now the poster boy of the company. The management had started taking note of me. They offered me a new cubicle right outside the unit head's cabin, which retrospectively became a nightmare because this unit head had no real business except to call me for ad hoc meetings that invariably began with, 'Let us do some white boarding so I can get some dope on what your thoughts are on a futuristic blend of best practices that can be leveraged against You Spin My Head Right Round Right Round.' All said and done, I was lapping up all this attention. Even Chirayu, the otherwise first class bugger of a manager, had begun to treat me with respect by inviting me home to play Foosball on Sunday afternoons. Speaking of which, one afternoon I swung the rotating bar of my player so hard, the damned ball went scuttling across the board, bounced off the edge and flew straight into Chirayu's open mouth as he watched my classy move with an expression of disbelief. I had to rush the poor fellow to the hospital. While on one hand it had deeply saddened me to watch tears roll down that fat, ghastly man's eyes as he was taken in for an endoscopy, I also noted that these tense moments were the only thirty minutes in Chirayu's company during which he did not offer me unsolicited tips on business strategy. Three hours later when he walked out, teary-eyed and all, he had transformed from bloody Michael Porter to Socrates, saying a small ball had just taught him that life was too short to be an asshole and that he would love to be a better human being.

The next day at work, he had switched back to being an asshole by asking me to transfer the hospital's bill amount to his bank. A week later when I asked him for the bills so I could claim the money back from the company, he snubbed me for trying to flout company policies by trying to stake claim to a bill in another employee's name. I think I should have stuffed a real football inside him to make him a better human being than he was gunning to be.

These minor sores aside, life looked pretty set on a smooth course. Mehek and I bonded a lot over prolonged phases of worklessness and pointless discussions about our ambitions. (I often exaggerated my ambitions to impress her; all I actually wanted was to somehow complete my mandatory five years at Bytesphere before being able to do something with the stock options offered to me at the time of my employment.) That year, I was also unusually excited about my due appraisal discussion. Given that I was in a bargaining position following that Young Achievers' Award, I had reason to believe a promotion (maybe two levels up!) and an astronomical rise in my perks was in the offing. Then I could go to Mehek and ask her to marry me because I would have totally become a stud with such phenomenal success at the raw age of...anyway.

Just when I was beginning to think I was scripting the perfect inspirational autobiography for every aspiring corporate slave, I was greeted by a very queer event. I got a call from one of our HR associates saying that she had seen my profile on Monster and would like to confirm if I would be available for an interview with Bytesphere that week. I first laughed very violently to acknowledge her sense of humour. Then she went on asking ridiculous questions about what salary I was expecting and what notice period I would need to give my current company before joining Bytesphere.

I can't tell you how upset I felt that day. Such abysmal levels of proficiency in the recruitment department, and then they hold weekly conferences in fancy hotels to discuss what can be done to plug employee attrition. When I reminded her I was the consultant who had brought Bytesphere all that goodwill with that telemedicine project in Dhokli, she apologized profusely, saying she had heard of such a project but did not know it was true. She had thought it was only a story floated around to be included in the annual report and oh how silly of her. I told the foolish woman that her ignorance was still pardonable if she could at least read what my CV stated as my current employer.

I don't remember putting up my profile on Monster ever. But this incident spurred me to think it was time for me to move on. I enthusiastically started applying to various companies. The only company that offered me a role stated in its job description 'Exciting role of senior telecom consultant located in growing Southeast Asian metropolis'. Fuckers meant Dhaka. I figured out one hour before signing the offer letter. Thanks, but no thanks. Plus, there were those stock options to exploit too. I had no option but to shut up and watch my aspirations die a slow death in the name of stability. Almost two years later, I had resigned myself to a fate of a miserable, stagnant career with nothing to write home about. I was also conscious of my responsibility towards everyone who was waiting to hear my story. But frankly, at that point I was so empty I could have written a story about some rancid attack of indigestion and called it *Jannat 25*, and no one would have cared.

Then one day, the inevitable happened. Bytesphere got screwed over for its arrogance and its habit of treating everyone, from its shareholders to its deserving, talented yet frustrated employees, like shit. We started losing our share in most international markets to the more grounded, cost-competitive players who did not have a chip on their shoulder. A sensible reaction from the management would have been to put their heads together and start retaining clients with the help of their able employees. Instead, they started cutting corners by axing half the workforce while continuing their obnoxious high-handedness in charging their clientele. Soon enough, we were on the verge of bankruptcy. At which point, our bird-brained board of directors called an emergency conclave at Four Seasons in Mauritius to deliberate over cost containment and optimum talent utilization. A week later, they came back to India and axed another twenty per cent of their employees and immediately asked the marketing team to decide a budget for the company's brand rejuvenation (which, by the way, only ended up changing the company's logo to a phoenix). If that weren't enough, they shamelessly announced they would be scrapping the policy of stock options with immediate effect, and all employees who had been wagging their tails in anticipation would be given two surplus annual leaves that year as compensation. In what was left of our company's employees, I saw pure rage and frustration. An impending revolt.

Amidst this chaos, I sensed a delicious opportunity when I was offered a chance to resurrect a dying relationship with Australian client Oz-Mobil, a cash cow turned hostile. Given its own dire straits, the client had given us a last chance to redeem our pride. But it wasn't going to be easy. We faced formidable challenges from Lex Technologies, our competitor who had gone on the verge of bankruptcy just like us, and was just as desperate to make money. In the face of this adversity, my business unit placed its implicit faith in my ability to show us the way out of this muck. Chirayu insisted it was only because the business unit had few other options. Anyway, I did not think much of his opinions. I had to get down to work NOW.

And here was where I began building my dream team to help revive my company's dying business. And here I was, moving one step at a time, towards a landmine of chaotic adventures…

# 1.

# Priority Zero Huddle

What is the whole point of classroom training, really? You first induct a new recruit into assignments he knows nothing about, waxing eloquent about how hands-on experience beats theoretical knowledge any day. The poor chap struts along, and by the time he begins to make sense of what his job is all about, you run out of work to assign him to. And then you conveniently shove him into a classroom session on 'Elementary Consulting—A Perspective' AFTER he has learnt all there could possibly be to consulting. How stupid is that?

I have written many a note to the senior management in the past, making valid, profound points in favour of replacing mundane, ineffective classroom training sessions with more interactive offsite programmes like white water rafting or mountaineering, or foreign junkets, wherein employees get to know and communicate with each other better alongside having some fun for a change. Most of my messages met with automated replies thanking me for my mail (and doing nothing about it thereafter), except a recent one which was read by some overenthusiastic chap in the resource monitoring department. The little twit wrote to my line manager, suggesting I be enrolled in the upcoming three-day session on 'Interpersonal communication, leadership and teamwork in new age enterprises' because my series of emails to his team suggested I had a lot of time to kill.

By the time I could get to Chirayu, my line manager whom I cannot hate enough for his stark managerial incompetence that becomes more apparent when one sees him grinning his way through the office gates in his Audi, my name had been registered with the training organizers. I reasoned with Chirayu on the pointlessness of training a seasoned resource, who had carved a niche for himself in the organization over three years of intense perseverance and incidental brilliance. I mean, it was a little like teaching Sachin Tendulkar how to load a rubber grip on the handle of his bat *after* he had scored his hundredth ton, right? But Chirayu did not see sense, which was hardly surprising to me. Instead, he offered me a counter analogy between baking fresh, sloppy manure to preparing it as a fertilizer and grooming young resources like me as part of organizational giveback. He then pulled out my report from the company portal with a graph that showed how my utilization had dipped over the last six months which wouldn't bode well during my appraisal. I have never ceased to wonder where he gets the time to analyze all these reports from. He always pretends to be so busy he can't fetch his own prints from the printing room, but he had all the time in the world for graphs. The freak had a ready graph to go with any and everything he ever talked about.

He reminded me that honing my leadership skills by way of wilfully engaging in training programmes was part of my key result areas for the year, and so I had no way out of it.

So here I was, registered for a three-day long workshop on 'Interpersonal communication, leadership and teamwork in new age enterprises'. For whatever it was worth, I had hoped the venue would at least be a nice hotel with a proper buffet meal as compensation for all the mental infliction. At the last minute, the stingy organizers revised the venue to a large spare conference room in our office itself—the lunch would be served by the obnoxious office canteen, and that, too, would not be free. I couldn't sleep the previous night at all from the thought of consuming that food. In fact, I recall getting an advance attack of food poisoning in anticipation.

My last hope was that the training instructor be an inspiringly hot woman, so that I could at least chat with her post-session by way of ridiculous but engaging questions like 'Does Bass's Theory of Transformational Leadership hold well in decentralized organizations with flat hierarchy?' Amazed at my inquisitiveness on such an exciting subject, she would discreetly hand me her address and suggest that the question be amply debated over a cup of coffee at her cozy apartment. Exciting things would follow...

'I am Gopinath Padgaonkar,' a bald, stout man with a razor-sharp moustache announced as he walked into the room. 'I will be your trainer for this programme. May I introduce myself first?'

I guess hot women as instructors existed only in pornographic films. What rubbish. I would never watch porn again. (I mean, I never did anyway).

Worse, this Gopinath Padgaonkar was so overly qualified I think it took him until the tea break to finish introducing himself to the class. Following the tea break, he asked the class to throw up various topics they would like to be covered in the day's session. A bunch of enthusiastic high-flyers spewed out one topic after another—ranging from *persuasive techniques* to *seeking holistic closed-loop communication from stakeholders*, all of which Gopinath jotted down on the whiteboard. I dedicated the rest of the day to imagining visuals of hot female instructors and to scribbling the word 'leadership' on my notepad in various creative fonts and sizes. At the end of the day when I looked up, Gopinath had sufficiently abused the whiteboard in the training room through a multitude of stick diagrams, names of theories you would never remember if you had a cat's nine lives, and all the requested topics proudly ticked as completed.

Day two of the ordeal was relatively better. Gopinath relinquished his passion for stating theories from HR manuals and had us participate in childish yet entertaining role plays to foster our *esprit de corps*. (Gopinath spoke this phrase out loud and added it had nothing to do with an apparel brand. Score one for sense of humour!) But the teambuilding activities didn't last beyond lunch. The post-lunch session was hardly difficult to tolerate. I had picked up a piece of rubbery paneer from the canteen's fancy buffet and had carried it to class. I spent the rest of the session secretly making clay formations from that piece of paneer. It wasn't as malleable as real clay, but it kept me busy until Gopinath announced the end of the second day.

Day three was like participating in a Roadies episode. Without the occasional thrill, of course. I don't think I have ever endured more pain than what I did trying to sit straight as we were meted out a thesis on the history of Organizational Behaviour as a science (don't ask). I think it was around the time I was about to fake a convulsion when a peon stormed in and asked for Nakul.

'Nakul,' he hollered. 'Who is Nakul out here?'

Little surprise, this, but five of us in the room stood up. Gopinath Padgaonkar looked at us blankly, presumably trying to come up with a prompt quote alluding to *the hazards of partial communication.*

'Chirayu Sir has called for one of you in C-304,' said the peon, looking at us.

'That must be for me,' I said excitedly as I packed my belongings to get the hell out of there. I don't think I had ever been so thrilled on being summoned by Chirayu.

I excused myself from Gopinath after dutifully asking him if his lectures were available online so I could browse them for future reference. To my surprise he actually mentioned a portal where he had a collection of four hundred and forty-seven blog posts pertaining to various forms of leadership, corporate communication and transparency in consulting. He fetched a piece of paper and wrote me details of where I could download videos of his earlier lectures on the subject from. I thanked him profusely and walked out in the open air. It felt like I had been in that room since 1936 or something.

I walked up the spiral staircase to C-304. Chirayu was in the room chatting with Anand, the company's business head for the telecom vertical, about the spiritual transformation he had undergone at the recently concluded annual vipassana conclave.

'I must say you are looking sharp, old chap,' Anand winked, slapping Chirayu on his somewhat deflated stomach.

Chirayu blushed like a bride. 'I could give you some health tips, you know.'

'Some day, some day,' Anand nodded, and then turned to see me standing at the door. 'Yes?'

'Ah, come in!' Chirayu beckoned, and then turned to Anand. 'I called him to join the meeting. I could use some help right away.'

'Oh well,' Anand nodded, and stood up to shake hands

with me. 'New employee, are you?'

This was not the first time he had asked me the question. Either he had a disgusting sense of humour, or I needed to look for a new job.

'I've been around for three years and more,' I replied with a plain smile.

'Why haven't we met before?' he asked, beckoning me to take a seat.

What was wrong with this man? How could he forget the numerous times I met him in his cabin here before he shifted to Bengaluru for better climate? How could he forget I was that ass-licker who drove him eighteen miles out of my way to What The Fish because he was craving fish curry on a Friday evening after work? I paid the bill too!

'He spearheaded the project in Dhokli in 2009,' Chirayu reminded him. 'Of course you have met him before.'

'Oh, it is coming back to me,' he blinked his eyes rapidly as though I were a Pythagorean Theorem he was trying to solve. 'Akhil! Right?'

'Nakul,' I replied dully.

'Yes, yes, same thing,' he clapped excitedly. 'Come, sit. I have something to show you guys.'

He fetched a PDF document on his laptop and connected it to the projector. The title read 'Statement Of Work For Oz-Mobil's Billing and Customer Service Transformation Programme'. A rush of blood flowed through my consulting veins.

'I have good news and bad news,' began Anand, flipping through the slides. When none of us reacted, he proceeded with the good news. 'We are among the top contenders to provide Oz-Mobil with the testing deliverable of this transformation programme. In fact, I am nearly convinced we will win the contract.'

Chirayu flashed his calm, vipassana smile. 'Sweet! What's the bad news?'

'Oz-Mobil has already hired Lex Technologies for the design of the application,' Anand added unhappily. 'We were kind of hopeful we'd win *both* the design and the testing segments. But those Lex assholes slashed their consulting prices at the last minute...'

And we continued charging prospective clients with fat margins, I said to myself with disdain. How old school! I wasn't surprised. This wasn't the first time they had scored over us.

Anand's primary fear stemmed from the famous rivalry Bytesphere shared with Lex in the consulting services market. Basically, both companies had weakened alike, were on the verge of major crises, and were fighting intensely to stay alive somewhere on the bottom rung of the market by winning whatever scale of business they could lay their hands on. Both companies usually fed on leftovers—client accounts other vendors would not be interested in because they would not forebode sufficient profitability. We had locked horns with them during past projects, and the hostility was always evident.

'It will be more evident now,' warned Anand, 'if we are pitted as the team that will test the application designed by them. In fact, I know Lex is trying to throw us out of contention in the testing contract as well. But no, we won't let them get away with it. We have made Oz-Mobil an offer they can't refuse.'

He fondled his scraggly beard, expecting us to roll our eyes at the dramatic pause. After that Gopinath marathon of three days, I could barely keep mine open. Chirayu, meanwhile, continued to smile, as though he were pre-empting everything Anand was about to say.

'We ran them through our past record with telecom clients!'

Anand declared jubilantly. 'They were suitably impressed. And as always, of course, we will over-deliver with our promised pool of six top class consultants.'

Chirayu's smile dissipated like vapour. 'Sorry, what did you just say?'

'Six top class consultants,' Anand repeated, less happily this time, as he watched Chirayu transform from a smiling sage to a petrified rabbit in the blink of an eye.

'Uh, well...' Chirayu began with a stutter.

Anand leaned forward and menacingly placed his hand on Chirayu's dampened collar. 'You might remember I had consulted you before committing to the client, yes? My job is to get us business. Your job is to tell me we have resources to handle the business.'

Chirayu broke into a throaty chuckle again. 'And that's exactly what I do, don't I?'

'I hope so,' Anand said, withdrawing into his chair with some relief.

'How long have you known me, Anand?' Chirayu asked with his eyes closed, as though in some sort of meditative trance. 'Ten years? What do you think are the strengths I can play to?'

'Licking ass,' I wanted to say. But I did not.

'My biggest strength is my resilience in shitty situations, Anand,' explained Chirayu when Anand refused to hazard a guess. 'You throw shit at me, and you can be assured I will turn it to gold.'

I seriously don't know how Chirayu ever made it to Bytesphere. A company that trained new recruits on the importance of concise and sensible communication had employed a resource manager who spoke so much he could gag on his own words.

'Are you trying to tell me I am throwing shit at you?' fumed Anand.

'Not exactly,' Chirayu reclined further in his seat, making some strange breathing sounds as he spoke. 'But the situation is shitty nonetheless. Because we don't have the resources in our team we have promised the client about.'

'Guess how many fucks I give about that?' Anand asked him this time. 'Trick question: None. Go figure out how you are going to manage the resources, Chirayu. We will have clinched this deal sooner than you might imagine. I want no glitches thereafter.'

Chirayu nodded, smiling as calmly as ever. 'I am the man you can count on.'

And then, just before leaving the room, Anand left us with the most cryptic message ever.

'In the meantime, please start engaging with the client.'

I presumed Chirayu had understood every word of that instruction, because he continued to nod in response. And then he told Anand he would hold a 'Priority Zero Huddle' with me soon after and would come up with a war footing strategy for the project. I swear my stubble grew a little in the time Chirayu took to finish that sentence. I feared it would turn into Moses' beard if he actually held a Priority Fucking Zero Huddle with me now.

'Talk in English sometimes, please,' Anand muttered to Chirayu as he swung the door open and walked out.

Chirayu looked on through the translucent walls of the room until he saw Anand glide down the staircase. Then he turned to me anxiously and asked me to shut the door. When I turned back, his vipassana smile had disappeared for good. He was now sunk in his chair, hyperventilating; his hands nervously ran through his sparse hair causing a rampage in there.

'What did he mean by "start engaging with the client"?' he asked me worriedly.

'I thought you knew what he meant,' I shrugged.

'What am I supposed to engage the client with when we haven't won the project yet?' he asked, ready to tear at his hair. 'And firstly, we need to worry about where we are going to get those six consultants from—more so, six guys who have some experience in testing practices.'

'Why, then, did we commit six subject experts to the client?' I asked.

'Elementary, Nakul,' he sighed. 'We know we don't have six subject experts. But the client doesn't know we don't have six subject experts. So we tell the client we have six subject experts while we set out looking for six guys whom we can train to become subject experts. Simple!'

He stifled a laugh at his own cheap joke. What sort of example was he setting before honest, hot-blooded professionals like me? Some day when I would write a bestselling book on the filth at my workplace, I'd let him know what I thought of him and of corporate ethics.

I told him we were in a very formidable situation if we didn't have a sufficient pool of resources to staff on to the project immediately. He suddenly started laughing and clarified it was *I* who was going to be in a formidable situation, because he had instinctively decided to let me try leading this assignment for a change, for two good reasons. One, because he was busy with 'various other deliverables', and two, because he thought I would never grow unless I started shouldering some of my seniors' responsibilities. I thanked him for his generosity but added he had rather show this gesture *after* getting me the resources for this project, instead of leaving me in the lurch like that.

'A consultant doesn't ask for solutions,' he told me, not for the first time. 'He provides them himself.'

Which meant he had no idea where those resources were going to come from. I didn't worry myself with it much then, for the deal was yet to be signed. So I patiently sat and listened to his discourse on consulting principles in crisis management, until I could not conceal my detachment any more. I quietly messaged Mehek (I could go on talking about this wonderful girl), asking her to call me on my phone in exactly five minutes. In the space of those five minutes, Chirayu had spoken further worth around two hundred and ninety-nine rupees of talk time.

'I must take this call,' I held up the beeping phone finally, much to his disappointment and my relief. 'Shall we connect later?'

'Oh yes, of course,' he nodded. 'I will text you in the evening once I have something figured out about the resources. And don't worry. There is no problem in the world that Chirayu Chaudhary doesn't have a solution to.'

'Perfect,' I said, getting up to leave.

'And listen,' he stopped me. 'In the meantime, set up a call tomorrow to start engaging with the client.'

'I thought you said you didn't know what that was supposed to mean,' I said uncertainly.

'Yes I don't,' he nodded. 'But Anand wants us to engage with the client. So you call the client tomorrow and figure out what that means.'

I sighed and thanked him, saying I would have been totally lost if it weren't for his able guidance. He grinned happily and assured me I would learn the ropes from him very soon.

I stepped out to answer Mehek's call. 'At the cafeteria in five minutes?'

'I don't think so,' she whispered on the phone. 'I am snowed under right now. Let's meet for dinner?'

'Dinner at eight?' I asked. 'At Vaishali?'

'Absolutely,' she affirmed. 'And oh, by the way, I have something very important to chat about.'

'I will wait for you,' I said, hanging up.

I can't stop talking about Mehek. I met her more than two years ago, and I knew right then she was the one. Actually not exactly then—I was seeing Kavya Mehra then. But I broke up soon with that materialistic, self-centered, inferiority-complex causing woman and moved on. Then I met Mehek again when she joined our company and I knew right then that she was the one. She worked with me on a project that caught the entire company's attention and we both turned into overnight stars at Bytesphere. That the glory lasted shorter than Harman Baweja's career was another matter. What matters is I was in love with her, and she did not reciprocate half as much when I told her so. She only thought we were...wait! Did she just tell me she had something important to chat about tonight? Goodness gracious, how did it not strike me! My perseverance was finally going to pay off!

After she had first jilted my suggestion that we made a fine pair, I ensured my self-respect superseded my overwhelming emotions. I hardly ever broached the subject again—except if you count the time I sent her a heart-shaped box of rum chocolates on her last birthday. I swear the shape of the box was a coincidence. Also, she claims there was this time in the middle of the night when I stood drunk outside her society gate and sang 'Last Christmas'—and that too, the Anu Malik version, not the George Michael one. Again, I cannot for the life of me remember any of this, and so this claim cannot be validated either. I will admit, though, that I have been dropping subtle and clever hints time and again, to remind her I am still available. For example, the other day I told her the HR team at Bytesphere had introduced a new and exciting employee-friendly policy wherein two Bytes who got married to each other would be eligible to win a company-sponsored Maruti Alto with a subsidized car loan. She reminded me of another policy with equal subtlety, which stated that repeatedly pursuing a colleague with matrimonial proposals amounted to employee harassment and could have grave consequences.

I hated these HR people in my company. They were such sticklers for lame policies, but took ages to approve of my official reimbursement claims to taxi fare. Also, why couldn't they recruit a good administration team that ensured we were served REAL food in the cafeteria, and not just fancy names like White Wonder Pilaf which was nothing but egg white beaten about in horribly pasty rice?

Anyway, I could go on about my problems out here. The truth is I should have left Bytesphere long ago and begun working on that dream business plan of mine which is still a well-guarded secret—mostly because I am myself not sure of what the business plan is going to be. At that moment, all I could think of was the important chat Mehek wanted to have with me. My rants could wait. I took a taxi back home to get ready for the big dinner coming up. En route, I stopped and purchased a super saver pack of three chocolate scented deodorants at the price of two. I sprayed some on myself right outside the store. Right then I saw a gorgeous young woman—that Axe deodorant advertisement kind—smell me from a distance as she cocked her head in my direction. She crossed over to the side of the store. And then she walked right past me.

Shy type, maybe. Anyway, I couldn't wait until dinner.

# 2.

# Partly AC

An epiphany hit me when I reached home: Chirayu was not so much of an ass after all. He had a heart too, glimpses of which he displayed at times. I got this message from him around seven in the evening.

Like I said...everything under control...will send in a plan over mail tonight, do read it before you come in to work tomorrow.

It was kind of heartening to see him leading a cause from the front, for a change, instead of relying on my skills and presence of mind all the time. I replied thanking him for his usual ingenuity in dealing with complicated matters, and that I looked forward to meeting him the next day. I briefly considered reading his mail, then decided against it. Long since I had experienced the futility of dogging around for the employer, I had come to value my work-life balance too much to part with it. I had been at the receiving end before—those terrible, insufferable phone calls in the dead of the night that compelled me to feel I had sold my soul to the company—until I decided one day I had had enough, and switched my phone off. Thereon, it became a habit I prided myself on. I had learnt to be at peace with myself, at least when I got home every evening.

Well, almost. You see, I shifted out of my plush one-bedroom apartment in Bandra about a year ago. Someone told me of a fantastically cheap apartment of nearly the same size in Dadar's Chamunda Co-operative Housing Society. It was a stone's throw away from work, which was a big relief. Also, in what was a pure coincidence, Mehek happened to live just two blocks away from Chamunda. Contrary to her suspicions, I did not know about this until I shifted to Chamunda. But once I did, it was comforting to know I could share my glum evenings with someone whose beauty was the purest inspiration to my life, someone who could cheer me up, someone who...

Actually, anyone who stayed in Chamunda Co-Operative Housing Society could actually do with a whole lot of cheering up. The low rent had so caught my fancy when I had taken it up that I ignored everything about the building that returned to haunt me later in time. For example, the building did not have an elevator. So what, I thought—climbing six floors up and down is great exercise. I cannot help but feel, in retrospect, that it was a pathetic idea. Hearing my knees creak louder by the day was not my idea of exercise. I began pestering the secretary of the society ages ago to get an elevator installed in the goddamn building, or I'd need a knee transplant. It turned out that the secretary privately practiced Ayurveda at home. Instead of understanding my agony, the bugger forced me to buy three bottles of Ayurvedic medicine which were supposed to make my knees strong enough to climb the Andes. The shameless guy didn't even offer a discount out of neighbourly love. I took that bill worth five hundred and seventy rupees for medical reimbursements to the Bytesphere HR department. Two weeks later, they mailed me a rejection note that said lifestyle consumables did not fall under the purview of medical drugs—whatever the deuce that meant.

That evening when I got home, the secretary met me again

and offered me a magic potion that would make my hair as thick as a haystack. I told him my hair was perfectly fine and he had much rather focus on making the society look a little cleaner and more organized instead.

He took umbrage at my suggestion. 'Show me one corner of the society that is not clean—now.'

I led him up the stairway so he could take a good look at the variety of designs left on the walls by oral sprays of betel nut. I had barely spoken when he shot out a generous spray himself, which landed on the wall and smoothly blended into the patterns being formed there.

'Yes, show me, Sir,' he challenged me, meticulously wiping his reddened mouth with his handkerchief. 'Look at the stairs, Sir, aren't they sparkling clean? They are so clean I can see my face there. Look!' He peered into one of the marble stairs to show me evidence.

I skipped the topic and moved on to rant over the intolerable ruckus the kids made while playing in the compounds downstairs every evening. Why did they have to shout and laugh so much while playing? Couldn't they just play quietly like mature adults? Did they not know that ten years later they would all be in jobs they would hate and these days would vanish in the pages of history? WHAT WERE THEY SO HAPPY ABOUT?

The secretary looked at me like I needed help. 'You seem to have a tough job.'

I nodded, hoping for some sympathy. Instead, he led me into his house and slammed a bottle of Ayurvedic capsules in my hand. 'They release stress hormones.'

I declined the offer and went back to my apartment, realizing there were issues about Chamunda that I would need to live with. I needed to look at the positives instead—such as the important chat Mehek wanted to have over dinner. I was so excited about it all evening I think I bathed thrice by mistake.

I finally got to Vaishali Restaurant & Bar (Partly AC) about half an hour behind schedule. As was always the case, she didn't throw a fit about having been made to wait that long. See? That is why she was so special—one of those rare girls who didn't derive energy from nagging the hell out of others or taking people for granted. And while she may not exactly be what you'd call hot—she was a little short, rather thin, and didn't bother much about her hair—she had the prettiest face I had ever seen, and enough spunk to make up for the geek look.

'Let us take the air-conditioned hall today,' I insisted.

'Why, is it a special occasion?' She turned around, surprised.

Why, what a tease! As if she didn't know what was special! I nudged her playfully and insisted we take the air-conditioned hall. We bypassed the non-AC hall that was teeming with around fifty men guzzling pitchers of beer and talking in loud, tired voices after a hard day's work.

'So what was the important chat you needed to have?' I asked her as we settled down in our seating booth. I could hear my heart throb.

She rolled her eyes inquisitively for a moment and ran her hand through her hair. 'Important chat? Oh...of course, well it was not that important after all.'

What the...Make up your mind, woman! The air-conditioned hall has a twenty per cent surcharge! I wonder what's with women taking time to open up to their true, inner feelings. It's not even like they are faced with situations as complicated as ours. We guys are the ones who go out in the open with a well thought out strategy on when to make the right pass at a girl at the right time. They only need to respond, yes? It is a simple binary response we expect: yes, or no. How long must that take?

She fetched a piece of paper from her bag and handed it to me. 'There is this profile Dad asked me to pass around. Can you take a look and see if it is a fitment in our unit?'

I flipped the paper open. The profile belonged to some Sameer Kashyap. Villain alert! I felt my pulse race. I knew these Sameer types. They were never any good. Sameers are your typically handsome, fair-skinned, six-footers who can't get enough of displaying their chivalry and awesomeness before every woman and make guys like me feel miserably insecure. This Sameer chapter needed to be closed before it made my life any more complicated.

'Who is he?' I asked, trying hard to control my anxiety.

'I don't really know him,' she said.

Phew! That was close.

'But his father is an old timer with my father since their days in police training,' she added. 'Dad has asked me to help him out with any available openings in Bytesphere.'

By the Holy Cow, it was a police fraternity connection! I could see everything now. Daddy Dearest Gupta had his eyes set on Kashyap Junior as a prospective son-in-law. The first step of the plan was to get Mehek to bring him to Bytesphere so they could get to know each other better. Then Sameer Goodboy Kashyap would download all the chivalry he had sourced from his cop pedigree and get the Gupta parents to start calling him over for a drink every weekend. One such evening, Smartass Kashyap would get Supercop Gupta all overwhelmed with his hardliner views on the Aksai Chin wasteland bordering India and China. Before I would realize it, Mehek would be married off to this guy in some grand sarkari club even as I would struggle to mop up the scattered pieces of my broken heart.

I sat calmly for a while and assimilated all the lovely, inspirational gems of advice I had ever gathered from books like *Guerrilla Warfare*, *How To Stop Worrying and Start Living*, and *Get a Life, You Sore Loser* (I could have got the title of the third book slightly wrong, but it was something to that effect). I mentally sorted all instructions from the books in descending order of the probability of their usefulness, and pulled out *Solve Your Problems 1.1* to play: Nip the source of your tension in the bud. This sounded easy.

I pushed Sameer's profile back towards Mehek. 'I am sorry. I don't like discussing work after hours.'

Ok, that was very lame and unbelievable. But what the hell—it was Advantage Nakul over Sameer Kashyap. The steward stepped forward to take our orders.

'The regular,' Mehek instructed him. He nodded and walked away.

'And get something to cool him down a bit,' she shouted after him, gesturing towards me.

'Whatever does that mean?' I asked, miffed.

'What exactly is "after hours" anyway?' she asked. 'Stop pretending like you have a life after work hours.'

'Well, why don't you post the profile on the recruitment portal yourself?' I snapped. *Pow! I could pack quite a nasty punch or what! You tell me you have something important to chat about, and then you introduce me to Daddy's candy boy and ask me to help him out? Well, fat chance! I am very clear where I must draw the line. You don't get to romp over me and…wait. What is that I see? She is looking away; lips twitching in dismay, eyes rolling over with disappointment, arms crossed over the chest in defiance…ok, ok, whatever. Quit the drama!*

I took the profile from her again and pretended to read it with considerable interest. Score: Deuce. Just my luck.

'I asked you to take a look because I was not sure where we can position this CV,' she said. 'And a lot of profiles get lost on the recruitment portal. We had much rather try sourcing him directly if his experience is of any use.'

I need not specify that I had lost all appetite for dinner by then. Reluctantly, I glanced through the first few lines on the CV that read something like: *Sameer Kashyap is an enterprising consultant with vast experience in blah and handling critical project positions in blah blah and having displayed blah blah blah leadership skills*...Why, the pompous brat! He was like one of those students in school who just HAD to ask the teacher an elaborate question right before the recess bell went off, or the kind who asked teachers to conduct extra lectures on Saturdays on behalf of the entire bloody class, BECAUSE THERE WAS ALWAYS SO MUCH MORE TO LEARN!

'He has written an entire story out here,' I mocked.

'You need not read it right now,' she said, pushing the CV away. 'Just think about it when you get the time. Dad told me he is a bright guy—MBA and the works.'

'Bah!' I smirked. 'MBAs are no great shakes any more now, are they? We have twelve hundred business schools in ...'

'From the Indian School of Business,' she added.

Goddamit! I felt the earth below me slip away. This was getting too dangerous to handle. Why was the fucker trying to get into Bytesphere if he was so smart? This company didn't even offer stock options any more. Couldn't he simply don a black suit and go offer his enterprising consulting skills in McKinsey or whatever? Surely he must have been the lowest grader of his batch. Loser.

'You never told me your father is a police officer,' I deftly changed the topic on reaching that Indian School of Business dead-end.

'Never got a chance to,' she said, serving us portions of the luscious gravy that had just got placed on our table. 'My parents are in town next weekend, by the way. Why don't you come over if you are free? We can have lunch together.'

'Oh, I am not so sure I must disturb you guys,' I said weakly, gunning for some sympathy votes against the poster boy of Indian School of Whatever.

She broke off a molecule from her roti and chewed on it laboriously for an entire minute while I waited for her to respond. She did not.

'Or maybe I can come after all,' I said finally. 'What do you think?'

'Yeah, why not?' she said, without looking up from her plate. 'Lunch on Saturday?'

'Lunch on Saturday,' I agreed. 'Actually, why don't I take you all out for lunch on Saturday instead? What food do your parents usually like?'

She looked me in the eye and smiled shrewdly. 'Why are you being so nice?'

I told her in all earnestness that I was just a compulsively nice guy and she hadn't noticed it so far, to which she replied with a very loud laugh. Then, very artfully, and without coming across as desperate at all, I managed to weasel out from her useful tips on how I could impress the policeman over lunch.

'A pinch of patriotism, and a dollop of discipline,' she said. 'What else can a solider expect from a fellow citizen?'

That sounded easy as pie. I got home and downloaded some gazillion web pages on the Kargil War, The Lahore Agreement, and for added measure, some kickass links on Just In Time too. I would ask someone at leisure later what JIT was all about and whether it actually had anything to do with punctuality and discipline. I was not very sure, but in any case I could always come up with some nice analogy between productivity due to JIT and the importance of punctuality in fashioning a stellar soldier. That's what we consultants were supposed to be so skilful at, after all—speak first, apply logic later.

While I was online, I also did a casual search on B-school ratings provided by multiple sources. You might think there would have been at least one bloody magazine that might have rated my B-school—Excel Institute of Management (why did they name it thus?) above this Indian School of Business, right? Wrong. This was because all these lacklustre surveys relied on common old knowledge of the pedigree of institutes, the kind of courses they offered, the plethora of jobs they grabbed every year and the kind of salaries their students demanded during placements. Whatever happened to soft skills like the students' street smartness, glibness and…and…innately positive tendencies towards corporate ethics, etcetera? We at Excel could have beaten the living hell out of any B-school in these aspects, couldn't we? But the damned surveys just wouldn't see the paradigm shift such softer skills were bringing to the world of management (For the record, I have a feeling the phrase 'paradigm shift' was also first invented in my institute, but I can't really prove it).

I finally chanced upon a rare interview our dean had given to one of these magazines, explaining why his institute did not feature in any of the B-school rankings. He said his college was an institution in learning and spreading knowledge, and not in pimping its way above other institutes by way of meaningless surveys. With all due respect to Mr Dean, I would have respected him a little more had he cared to invest a little money into a good public relations firm instead of selling this whole cock-and-bull stuff about educational evangelism. Anyway, I forwarded that link to Mehek that night to subtly imply that a degree from an elite B-school did not necessarily make an ideal consultant, and it needed wide experience, passion on the job, and suaveness (guess who!) to supplement whatever you earned out of your education. I wanted to proofread my mail before sending it to her, but it was too long and I decided against it. I haven't got a reply on that email till date. Maybe it went into her junk folder or something. But I conveyed my message anyway.

It had been a long day, and I was just about to plop into bed when the doorbell rang. It was ten in the night, but I didn't really mind. Each time my doorbell rang, I was gently reminded that my social life in the city had not come to a complete halt. There were people who still bothered to come meet me, even if they were only the drycleaner and the maid.

I found a wiry, bespectacled man at the door, probably in his mid-sixties. 'Yes?'

'You are IT fellow?' he asked, jabbing his finger in my shoulder.

I looked at him, nonplussed. 'Sort of.'

'Come with me,' he grabbed my wrist suddenly. 'Please come.'

I was so scared I couldn't even shout for help. 'Where are you taking me?' I croaked.

'You are an IT fellow, no?' he kept repeating. 'Come with me.'

For the life of me I had no freaking idea since when being an IT fellow amounted to a crime. Where the hell was he taking me? Maybe the neighbours had suspected I was downloading porn from the broadband set up in the society? Fuck… I mean,

I never downloaded porn. But you know, sometimes when one is browsing innocent, harmless sites on weight loss and vehicle insurance, those annoying, vulgar pop-ups of nude chicks come up from nowhere and force you to click them open? Yeah, that was a common way to snare upright and well-behaved bachelors like me into vile content like porn. But I'd have been darned if the society had been keeping a watch on me and invading my privacy.

He led me up to the floor above and into his modest apartment, and directed me to a chair next to a small dining table. 'Please sit, IT boy.'

I wanted to ask him to stop calling me that. I had a name as well, in case it hadn't crossed his mind. Social appropriateness, hello!

'What will you have?' he asked.

I was partly relieved on seeing his hospitality. At least this was not about porn downloads. I told him without sounding rude that I was very full and didn't want anything except a good night's sleep.

'Ok, I will take all of five minutes,' he hurried into his room and came running back with a parcel. 'My daughter has sent this camera to me from the States. I want you to fix it to my computer so that I can talk to her. Ok?'

He handed me a heavily taped parcel signed by a certain Nandy Shaw from Dallas. I fetched a pair of scissors from his kitchen and cut it open to bring out a brand new Logitech webcam. The man looked at it in mild astonishment.

'Where is your computer?' I asked, unpacking the webcam.

He led me to a room inside and undid a dusty old tablecloth to reveal an archaic computer from the era when I had learnt to use Logo and Basic in school. I had almost forgotten such computers existed. But Mr Shaw was peering above my shoulder.

'You guys work with computers, no?' He examined me as though I were some relic.

'Kind of,' I replied listlessly, looking for the open ports in the system I could plug the webcam to.

After fumbling forever with the computer's programme settings and decoding its complicated hardware, I finally managed to install the webcam and get it up and running.

I looked at my watch, yawning. 'It is almost eleven. I must head home now, if we are done.'

He shook his head obstinately. 'First show me how to use it, no?'

I offered him my seat next to the computer and held the mouse to guide him through the setup.

He slapped my wrist suddenly and snatched the mouse from me. 'No! I will do it myself. You just tell me what I need to click.'

'Drag the mouse over to the Start button,' I instructed, and then yawned a little, hoping he'd realize I was in no condition to stay up any longer. Instead, he asked me if I'd like to go to the kitchen and make myself some coffee so I could wake myself up.

I gritted my teeth and declined the offer again, observing that he had taken the 'drag the mouse' part of the instruction a little too literally. The pointer crawled painfully all over the screen even as he scanned the screen looking for the Start button. I quietly brushed my hand over the mouse and quickly dragged it towards the Start button.

He slapped my wrist again. 'No! I will do it myself.'

Defiantly, he dragged the mouse a foot away from the button and then brought it back himself. He looked at the screen for the longest minute of my life and then finally clicked the button. I tottered around his seat impatiently while the webcam application took its own sweet time to appear on his abnormally slow machine.

'You must clear up some disk space,' I advised him.

He proceeded to clear some old books and magazines scattered on his desk. 'Here. Cleared. But why?'

'Never mind that,' I shook my head, and then looked at the screen which was showing us a close-up shot of the insides of his nostrils.

I asked him to recline a little. 'Now look into the camera lens.'

'Oh-ho!' He exclaimed with short, staccato claps on finally seeing himself on the screen. His eyes wandered curiously all over the screen. 'I can't see my daughter though.'

'You will need to connect to the internet and wait for her to come online,' I told him.

He rose an inch or two from his seat and strained his eyes to read the time on a clock placed on a mantelpiece. 'It is eleven already!'

Ask me about it! I could see two of everything around me by then, and he was not in a mood to let go.

'She told me she'd be online by eleven,' he smiled gleefully. 'Would you like to say hello to my family?'

I shifted uneasily between my feet. 'Some other time, Sir. I'd like to leave now.'

'Oh alright, I won't hold you up,' he relented, getting up to walk me to the door. 'Do come over whenever you feel like a nice drink, ok?'

I stopped near his door and scanned the interiors of his house—a rather modest décor, meager furnishings, some of which were peeling off their edges. And the photograph of a very angry-looking woman, probably his wife, hanging over the foyer.

'I feel like a nice drink almost all the time,' I laughed.

'So do I!' He shook hands with me with gusto. 'Good night, and do drop in again!'

'Good night, Mr Shaw,' I said.

'Mr Shah,' he corrected me. 'Suresh Shah.'

I smiled once again, and took his leave. Back home, I spent some time declining friends' requests to play online Poker. Which is when I received an email alert from Chirayu. And just like that, my firm-as-a-rock work-life balance credo went for a toss when I read his email.

From: Chirayu Chaudhary
To: Anand Rai, Cc: Nakul Kapoor
Subject: Project Kickoff

*Dear Anand,*

*Thank you for giving us this exciting project opportunity with Oz-Mobil. I can assure you while our team may be young, it boasts of the kind of passion that is needed in building a sustainable relationship with this client. Needless to say, the project throws up exciting opportunities ahead. We will be looking to leverage them through a stellar and committed effort at regaining the client's confidence through our three-pronged strategy and Where Did You Come From Where Did You Go, Cotton Eye Joe...*

[Approximately eight hundred words later...]

*...I have prepared a plan to engage with the client, wherein*

*we will share a kickoff plan with them on an introductory call tomorrow. Nakul will be joining me with effect from tomorrow itself, and as the work builds up, I will get the rest of the team ready. I will also ensure a delivery of daily status reports on the project to you. Do let me know if you need any modifications to the plan. Else, we are good to go.*

*Chirayu*

He may be intolerably verbose and self-indulgent, but Chirayu had pleasantly surprised me that night with his presence of mind to come up with that three-pronged strategy (which I was yet to read about) in such a tense situation. I was in absolute awe of him.

# 3.

# What's in a Smiley?

Chirayu is a scheming bastard! I am yet to come across a man so unscrupulous and brash about it at the same time. It all started the next morning, when he called and requested me to get some important printouts from the printing area on the fourth floor, on my way to his cabin. I presumed they were some important project documents and so I ran up to fetch the printouts. When I picked them up I saw they were actually his personal banking transactions and a couple of salary statements that looked as fat as his hide.

I slammed them on his table in evident anger. 'I am not sure I'd like to run your personal errands again.'

Now, you would think there could not be a sterner and colder message shot by an employee to his boss—closed loop, and with little room for negotiation and debate. Instead, he middled my delivery targeted at his middle stump and flicked it to the boundary by launching a counter-attack about how teamwork and a compassionate spirit towards co-workers was the only metric I had underachieved on in my last appraisal. He said I really needed to let go of my ego at times and proactively offer a helping hand to colleagues who kept busier than him. Then he forced me to watch a Youtube video of an army of worker bees working their asses off in a beehive while the queen bee sat smugly and watched the proceedings.

'There is only one queen bee in every colony,' he winked. I felt like shoving an entire beehive up his buttocks.

But that was not all. He then told me he couldn't join the introductory call 'to engage with the client' because he had some conflicting meetings with other account teams that he had totally forgotten about. As always, he made a big deal about how disarrayed and hectic his schedule was, by pacing up and down the room exaggeratedly.

'All the other accounts in the unit need a piece of me,' he sighed.

'I am sure,' I sighed back in response. 'So what do we do now, postpone the call?'

'Of course not!' He exclaimed. 'You join the call. And brief me in the evening on how it went.'

'I can't join the call alone!' I said, horrified at the prospect. 'I haven't even read the proposal document carefully. I don't know how to engage with the client.'

'You should have read the proposal document,' he retorted.

Of course, I briefly argued that he had mailed me the proposal only late the previous night, and he surely didn't expect me to stay up and read the document in the middle of the night. That argument was downrightly rubbished by smoothly dishing out some quotes from some consulting manual which could crudely be translated to something like 'your work-life balance can go take a walk'.

'Join the call anyway,' he insisted. 'I don't think there's much to talk about today. It's just a formal introduction with the client. Say hello to them, tell them how much you are looking forward to working with them, and then mail me the minutes of the meeting.'

I suddenly remembered my international calling code was no longer active. He handed me his code and asked me to get on with the call immediately. I walked into the adjacent conference room, wondering what social pleasantries or nuances about the Australian culture I could fall back upon if the client decided to get overexcited about our deliverables already. After a dozen failed attempts at getting through, I learnt that the call code had been deactivated. I looked at the watch—it was time already. So much for a professional start to the project. I called the IT helpdesk to have them sort out the call code mess for me. The analyst on the phone told me that the user's call code had been disabled due to violation of the company's professional commitment guidelines. It had been found that the code had been used to make frequent calls to toll free numbers that belonged to shady spa and massage agencies. I quietly asked the analyst if there would be a provision to take disciplinary action against the worthless abuser of this international call code. There was confused silence at the other end. Disappointed, I had to hang up and call that international number from my mobile phone. I made a note to monitor the usage and send the reimbursement claim to HR later with a hope to get it reimbursed within the same calendar year.

When I was finally connected to the conference, I overheard a thick, male Caucasian voice mutter to itself. He heaved a sigh of relief on hearing me connect to the call. He introduced himself as Jerry White, our potential client lead—and then sarcastically added he was just beginning to wonder if the call was scheduled for the next day. I ignored the sarcasm and started engaging with him by chatting up on what laurels I had achieved in my short career that far and how excited I was to see 'the Bytesphere and Oz-Mobil synergies merge for a smooth, seamless transformation programme very soon'—a line I had stolen from—no prizes for guessing—Chirayu Chaudhary. He sounded like he hadn't understood a word of what I just said. Then after an awkward pause he told me the deal was nearing its final stages of getting approved and signed and that he looked forward to getting on with the project as soon as possible.

'We have had to go through some delayed decisions,' he explained. 'But more likely than not, we will be looking forward to you guys working with us.'

I didn't bother myself with the fact that he was under the false impression we had a team ready at his disposal already. But only until he mentioned how glad he had been to be informed by the Bytesphere management that the project team was all good and ready and could not wait to start working on the project. I thought it best not to utter another word for as long as I could help it.

And then, in a moment of very bad timing, I uttered words I shouldn't have, right when it looked like the call was on its way to ending peacefully. Jerry told me his management would take another two days to approve awarding the contract to us. I thought it would be very unbecoming of me as a mature, seasoned consultant if I did not show keenness to utilize the two days in contributing handsomely to the client's business in some way. Thus, I asked Jerry very enthusiastically if he could pass us any pre-project activity until then. I expected him to simply thank me profusely and decline my offer and maybe, at the most, write an email before my appraisal, appreciating my hunger to contribute. Instead, he got so excited on hearing the offer he began muttering incoherently about some research his marketing team was conducting on the feasibility of launching a product somewhere in the interiors of Bali and that he would be only too happy in receiving my help in that regard. He asked me if I could conduct a due diligence on the telecom market in the interiors of Bali.

'I would love to help,' I had no choice but to agree.

Obviously, I expected him to realize I could not possibly find much about Bali and its telecom market in two days, while sitting in India. Hence I thought he would, at the most, expect some secondary research using links that would easily pop up on entering keywords like 'Bali', 'telecom' and 'trends' in the Google search bar. On the contrary, he suggested I try conducting first-hand interviews with my telecom counterparts in Bytesphere's subsidiary in Bali based on a template he would email me in a minute along with 'a few other useful documents'.

Shortly, I heard a barrage of emails go ballistic on my inbox. Nine emails from Jerry in a span of six seconds—what a freak! And all of them had attachments of more than 2 MB each. Was this a research document or the Israel-Palestine peace dossier? Jerry made an unfunny joke about how my mailbox could crash any moment, which was not exactly a joke.

'Feel free to add more columns to the template,' he added.

I was utterly depressed about the proceedings. Research scared me. To relieve myself of the worry and also to break some ice with him, I casually asked him if it would be wise to have me travel to Bali for a week or so in order to help build this research with more authentic data and first-hand information on what customers wanted from their telecom services. Clearly, there was no desperation to go on a foreign assignment to an exotic island. It was purely in interest of the client, and maybe the least I could have demanded after all those gargantuan attachments they had emailed me. He laughed out loud and said that far from it, this assignment was not even going to be considered billable. He said he expected us to do it purely out of goodwill and to consolidate the relationship between the two companies.

I hung up and took some time to contemplate the pile of shit I had landed us into. When I did, I marched right into Chirayu's cabin and apprised him of what had transpired despite my best efforts at managing the show beautifully.

'I have good news as well as bad news,' said Chirayu, without looking up from his screen. 'The good news is I am very happy you took this proactive step at helping the client. I will remember this when I mark my feedback during your appraisal.'

'Thank you,' I smiled in relief.

'The bad news is I cannot involve myself in this free-of-cost assignment,' he continued. 'Also, it is a pretty silly situation you have landed us into, and now you will have to manage it on your own.'

'I will try my best,' I replied weakly. 'But there is only very little I can do in two days anyway.'

He did not reply. He just nodded absently and dug his face deeper into the screen of his laptop.

'By the way, Jerry thinks I am the programme manager,' I said casually, trying to gauge Chirayu's reaction. I was still not sure, but it looked like Jerry was a little confused about the designations out here. Then Chirayu laughed out loud, confirming my suspicion.

'Also, he was asking for the rest of the team,' I told him. 'Who else has joined this team already?'

He finally shut the screen of his laptop and stood up. 'Again, I have good news and bad news. The good news is you are, in fact, the programme manager for this project.'

My eyes were ready to pop out in delight. 'Indeed?'

'Easy,' he raised his hand. 'This is only for the client bills. Your actual designation does not change.'

I did not even react to that last line. For some reason, I was hardly surprised.'What is the bad news?' I asked.

'The bad news is there is no team,' he said. 'You are all by yourself as of now.'

This time, I laughed out loud, expecting that shameless admission to be his attempt at making a joke. It was not.

'Jerry thinks we have a team!' I said, exasperated.

He giggled. 'Ha! Yes, it has been put up in the proposal, hasn't it? We are supposed to have one.'

'And?'

'And we don't have one yet,' he shrugged casually. 'So what? We will have one. What are you fretting about like a baby?'

'Well, what am I to do now?' I asked him bluntly.

'Tell me, Nakul,' he frowned. 'Whose responsibility is it to get the team ready? The programme manager's, you think?'

'I think, yes.'

'Who is the programme manager?' he asked. 'You, I think?'

I looked at him blankly. 'So you mean *I* need to get the team ready?'

'Eureka!' He threw up his arms in the air like a crazy, obnoxious, flea-infested, ugly baboon.

I asked him what exactly his role was going to be in this project, given that he had gone all berserk before Anand about some three-pronged strategy bullshit. He said he would be overseeing the project 'on a high level' and would involve himself in 'strictly advisory matters'. I mock-thanked him for his kindness and he took the compliment seriously.

'I can also help you get a few team members,' he said as an

afterthought, almost like he was doing me a favour. 'Let me try pulling out a few people from some other projects for you, ok?'

He looked up a roster on his laptop that showed available resources. He clucked his tongue on seeing there was hardly anyone he could pick.

'What is Mehek working on these days?' He looked up at me.

I am not sure, but I may have blushed, because I saw him smiling at me very shadily.

'Some proposal, I heard,' I replied vaguely. 'But I am sure her time can be freed up.'

He smiled wider and winked, 'Of course.'

I harrumphed a little and murmured, 'Whatever.'

'Talk to her and get her on-board, then,' he said. 'What are you waiting for?'

'That would make two of us,' I said. 'What do we do about the others?'

He then bored into the roster again, and after pondering in vain for two minutes, he looked up and told me I shouldn't be expecting him to spoon-feed me any more.

'I am giving you a free hand,' he said. 'Go pick up your team from wherever you feel like. Use your judgement and take a call now. I can assure you support in terms of budget approvals also—in case you need to recruit someone from outside.'

'That wouldn't be preferable,' I mused.

'Of course it wouldn't,' he agreed. 'Provided we were left with some options within our team. Oh by the way, I see an available resource in our department. But they are in Saurabh's team. You will need to speak to him to have them commissioned.'

He turned the laptop towards me and showed me the profile of a certain Radha Murthy who had been recently sourced from the Hyderabad training unit of Bytesphere.

'There, I've solved half your problem,' Chirayu said proudly. 'Now go talk to Saurabh and get her over to the team.'

Saurabh, whose last name I may never need to know, was the jolliest person I had met in Bytesphere. Maybe because at that point in time, I knew all of six people in Bytesphere. But still, he was a jolly person. He actually asked me how I was doing when I called on him. I was touched. I told him I was doing hunky-dory, and would do much better if he could spare Radha Murthy for this major project coming up. He took some time to soak in this request.

'Radha Murthy, did you say?' he asked no less than three times.

'Yes, that's the one,' I confirmed each time.

Suddenly, he began sounding like I had offered to pay out his pending home loan. Like a seasoned salesman, he started dishing out redundant information about Radha—her qualifications, her family background, her socio-cultural value system. I asked him to come to the point and tell me why she hadn't been placed on a project in the three months she had been here.

He was quick to clarify. 'She appeared for three project interviews with clients last month. None of them clicked. But she is a very ambitious and committed employee.'

'That is all I need,' I replied softly. 'I guess. Can I meet her today?'

'Right away!'

I must have hung up and walked less than two hundred steps back to my cubicle, in which time I got a detailed email from Saurabh, marked to at least five other names I did not know of—confirming that I had commissioned Radha for the project.

*Dear Nakul,*

*Totally thrilled talking to you. Pleased to relinquish Radha for the Oz-Mobil project. I would like to confirm that I am allocating her time schedule to this project for the next four months (ballpark) and these details will be entered in the system in the next two hours. For any changes to the resource allocation plan hereon, you will need to give me at least a month's notice to reshuffle her into an alternate assignment. All the best for the project. Even as I write this mail, Radha is on her way to your cubicle. Please provide her with the necessary documentation and training support so she is on speed with the project soon.*

*Regards,*
*Saurabh*

He signed off with three smileys. I wondered what he was so thrilled about.

In fifteen minutes, a portly young woman stood before me. She looked rather unhappy and was least in the mood to exchange pleasantries. She introduced herself as Radha and promptly asked me to hand her a work station along with some work. Her body language was rather reserved and uninspiring, but I didn't care—I had someone I could offload that Bali research nonsense to! I was very thrilled. I got down to business immediately and told her of the criticality of that research from a timeline perspective. Surprisingly, Radha didn't look like she thought it was a big deal at all.

'What do I need to research on?' she asked.

'Practically everything there is to the Bali telecom market,' I gave as accurate a response as I could manage. 'I have sent you an email listing the client's expectations.'

She nodded coolly as though that were easy as pie. Then she asked me what recourse she had in the event that certain data points were not readily available from the sources of research. I complimented her for the intelligent question and in the same breath conveyed it may not be desirable to not have data points available; good research always yielded every data point on the face of this earth. I knew this was not true, but it felt nice to exert some undue pressure in early days, project manager style.

'Nevertheless,' I reassured her, 'you can mention constraints in your research document if you really don't end up finding exactly what you were looking for. But make sure you get closest relevant information.'

She nodded tersely, satisfied with this convenient arrangement. Then she scampered away to her work station, assuring me she would submit the report to me in the next hour. Surprised, I told her I didn't think it would be that easy. But she looked convinced, and so I chose to keep quiet. For the next hour, I breathed a little easy, hoping the research was progressing smoothly. So I whiled away some time chatting on the office intranet with Mehek, asking her what service batch and cadre her father belonged to, and other such important things. To my joy which I did not make overly evident, Mehek confirmed her availability for the project from the next day. I was very excited.

It was only at four in the evening that I realized Radha was yet to send me her findings.

'Five more minutes,' she replied from her cubicle.

In ten minutes, I saw the most bizarre response to a research assignment ever, staring me in the face.

From: Radha Murty
To: Nakul Kapoor
Subject: HELLO (What the…)

*Hello Nakul,*

*Pali is a district situated in the state of Rajasthan, India. It is surrounded from all corners by the Aravalli ranges. It has nine sub-districts and thrives on the industries of textile dyeing and printing and cotton ginning.*

*The literacy rate in Pali is 63.2% with 78.2% of that literate population being males. Residents of Pali are by and large fairly affluent and presumably own mobile phones.*

*CONSTRAINT: The research team could not provide documents relevant to the postpaid and prepaid usage by customers in Pali.*

*However, I provide you herewith the closest relevant information: the overall penetration of mobile phone usage in India is 38 per cent according to a recent census report.*

*Please find attached a map of Pali district as well as a graph showing the gender ratio in the district.*

*I hope this research is of use to you.*

*Regards,*
*Radha Murthy*

I felt a fire rage within me. A volcano of anger was waiting to burst at the seams of my shirt. But the mark of a true leader is to compassionately understand his colleagues' issues and solve them by way of open and transparent communication. So I walked up to Radha and compassionately asked her what her goddamn problem was, and what urged her to look up the gender ratio in Pali when all I had asked for was a handful of reports on postpaid and prepaid usage in Bali.

'Pali and Bali sound alike,' Radha explained, giggling for the first time.

I held my breath patiently and told her they at least did not *read* alike! I asked her what kept her from reading my mails before embarking on that ridiculous research on Pali's demographics.

'Large mails,' Radha replied in earnest. 'I thought I could save time by starting off directly.'

Continuing to be as compassionate and transparently communicative as I could, I told her it was a very silly idea to shoot in the dark without knowing what in God's name one was supposed to do. I was only beginning to express my disappointment yet, in the politest manner possible, when she started crying a little. When I first heard that muffled breathing, I just thought she needed some lozenges. Then the heavy breathing turned into systematic, scary sniffles. She brought out a handkerchief from a very large purse and harrumphed into it like a bugle. I patted her on the back, asking her if she was alright. Which she obviously was not. Far from calming down, she looked up at me sharply through her soda glasses. That cold gaze permeated through the thickness of her spectacles and injected my soul with unbearable guilt. Also, I feared that HR would give me hell if they found out I had managed to make a woman cry at work. So I immediately brought out the suave, jocular persona latent inside me and made a cool joke about how I had once mistakenly emailed the client a strategy document with its competitor's name in the slide footer. Firstly, nothing of that sort had really happened. I was just being nice to her. And the thankless woman did not even laugh at my joke. Anyway, at least she had finally stopped crying.

I connected her on a call with the in-house research team and got some documents arranged from where she could conveniently source some sensible information. Radha scanned the length and breadth of the dozen documents and told me curtly that she would notify me of the progress the next morning. She also subtly hinted that I should leave her alone and not try making any more lame jokes.

I went back to my seat. Worried, and thoroughly convinced that she would come to no good with the assignment, I bored into the documents myself—but not before writing to that scumbag Saurabh that I did not, after all, want Radha on my project any more. He replied promptly, once again marking every fucking person above him on the mail. That spineless creature. This time he *began* his mail with three smileys and followed up with reminding me that Radha could not be released from the Oz-Mobil project for the next one month. He also told me I should have thought about whatever issues I had with her before getting her commissioned on the project. He signed off quoting Henry Ford: 'Coming together is a beginning, staying together is progress, and working together is success.'

Now I felt like crying too.

I called Parul, a sizzling supermodel who once lost her way into our Human Resources unit. Some cheap rascals always kept waddling across to her desk under the pretext of random discussions on career alignment and annual reviews. And then they would check her out, full and proper, like desperate lechers. I would like to proudly mention I wasn't one of them. I conducted myself with dignity and poise before her at all times, never letting my hormonal instincts come to the fore. If at all they would come to the fore, I would only steal covert glances while pretending to saunter around the lobby, talking on my phone to no one in particular in an NRI accent. Maybe that is why she liked me.

'I need to speak to you about some profiles that have been referred for positions in our unit,' I began, but she cut me off in her husky, delicious tone.

'I am really busy,' she said. 'In the middle of a conference. Will call you back.'

Nonsense! How could an HR person be 'really busy', pray tell me? All they ever did was send us weekly emails on Friday celebrations in the office—traditional day, Diwali day, Halloween day, I-don't-know-what-but-let's-freak-out-anyway day. I was running out of time and patience. I needed to get new people on to the team, and I needed them fast.

'You need to take it easy,' Mehek said when I met her later for coffee at the cafeteria. 'That girl is new to the job. She will take time to learn.'

'She sure is good enough at downloading irrelevant information from Wikipedia,' I said wryly. 'And why did she have to cry?'

'You must have been mean to her,' she said, pinching my arm.

'Yeah, of course,' I said bitterly. 'I am the villain.'

'Probably not,' she corrected me. 'But you are the team leader, aren't you? Treat her as a leader would.'

'Maybe you need to get on-board real quick and give her a hug,' I snarled.

'I will, if that helps,' she smiled. 'Now stop being a baby and have your coffee. There's no problem without a solution.'

I got something that looked like a plausible solution late that evening. Parul called me after hours, telling me it had been long since we caught up. I asked her if she was sure who I was, because I had met her only the previous day at her desk to ask her about the revised policy on stock options. After a few seconds of awkward silence, she deftly changed the topic and asked me what I had called her for. I told her I needed to interview candidates for a couple of open positions on the project.

'I have three profiles,' she said. 'I will mail you their details once I get home. Take a look and let me know.'

'My only condition is I need them on-board immediately,' I stressed on the last word.

'That will be difficult,' she said. 'They all come with a caveat of a notice period.'

'That doesn't help much,' I said disappointedly.

'There is one more though,' she said. 'His name is Akshat Mehra. But I hadn't seemed inclined to shortlist him earlier.'

'Why not?'

'He quit his job two months before applying here,' she said. 'We are always a little wary about candidates exiting their companies abruptly with nothing else on offer.'

'Hmm, he could have been asked to leave,' I said sympathetically. 'Send the profiles in anyway. We will interview them and negotiate on the joining date.'

I went home, partly relieved. Hopefully, a team was on its way to being formed. Screw Chirayu and his evasive tactics. I was going to show him it took a self-believing leader to hold a problem by its horns and tackle it instead of offloading it to a hapless subordinate like a sissy. If only Jerry White wouldn't have been shameless enough to free-ride on my niceness. I would sit with him on a call soon and set his expectations for the rest of the project right.

# 4.

# A CNBC Report

Suresh Shah was Batman in disguise. I don't know what he did during the day, but he made himself visible to me almost every night. Every now and then, he would come over and force me to help him with an assortment of issues. I don't know who had driven it into his head that guys like me could fix everything from grainy television screens to flickering bulbs.

And he didn't know my name yet.

I didn't know how to put an end to this politely. But it wasn't fun at all. That evening, I saw him sitting on the stairs right outside my door. He looked like he had been a little upset for some time. He lightened up a bit on seeing me, which I was not happy about. I wondered what it was this time.

'IT boy!' He extended his hand. 'Where have you been?'

'At the factory where a million like me are made,' I replied, not bothering to tell him my name yet.

'Ok, listen,' he intercepted my path, not even allowing me to get inside the house. 'There is a problem. I have not yet been able to chat with my daughter over that camera.'

'Why not?'

'I don't know,' he shrugged. 'That's what I want you to find out. Come.'

'Why didn't you tell me when I came to check on your television?' I asked impatiently.

'I thought it would get sorted out on its own,' he said. 'Nandita was clueless too. I spoke to her on the phone. She told me there shouldn't have been an issue.'

'Can I freshen up and see you there in a while?' I asked.

'No,' he shook his head. 'Come now, please.'

Of course. Why waste time over physiological processes like taking a leak? How could I be so self centered when a friendly neighbour had invested his faith in my IT skills so that I could solve his internet chat problem? Peeing could wait. I went up to his apartment and examined his computer. After thoroughly beating around the bush we discovered he did not have an internet connection. I asked him what exactly he had in mind while trying to chat over a computer without a basic internet connection. He told me his daughter told him all he needed was that webcam she sent him.

'She may not have known you don't have an internet connection,' I told him. 'You will need to apply for one.'

'That might take awfully long?' he considered me with a frown.

'Two days,' I replied, 'if you have all documents in place.'

He pondered for a while and then excitedly asked me if he could simply borrow my internet connection instead. I told him that wouldn't be possible because I had a wireless setup at home that I couldn't really lend him. He asked me why that was such a big deal, when he used to easily hack his neighbour's cable connection and plug it to his own television in earlier years. I didn't have an answer to that, but I insisted anyway that he needed to apply for an internet connection independently. All he needed was to submit a handful of documents for verification and purchase a data card. Simple. He somehow felt very overwhelmed by the entire rigour of going to a retailer and handing him the documents and filling up lengthy forms and the works. So he asked me if there was an easier route he could work his way through. I idiotically told him the easiest way to work his way through would be to take along someone proficient with the entire mumbo jumbo of purchasing a connection. I soon realized I shouldn't have spoken so much. He smiled at me. I quickly stood up and tried to take leave of him, citing reasons of tremendous workload and a premonition of imminent pneumonia. But he got the better of me and began persuading me to submit his documents to the retailer the next morning. I told him he needed to go to the store in person to sign a form, but he wouldn't listen to logic. He ran down to the photocopier outside our gate, got copies of an identity and an address proof, and forced them into my hands.

'Won't you do this for me?' he looked at me hopefully.

Compassionate as I innately was, I agreed. He was so happy he handed me an unused bottle of scotch as a token of gratitude. I was so excited about this free alcohol situation that I sat up through the night and got myself drunk silly, and then woke up after nine the next morning when Chirayu called asking for a status report on the project—ON PRIORITY. I was so hung over for about half an hour that I actually sat down and began furnishing a status report. Then I realized the project had not begun, and so there could not have been a status report. I emailed Chirayu, asking him to hold his horses and to stop bothering me with such ridiculous requests. I had lost good time already, so I chose to skip certain unproductive activities like shaving, getting into a shower, and such. Instead, I doused myself with liberal portions of an expensive perfume from Bangkok once gifted to me, and then set out to work. En route, I dropped by at the retailer and chose an internet dongle for Suresh Shah. As expected, the retailer refused to sell the dongle until the user came personally and filled up an application form.

'We will be back in the evening,' I said tiredly as I left.

By the time I got to work, I had concluded with reasonable evidence that stepping out to work without a shower and with a hangover from the previous night was a pathetic idea. I realized to my dismay that I had ended up spraying too much cologne, and it only ended up dampening my shirt rather than doing me any good. Also, this perfume had kind of mixed with my sweat and had now spawned some weird, inexplicable smell—hardly pleasant. This was ridiculous, yes. I made a mental note never to accept gifts from people returning from Bangkok. They always had to be cheap fakes.

Anyway, I contended with the thought that there were not too many people out at work who really cared about what I looked or smelt like. Also, I needed to get down to work soon. And so I did. But then Murphy's law caught up with me when Parul strolled up to my desk and began chatting about the profiles she had shortlisted for an interview with me. I mean, who does not want a Parul to walk up to his desk? But did she really have to choose that very wretched day of all the three years and one hundred and forty days I had been in that office? Of course not. But then that is what happens to you when you get up on the wrong side of the bed. I froze for a few seconds, not sure of what to do. Then I saw her twitch her nose uncomfortably. I was thoroughly embarrassed. Also, there was no one else in the cubicle whom I could in turn twitch my nose at and pass the blame. So I excused myself from our conversation for a minute and quickly called the Facilities helpdesk, complaining about an unknown stink emanating from some corner of my cubicle, presumably because someone had left an unfinished bowl of spinach out there the previous evening. The confused guy at the helpdesk pondered for a while and promised to send some air freshener immediately. I looked up at Parul, who at least SEEMED reasonably satisfied by the spinach story. I mentally patted myself on the back for my ingenuity in times of crisis, and then resumed the conversation which now looked a little more hurried from her side than before.

'Can I put them on for telephonic interviews today?' she asked.

'Put them all on, one after the other,' I said. 'If they are good, I want them right away. Let's do this in the second half of the day please.'

'Will be done,' she assured me, walking out of my working bay.

I thanked her and subtly offered once again that we meet for coffee some day. (This was, at best, a fallback option in case Goodboy Kashyap played truant with my chances with Mehek). She giggled and walked back to her desk. I guess I've had this thing of embarrassing women with my playful charm. I try containing myself, but I guess it just comes out naturally.

Soon after, I joined Radha in the conference room to catch up on whatever semblance of progress there may have been on that research. When I walked in, I saw Mehek had already introduced herself, and they were getting rather chatty and comfortable. Also, Radha was smiling, which was a big relief after the way she had scandalized me the previous afternoon with all that sobbing. She stopped smiling once again on seeing me and dug herself sulkily into her laptop.

I ignored the body language and got down to business.

'What updates do we have on the research work?'

'Check your email,' said Radha bitterly, pushing her thickly oiled ponytail to the back of her head.

I went back and checked her mail. The good part of the work done was that this time the focus of research was actually on Bali. The bad part was that the content delivered was still pointless—a little like bringing me an entire mountain when all I had asked for was the Sanjeevani herb. I scouted through the tonnage of text she had sent me, sourced from analysts worldwide, on what she thought of the Bali telecom market and its future. When I realized it would take me forever to handpick any relevant information, I discarded those documents and downloaded from *Harvard Business Review* a simple, colourful PDF that offered a very straightforward analysis of the market's strengths and weaknesses. Now that is what I call a report! And, wonder of wonders—I noticed that document also contained comments by industry experts in Bali on their assessment of future trends in the sector. I prepared an exhaustive report, carefully pasting information from this discreet document and a few other purchasable reports I had managed to discover online. I bought the reports, applied for reimbursements (which I knew would not be reimbursed for some obscure reason) and prepared a fresh, comprehensive report which essentially was a collection of all those downloaded reports. I was still worried about that primary research nonsense Jerry had requested for. The last thing I'd fancy would be to interview counterparts in Bali on a topic I was hardly interested in. Which is when a brilliant idea hit me like a wave. I had stumbled across names of some telecom industry experts in those downloaded reports, who seemed to know plenty about the market. I carefully replaced their mentioned designations with some random designations provided in the Bytesphere organizational structure in Bali. Quickfire primary research, that!

'That is a big risk you are taking there,' Mehek warned me when she discovered what I was up to.

Yes, it was a little bit of a risk, but then, if I were Jerry White, I wouldn't bother validating trivial details around my vendor's resource database.

'The practical question we need to ask ourselves, Mehek,' I smiled calmly, 'is whether we had the time to conduct that primary research with our Bali counterparts in such little time. We did not. So I made these analysts in the report our Bali counterparts for one paltry report. It is a no-loss situation.'

'What if he were to find out no one by the name...' she peered into the report to read the analysts' names. '...No one by the name Moses Sveltekarlo works in Bytesphere Bali? That name doesn't even sound like it belongs to Bali.'

'That is not even important,' I winked. 'Don't worry. I have got it all under control. There is plenty of other text they will have their attention diverted to.'

Of course I was right. Why would they choose to hover specifically over tongue-twisting names across a report of over sixty pages?

There were some handsome graphs in there too. But they contained data only most recent to 2008. So I retained the same information in the graphs but changed the timeline from 2004-2008 to 2010-2014, and multiplied the per year value provided in the graphs by around four per cent extra and brandished new, relevant graphs in the report. Some of you might call this fabrication of data. But I call it making the best out of waste, or something like that. Who would have thought graphs half a decade old could still be analyzed to get ballpark projections of a country's telecom market? I came up with that solution. Moreover, I needed to be credited with the assumption that all per year values be multiplied by four per cent extra to come up with reasonable values. This stroke of genius resulted from a report I had read almost a year ago, which said that the Asia Pacific telecom market was growing at a compound annual growth rate of one per cent. Then I gave a fairly analytical shot at the percentage of market value a small island like Bali would be providing to Asia Pacific, and then I divided...do you really care about the details any more? Let it just suffice to say that in view of insufficient data availability, a consultant must use his systematic reasoning capabilities to arrive at safe estimates rather than putting a footnote in the report cribbing about inadequate information.

In less than two hours, a beautifully documented report, complete with all formatting and indexes was lying in Jerry White's inbox. In less than three hours, a note of thanks with an appointment to discuss the report 'at length' was lying in mine. It all seemed to be positive and pleasant for most part of our discussion. But that was mainly because Jerry White could not give up being diplomatic to save his life. In retrospect, I feel really grateful I kept the rest of the team out of this embarrassing conference call.

'It looks like a wonderful CNBC report,' Jerry started slowly.

I was about to thank him, when he added. 'Maybe because it is very stylized and has very little relevant content.'

What's with sly remarks in the world? All he needed to tell me was he was not satisfied with what I had sent him. I wouldn't have been entirely surprised, knowing that clients often tend to behave like cranky and overbearing girlfriends. Instead, he delved into this entire foreplay of how I had formatted and version-controlled the document well, but otherwise, in sophisticated terms, the content was all hogwash.

'Nakul, I will first tell you what I liked about the report,' said Jerry. 'I think it is very exhaustive and I thoroughly appreciate the intent of putting together so much data for us in just a day.'

'I also appreciate you have got us some useful numbers on the projected market volume over the next five years,' he added. I heaved a sigh of relief. Thankfully he hadn't noticed the partly fudged data. 'But I think we really need to prune out some information. For example, I am not sure why we need the analysis of Bali's political landscape.'

I tried explaining to him that Bali's government regulations on tariffs would have a bearing on the way companies would price their products, but Jerry was on a trip of his own, marking most of whatever we had provided him for deletion.

'We only needed the usage patterns of customers in Bali,' he repeated mechanically, frustrating the hell out of me.

I stopped him before he could further paw his opinions all over the report, and told him I'd send in a preened version by the end of the day if that is what they wanted. For all the pain that it had caused, I was at least relieved it was almost over. Or so it seemed. For just when we were preparing to wind up the call, something in the document caught Jerry's interest.

'I like what I see here, Nakul,' said Jerry. 'This, er…your colleague Marlon Pacino has something interesting to say about the data services segment. What was that again, can you please tell me a little about it?'

I panicked. Yes, yes. Go on. Tell me I was told so! But the likelihood of such a holocaust is always so low I thought I could have fancied my chances. How was I to know this chap would get so horny about one Marlon Pacino comment in the entire bloody report? Sweating profusely, I moved the mouse with my trembling fingers over to this Marlon Pacino comment. As I had feared, I could not make sense of it at all. So I began breathing heavily into the phone and rubbing my stubble against the mouthpiece, sending an annoying, jarring noise over the line.

'What's that disturbance?' I asked irritably, desperately trying to buy time.

'A minor glitch, maybe? Go on, Nakul.'

'Hello?'

'Yes, Nakul,' he said, a little louder this time. 'I can hear you. The Marlon Pacino comment, please.'

I ran through the Marlon Pacino comment.

*We downgrade our industry expectations from Outperform to Neutral basis the satiated market for fixed telephony which saw a meager growth of 0.8 per cent in 2010. On current valuations we see the volume growth step up over next year, leveraged by increased usage of data and cable services. While there is clearly value unlock potential, we believe a spin-off of the data services blah blah blah...*
*—Marlon Pacino, Senior Telecom Consultant, Bytesphere Corp., Bali.*

Fucking verbose Marlon Pacino! What kind of freak writes stuff like that? I felt like calling Mehek over, apologizing for my misfired cleverness and cradling my weeping head in her lap for comfort...

And then I put a skill mastered in the MBA days to play. I began reading Pacino's comment verbatim, inserting crucial phrases like "as you can see" and "self-explanatory" where deemed fit. Then I started doing the same thing over and over again, tiring out the client thoroughly.

'We would like to speak to Marlon some time this week,' said Jerry, giving up on me finally. 'Can you help fix up a call with him so that we can flesh out some more details?'

You know those moments in life when you feel everything around you is a bad dream? That is exactly how I felt at that moment. Rows of sweat beads were trickling down my legs, sending a tingling sensation all over.

'Oh, Marlon said he is keeping extremely busy these days with a global assignment,' I sputtered. 'That could take some time.'

'I think we can wait,' Jerry said. 'I will check with you next week again. And oh yes, I almost forgot to mention— congratulations! You will, indeed, be our chosen vendor for the testing service in our programme!'

Thankfully, this time he didn't ask for details on team readiness. I thanked him for the wonderful opportunity and promised him a prompt project strategy document.

'Sure,' he said before hanging up. 'But don't forget about Marlon Pacino.'

Fantastic. So now besides all the shit that was expected to come to us over the next three months, I now had this added responsibility of creating a certain Marlon Pacino out of thin air and get him to speak to the client. And all this for a non-billable assignment!

I also wanted Marlon Pacino's postal address now, so that I could gift him a *Brevity For Dummies* handbook at the earliest before he screwed up someone else's life. But that could wait. What I was more worried about at the moment was building a real team before even thinking of giving the client an unrealistic work plan for the project. I connected with Parul once again, this time over the phone. (Thank God for small mercies).

'Have you considered campus recruitments?' she asked me. 'There is a team travelling to Madurai to recruit some software engineers next week.'

'Our unit won't give us the budget to travel to Madurai, I know,' I said. 'We could look up colleges in Mumbai itself, though.'

'What timing!' she said. 'Most colleges in Mumbai have their placements starting in a week's time. We can get us a few slots in some colleges.'

'A week?' I asked disappointedly.

'That is the soonest we can reach them,' she said.

'Alright, put me on to two colleges,' I said after some thought. 'Let's get this over and done with.'

'Sure,' she said. 'Let me slate the schedule and call you back tomorrow.'

I met Mehek at lunch and briefed her dismally on the Marlon Pacino situation.

'I told you so,' were her first words.

'Stop that already,' I cut in, 'and tell me what I am supposed to do now.'

'Come clean.'

'Yeah right, thanks,' I snorted. 'And have myself thrown out of the company!'

We lined up with our plates in the queue leading to the food counter. The levels of gravies and rice in the containers were fast depleting, and it was only one thirty in the afternoon. That wasn't surprising, though. The catering vendors had themselves expressed amazement and anguish at the sheer rise in employment here over the years against their inability to supply food in accordance. As a result, they had begun to resort to the very predictable option of mixing water in the gravies—and that too rather liberally.

'Can I get a straw please?' I winked at the server who was pouring a yellowish liquid in one of the sections of my plate.

Much against my expectation, he actually placed a straw in it as well.

'Stop being grumpy,' Mehek hissed from behind.

'I can't eat this stuff any more,' I put down my plate resentfully. I turned to one of the servers. 'Please call your manager.'

The manager emerged from right behind the server with a clearly disinterested look. 'Yes?'

I swung a large spoon around a container with thick gravy. 'This is supposed to be Paneer-Corn Delight.' I pointed at a board on which they had scribbled the menu. 'I completely understand that the delight is missing but where is the paneer?'

The manager peeped into the container and then walked over to the board with a duster. He rubbed off the name of the gravy and changed it to Corn-e-Crunchy.

'There you go,' he said and smirked again.

We resigned to the misery of yet another shoddy lunch and settled down at a table.

'Your honesty will pay off,' Mehek continued later. 'I really think you must undo this Pacino screw-up before it becomes harder to tackle.'

'I have a week to figure this out,' I said finally. 'We will have a solution, don't worry.'

'Why would I worry anyway?' she shrugged.

Violins were heard somewhere in the backdrop with a sad, melancholic tone. Why would she worry? I was nothing to her but a charismatic, charming senior colleague whom she could learn tricks of the trade from. And at the very most, I was the geek who was madly in love with her in spite of the undeniable fact that she wasn't even a patch on Parul Parkar in terms of hotness. But of course, my genuine feelings were overlooked as always.

'Wait for a week,' she suggested again. 'And then tell them Pacino has resigned from the company.'

For a moment or more, that looked like a plausible option. But I realized Jerry was way too insistent when he desperately needed something. He would ask for the contacts of the other four 'consultants' whose names I had listed in the report with similarly verbose smart-ass comments. And even those evil conglomerates in Sidney Sheldon's novels probably never had four employees resign together in the space of less than a week.

'Ruled out,' I said. 'That was a near smart option, though, I will admit. Forget about it. We have other things to talk about.'

'I know,' she said. 'I got your email on the project strategy document. We have an awful lot on our plates. Don't worry, I will get Radha started. You need to worry about getting more people on.'

'I like you for your proactive style of working,' I giggled and looked at her meaningfully. Screw proactive styles. I liked everything about her. 'And that is why I am taking you along for a campus recruitment initiative.'

'Really?' she asked, wiping residuals of buttermilk from her tiny lips.

'Yes, we need new recruits for the project,' I explained. 'Also, that will give us to spend an entire day together...'

I don't know why I said that. It was most inappropriate, coming from a project manager. But some emotions just cannot be contained. She was polite enough to ignore that part of the conversation and to switch to something more comfortable— that of the pending telephonic interviews for that afternoon.

'I have four guys I am going to speak to,' I told her. 'But the last one is only a fallback option. I noticed a gap in his employment.'

'So what?' she asked.

'I suspect people with gaps in employment,' I shrugged. 'I can't seem to help it.'

'He might have had some concerns,' she suggested. 'Talk to them all. You never know when you pick a jewel from a coal mine.'

'Whatever,' I said, forcing the last morsel of Corn-e-Crunchy in my mouth. 'Our lunch with your parents on Saturday is on, isn't it?'

'Totally is,' she said. 'Let us know where you want to go.'

'We will let your parents decide,' I offered graciously.

To which she thanklessly added, 'By the way, Sameer is in town too. And Dad wants him to come over one of the days. I might ask him to drop by on Sunday if we are lunching with you on Saturday.'

'Congratulations,' I remarked curtly.

'What?'

'Why are you mentioning Sameer to me in the first place?' I asked her rudely. 'Do I need to go receive him at the airport?'

'You are acting strange,' she said, getting up. 'Anyway, time to get back to work. Shall we?'

There she went with her cryptic ways again. Drop a vague hint about seeing a family friend's son over the weekend, and then quickly chuck the discussion and leave. If she was looking at driving me out of my mind, her plan was working. But this time, I was not going to let my guard down. I was vexed inside at the very concept of the existence of a Sameer Kashyap, but I decided to not let it show.

Moreover, I was a little excited about conducting interviews for the first time in my life. Ever since I was first interviewed for a potential job during grad school, and seeing the way

I was stress-tested with obnoxiously difficult questions on microprocessors, I had this burning desire to get even by moving to the other side of the table one day. This was my chance to throw some weight around.

Nothing of the sort really happened. The first three candidates I interviewed were actually pretty sharp and I hardly got a chance to take their case. In fact, the second candidate was a little too hyper. He had more questions to ask me than he had answers to give.

'Where do you see Bytesphere in the next five years?' he asked me! What cheek!

I think he had been watching too many of those Fair & Handsome adverts on television—must have got carried away. I nearly told him no one here really gave a damn about where Bytesphere would be five years hence, as long as we were making good money and had a job on hand at all times. But on the whole, they were all pretty smart, save for the conditions they put forward. The first one could not negotiate on a notice period of three months with his previous company. The second one persisted on challenging me with questions like 'But why should I join Bytesphere only?' till I had to tell him maybe we both needed to mull over that question for a decade or so and reconvene. The third one gave me an attack of acidity by demanding a salary higher than mine, and he also wanted to know if Bytesphere had any kind of clause against its consultants quitting and joining the client organization at any point in time of their service.

I considered the fourth candidate's profile finally, a little reluctantly though. Akshat Mehra—read the header. He looked alright to me, except for that one blip on the screen of a gap in employment. I asked to be connected to him as well. When

I finally got to speak to him, I was taken in completely by his glibness. He was the smooth, cool operator I always wanted to be but was far from being. And he was so candid in the way he spoke he almost unsettled me with his honesty. When I asked him the clichéd question of where he saw himself five years hence, he told me he saw himself leading his father's business in ball bearings.

'What happens to Bytesphere then?' I tested him.

'It will help me grow as I learn,' he said. And then, he stumped me with a bit of an anti-climax. 'Moreover, I need to keep myself busy with something till the time my Pop thinks I am fit enough to join him.'

So he thought Bytesphere was mere leverage. Well, I couldn't hold it against him. Bytesphere was not exactly what we'd call aspiration worthy. It was an old, tiring company that was getting increasingly bureaucratic and it wasn't a very pretty paymaster either. In fact, at some level, all Bytes treated Bytesphere as mere leverage. This guy was at least honest about his intentions. The only thing that worried me a little was he seemed to talk a little too much. While that was the primary skill sought in a consultant, it could get on one's nerves in the long run. But then, what did I have right now in my team but a girl who despised me with her whole heart and another with whom I experienced awkward undercurrents of blooming romance? One slightly boisterous addition to the team wouldn't hurt in getting the team dynamics in place.

I finally got down to my real concern. 'Why did you quit your previous company? I see a huge gap in your employment.'

For the first time in that conversation, Akshat went completely silent. And then, slowly, he came up with a completely predictable response.

'I had grown out of that role.'

'So you left it?' I asked suspiciously. 'With nothing else on hand?'

'I like taking risks,' he got back to being enviably cool.

Mentally, I had recruited the guy already. But I poked him a little longer to satiate my desire of stress-interviewing a smart guy some day. To my disappointment, nothing stressed him out—not even my stated perception that rich Delhi boys were only meant to drive swanky cars, listen to loud music and get on the turkey. Besides, he seemed sufficiently well-versed with testing as a software practice for me to let him in. I couldn't care less about his longevity in the company as long as he fitted the bill on this project.

'You can leave it to me, Nakul,' he said in a sing-song tone. 'Trust me with working around clients and their whims. If I may—I have the single biggest strength a consultant can possibly play to—that of building relationships with people who matter.'

It would only be very late in the day that I would realize what grave insinuations his claim really had. Building relationships with people who matter—for then, I was duly impressed. I only wish I had asked the guy to elaborate a little on that point before jumping to hasty conclusions about his abilities.

I headed towards Parul's desk, took a small detour towards the restroom and emptied some air freshening spray under my collar. I smelt like a bouquet soon after, but that was better than smelling like decayed spinach any day. I walked into the HR cubicle, where Parul and her equally hot colleague—whose name I had never got an excuse to find out—were wired on a conference call, and were liking each other's Facebook pictures alongside.

Parul muted the speakerphone button and looked up at me.

'Akshat Mehra,' I confirmed.

'The underdog!' she cried out. 'That is interesting, eh?'

I told her it was not the size of the dog but the size of the fight in the dog that mattered at the end of the day. I realized a little late that did not even make sense. Parul and the other hot HR woman looked at each other perplexed. I was steadily losing points in the sense of humour department. I probably needed to read more Dilbert.

'Yes, the underdog,' I said, and then got on to a heavy discussion around the completion of on-boarding formalities so there was a fair chance they would forget all about my joke. 'Can you email me Akshat's completed application form? I need to make a few reference checks, just in case.'

'Will do, this evening,' she said and smiled. I must contend there was something fatally attractive about the way she smiled.

As I walked away from her, I am pretty sure I saw her sigh deeply and whisper to her colleague, 'Such a hunk!'

Whoa! Ok, fine. I understand where she was coming from. But this was so teenager-ish. We were mature adults, for God's sake. I'd have much rather appreciated her come forward and tell me so, one on one, instead of pining over me in front of some random colleague. I pretended to not have heard the comment, and slinked away in candid anticipation of her following me down the corridor and asking me if I was free that evening. She did not.

Meanwhile, not very surprisingly, Chirayu had emailed, asking me to mail him EVERYTHING pertaining to the project that had transpired during the day WITHOUT marking anyone else on the email. I did so, and half an hour later, he had recreated exactly the same email with the only addition being a line ahead of the rest of the text that said: 'Dear Anand, *I* have prepared below the following details of the project status so far. Please let *me* know if you'd like to discuss anything before *I* begin the work allocation to the team starting tomorrow.'

Numero Uno Cretin, Chirayu Chaudhary. It was surprising he never cared about what I'd think of him when I saw him stoop low thus. He was clearly as thick skinned as he looked.

Some time in the evening, a guy in the HR department whose name I have never bothered to know, met me at the coffee machine and told me what Parul had whispered to her colleague behind my back was, in fact, 'What a skunk!'

Insecure fellow. I think he was just trying to create a misunderstanding between Parul and me. Or maybe he was just plain frustrated because he was the only guy in the HR department in this office. I asked him to shut the fuck up and go back and remind Parul to email me Akshat's application form.

I received the form an hour later. I quickly picked up the number of one of his mentioned references from the earlier organization. The call was answered by an enthusiastic corporate voice. 'Go for Vikram!' he boomed.

'I am calling from Bytesphere,' I began. 'My name is Nakul Kapoor, and I am calling in regard with Akshat Mehra, who has just appeared for an interview here...'

'Akshat Mehra!' he exclaimed. 'Wonderful, wonderful.'

'I'd just like to conduct a quick reputation check,' I said. 'Vikram?'

'Wonderful,' he said again. 'Except...'

'Except?'

'Oh wait,' he said as an afterthought. 'Who am I to pass a judgement on someone?'

'Your judgement is exactly what I have called you for,' I said impatiently.

'I am not sure I'd like to play party pooper here,' he said slowly. 'But did he tell you why he had to leave our company?'

∽

I was disturbed by what Vikram told me. But I was distracted soon enough, when I received a very heartening email from Anand: the contract for the testing assignment had been awarded to us. Jerry had added a note mentioning he was pleased to see how I had proactively helped his team with a beautifully researched report, and that he looked forward to similar gusto from our team during the entire project. Chirayu followed up with another email marked to Anand and me, mentioning he was very impressed with me for having toed his line and having gone out of the way to the client's aid, like he had always advised me. Such a son of a gun, this fellow. He further added that the management would be watching me as I led the team hereon, for this was a challenge very few people at my level were exposed to.

I had no idea what he was talking about. From my point of view, this project looked easy as pie. I had won Jerry's faith already, after all.

# 5.

# Thank God It's Friday

Mehek called to let me know she wouldn't join me for dinner that evening. That prick Sameer was in town and wanted to be shown around Nariman Point. Just like a small town boy to get enamoured by an ordinary road next to the sea, I told her.

'He is from Delhi, which is not quite a small town,' she quipped.

I rudely replied that I didn't care, and that I wasn't hungry anyway, expecting her to indulge me a little with some concerned questions on my lack of appetite. Instead, she asked me if I had tried the buffet at The Intercontinental, because Sameer had mentioned he was a privileged guest at the hotel and could get them a nice deal. Basically, he just wanted to let the whole world know he had a lot of money to throw away at luxury hotel dinners. I curtly disconnected the call without bothering to answer.

This thing of hanging up really worked, I was sure. I had tried it once too often on girls back in college. I gave Mehek fifteen minutes to call back and apologize for her insensitivity.

Twenty minutes passed by even as Suresh Shah and I walked down to the retailer to get his internet dongle. She hadn't called back yet. Bloody network congestions. Fine, I'd give her another fifteen.

'You seemed to be pretty angry, eh?' asked Suresh Shah, impatiently tapping his fingers on the counter at the retailer's.

'Are we all done here?' I looked around irritably for the shopkeeper, who was in some corner of his store looking for the warranty booklet of the internet card.

'Girlfriend?' asked Suresh Shah.

'Not a chance,' I shot back.

'She sounded like one,' he beamed. 'I've had lots of them, son. I know how they are.'

Suresh Shah was like a cross between Batman and Sherlock Holmes, actually. And he was not only a little too nosy for his age, but unbelievably filmy too. He wielded some heavy lines on resistance being the inevitable in the pursuit of love.

The shopkeeper arrived finally, ending the long wait for the internet card as he handed Suresh Shah his dongle and the associated documents.

'Today, my son, I will teach you how to win a girl over,' Suresh declared as we walked out of the store.

'Thanks, but no thanks,' I resisted.

'We will discuss it over dinner,' he insisted, grabbing me by the arm. 'Don't worry. I overheard you don't have company tonight. I will come along with you. Think nothing about it.'

'I don't think I feel like eating out anyway,' I said helplessly. 'I am just going to stay indoors.'

'Even better,' he said. 'I have cooked some food at home. Let us eat at my place.'

Now, I know it was a Friday evening and I had nothing interesting to do. But this was no way to punish me just because my social life sucked. I'd rather stay at home and watch some old Hindi movie and order in pizza. No, I was not going to let Suresh Shah have me cave in under his adamancy this time.

No, no, absolutely not.

'I can't come, I am sorry,' I said, mustering some insensitivity.

'Oh,' he let go of my arm suddenly.

We walked back towards the society in deathly silence—the kind of silence that made me terribly guilty for no bloody fault of mine. I looked at him from the corner of my eye. He looked sulky and almost distraught. I felt strangled between my conscience and my peace of mind. And after all the chaos that I was trapped in at work, my peace of mind was clearly dearer to me, especially on a Friday evening.

We walked up the stairs, Suresh's gait painfully slow, reeking of depression, evoking sympathy. It was a little after dark, but I could see he was anything but happy. I tried making small talk about how he could peacefully chat with Nandita for as long as he wanted now, but all I got in return was a couple of short grunts. I finally sacrificed my peace of mind.

'You can join me if you like pizza,' I said slowly, and very unconvincingly. 'I have a couple of movies we can watch.'

'Oh no,' he shook his head and continued to walk up the next flight. 'I am really not that overbearing kind.'

Maybe he could have asked me for my opinion on that statement. He may be a sweetish kind of guy, but there was no way on earth he was not overbearing. Loneliness does that to us, I guess. I couldn't help but feel sorry for him, although imagining Mehek dining out with Kashyap made me feel even sorrier for myself.

Whatever.

If there ever was such a theory that stated the negative energies of two depressed souls could convert into a powerhouse of positive energy, there didn't seem much to lose in killing some time.

'Alright, I'll come over then,' I said finally.

He smiled so wide the whiteness of his teeth shone like a halo in the dark stairway. 'Come!'

We went up to his apartment, which, as always, was so messy I could hardly locate a seat to land myself on.

'Make yourself comfortable,' he said, tossing an assortment of towels and loose papers off the couch to show me a seat I could use. The couch had wires jutting out through its torn fabric, and the damp walls behind it had cement peeling off them on schedule.

'Dinner will be ready in ten minutes,' he said, striding into the kitchen.

I heard a loud clatter of utensils being upturned.

'You really did not have to bother,' I shouted out.

'Oh, I am used to it,' he shouted back. 'And I would have eaten even if you weren't here, wouldn't I?'

I stepped into the kitchen. Sitting on the couch like a hungry oaf was rather impolite while the host busied himself in the kitchen with what smelt like…burnt bread.

I walked in and opened my mouth in horror. The stove looked like it had gone up in flames. 'Oh God!'

He didn't in the least seem upset. He turned around with a smile. 'What? The lentils are ready. I am nearly done with the chapattis.'

I inched closer to see a lumpy, shapeless piece of dough lying helplessly on the cooking pan, as though screaming for help. The length and breadth of it were turning black by the second. He was nearly done with them indeed.

'Cooking is fun,' he laughed. 'My wife, when she was alive, never allowed me to step into the kitchen. A woman very possessive about her ownership of this department, I tell you.'

'I can see why,' I said under my breath, dismally picking up a chapatti from one of its many black corners and examining its thickness.

I returned to the living room with the lentils. He followed suit with a very large number of those chapattis and a jar of ghee in the other hand. He insisted ghee helped enhance the taste of a chapatti. Saying so, he smeared so much ghee on my rocky chapattis they now looked and felt like large mounds of grayish, pasty clay.

'Ah, nothing like a self-cooked meal!' he slurped even as I struggled to chew my first morsel.

The verdict was sealed. I was supposed to concur in my opinion of that food, which I did, like a well-behaved guest would. But my stomach was actually churning the way it did when our entire team was once taken to a free screening of *Agent Vinod*. I was still going to need that pizza to be delivered later in the night.

'So, what's the girl's name?' Suresh asked a few minutes later.

'Mehek,' I replied. 'But there is nothing on between us.'

'Of course there isn't,' he laughed. 'Girls don't dig guys who sit back and watch them being taken away by early birds. They like guys who slug it out with their competitors.'

For his generation, Suresh Shah was very vocal about courtship strategies. My father always told me pursuing girls was a waste of my time and an impediment to building a glorious career. I got so distressed with that advice that I landed in the middle of nowhere—a humdrum job and absolute lack of conviction while pursuing women. Not to mention that three years after having gotten a job, my father was the first one to sensitize me towards the importance of finding a nice girl. And when I stopped responding to that bit of conversation, he had begun asking me if I had a thing for women in the first place.

'I don't have a competitor,' I argued most unconvincingly.

'Who is the guy whom your girl took out to Nariman Point tonight?' he smiled sadistically.

I rolled my eyes. 'You have very sharp ears to be able to hear through my phone.'

He missed the sarcasm. 'Son, this is experience talking. I remember in 1968 when...'

In the time that he regaled me with his romantic escapades from the past, I had only managed to eat a quarter of my first chapatti, and I already had this awkward feeling I had chipped off portions of some of my teeth. My mouth felt a little emptier after I was done with the first chapatti. He tried loading the second chapatti on to my plate but I told him I was very satiated with the delightful experience and had no room for more food. He scooped up some more lentils and plopped them on to my plate. He explained it was a tradition in his household to continue eating until a conversation had ended. Basically, my intestines were destined to die a painful death that night.

'That guy she was talking about is not competition,' I said. 'I haven't even met him. And it is just a harmless dinner anyway.'

'That gives more reason to be worried,' he pursed his lips. 'It all begins with harmless dinners. The other guy needs only one large dinner bill to win her over.'

'Mehek is not what you'd call a materialistic girl,' I shook my head vehemently.

'But this guy is what you'd call the opportunistic prick?' he cocked a brow at me.

I looked agape at Suresh, stunned by his choice of words. He was beginning to look like he was my type after all. We both thought Sameer was a prick. But Suresh's sermons were not making my Friday evening any more exciting. Then again, he was a slow eater. I listened on as he made his way into the density of his next chapatti.

'So what do you suggest I do?' I asked after a pause, during which he had let out a few staccato burps.

'Show her you care,' he said, heading for the wash basin to rinse his hands. 'Show her you can give her what Mr Nariman Point can't even begin to think of.'

I nodded in agreement, but inwardly I curdled at the impossibility of that situation. Mr Nariman Point was the Raymond Man in the eyes of her family. I could so imagine him telling her right then how he once revived an impoverished, abandoned cat and won the award for compassionate treatment towards animals at some elite social club of Delhi. Moreover, he was from the Indian School of Business. Mr Nariman Point could give her anything. Of course, the downside to his awesomeness was when he expressed his desire to join a company like Bytesphere, but then who knew what tricks the devil had up his Armani sleeve?

'Showing that you care is contrived,' I laughed off the suggestion. 'And I don't think it works anyway. In *Casablanca*, Rick shows Ilsa he cares for her. And what happens finally? Ilsa runs off with Laszlo!'

'Hmm, I haven't seen the film,' he said. 'But I won't discount the possibility of such a thing happening. In which case, all you can do is *imagine* yourself to be superior to your adversary.'

'How's that?' I asked.

'I don't know,' he shrugged. 'Do whatever it takes. Play out the climax of a Hindi film in your head—you are the hero who's got to woo the heroine. The competitor is the bad guy in the film whom you have to whip the ever-loving life out of.

Play it over and over again in your head until you feel good about yourself.'

'How does that help me get the girl?' I asked, confused.

'It doesn't,' he laughed. 'But it gives you peace of mind. Trust me, I have tried it. It works.'

The futility of his theories notwithstanding, Suresh Shah could at least make me laugh. I thanked him for the hearty dinner he fed me and also told him I wouldn't be able to eat anything for the next two days. He laughed and said it wasn't all that great after all. I laughed in agreement and mildly implied that was exactly what I had meant, too, and that he should probably hire a maid who can cook some serious food. He said he had appointed a number of them in the past but they could not meet the benchmark of palatability he had been looking for.

By the time I got home and got through the ever-busy number of the pizza outlet, they had shut shop for the day. Tired and exasperated, I flopped on to the bed and tried to put myself to sleep. But I couldn't help thinking about Sameer. Maybe I should have spoken to him when Mehek showed me his profile after all. I could have called and informed him of a serious forthcoming financial scandal to be committed by the Bytesphere management that I was privy to. I could have warned him about an impending company shutdown or something and asked him to leave Bombay immediately. At least this Nariman Point drama could have been avoided. But I had little choice left now. I had to fight it out like a man.

I got up and downed some jasmine tea to soothe my nerves, handmade by the Chinese apparently. The China-returned vacationer who gifted it to me had said it had a levitating effect on people. I must admit that was true. It tasted horrible, but it did calm me down a bit. I lay down again and mentally geared up for the big lunch with Mehek's parents the next afternoon. If I could pull this one off smartly, I would never have to worry about the Raymond man again. Only time would tell.

# 6.

# Conference Calls

*I am accosted by two burly guards at the iron gates of the palatial wedding farmhouse. I am taken in by the sprawling acreage, but I don't let it deter my intent.*

*'You are not appropriately dressed,' remarks one of the guards with a smirk, pointing at my sleeves which clearly don't have cufflinks on them. 'You can't attend the wedding dressed like that.'*

*I roll up my sleeves and stand akimbo. Suddenly, two large boulder-sized curls jut out of my arms, leaving the guards stoned with shock.*

*'Who said I am here to attend the wedding?' I wink coolly. 'I am here to stop the wedding.'*

*The startled guards charge at me wielding their batons on my unremitting toughness and rip my shirt off to reveal my perfectly carved abs. I stand still and give them a fair chance to have a go at me. When I see they have tired out, I execute a stinging jab in each of their torsos. A fighter is born out of circumstances, not out of talent—I growl at them angrily.*

*I kick open the gates and storm into the party where Sameer has just brought out an expensive ring and is shamelessly waving it before the crowd. As I walk past the gentry with a bare torso, beads of sweat accentuating every muscle, a collective gasp escapes the audience. I march up to Mehek and grab her hand forcefully. Her parents watch in awe from the sidelines.*

*Mehek holds Sameer's hand and eyes me angrily. 'I walk where I smell the green, darling.'*

*I observe Sameer tipping what seems to be his convocation hat from the Indian School of Business instead of the customary wedding veil. He flashes an evil smile at me even as I struggle to speak.*

*'Civilians, bah!' curses an old but sharply dressed man, looking at me disdainfully. He is a spitting image of Sameer, only much older—presumably his Policeman Papa.*

*Dejectedly, I let go of Mehek's hand. I begin walking away but not before glaring hard at Kashyap Junior, who glares doubly in return. He glares so bloody hard his face begins to turn red. Gradually, we see a large eruption forming right in the centre of his forehead. It grows bigger in size and steadily turns yellow in colour, with a large drop of pus settling inside it. As he seethes further in anger, the eruptions multiply till Mehek shrieks in fright and jumps into my arms for safety. I comfortingly pat her head as we see his ears gradually transforming into those of a werewolf...*

*'Hey wait, can I still send you my profile?' asks the helpless half-man as I steal away his bride from right under his nose...*

I woke up a little queasy. No, it was not the dream. If anything, that dream made me feel a little good. Acne King Sameer Kashyap was damn ugly. At least in the dream, that is.

It was actually an upset bowel condition that had been bothering me ever since I got up. It must have been those chapattis. I'd reckon Suresh could use one of them as his mouse-pad. Now here I was, having guzzled heaven knows how many glasses of milk to be able to conquer an important mission in the toilet. But my system at that moment felt a little like how the Andheri East roads must feel during the morning traffic when four cars try squeezing into the space for two. An hour later I was smelling like a dairy, but I hadn't felt a tad relieved. So I walked up to a chemist and asked him if he had a remedy that was not exactly a laxative but would still hold effective enough to get my bowels some serious action. He smiled sagely and produced a powder with some obscure brand name. He told me one teaspoon was all it would take for me to forget what constipation even meant.

Bastard.

I mean, yes, the powder worked as it was probably supposed to. But the duffer did not tell me it was supposed to be administered only at night. In thirty minutes, I felt my system was on a rampage. It was like someone had installed an entire rocket propeller inside me. I freaked out like shit, no pun intended. As it is, a minute in a humid Bombay bathroom can get you sweating like a monkey. I was spending minute after minute in there, and this looked only like the beginning. On top of it, Mehek had been calling incessantly. Possibly a change in plan, I guessed. Actually, given my disposition at the time, I wouldn't have minded one bit had the plan got cancelled. I would answer it as soon as I got the time...

Screw my luck. The plan was not canceled. She had only been calling to tell me that they'd be reaching Global Fusion at twelve o' clock sharp, delicately reminding me towards the end of the conversation that her father was a stickler for punctuality. I told her I was well aware of that and I would be there on time despite whatever conditions might prevail, without sharing further details, of course.

When all hell had broken loose, I called my mother who told me to chew some cumin seeds in order to plug the menace, which I duly did. She also reminded me that such unusual triggers in the stomach had a lot to do with the games one's mind played, and so I should try forgetting I was suffering from any such condition. I followed her instructions and kept repeating to myself that my bowels were calm and dandy after all. The trick worked in most part, but not quite entirely so. I managed to get ready anyway, and then darted off to Global Fusion as fast as my car could take me. Given the way fate always managed to conspire against me, I was hardly surprised to not find a parking spot at the restaurant. So I got off at the closest available parking spot which was like almost in Ahmedabad, and then began that hurried walk to Global Fusion. It was during that distressful walk that I realized the cumin seeds as well as the mind game theory worked only so long as I limited my bodily movements. But that walk was messing it all up again. A walk that should have taken no more than three minutes took fifteen instead, what with the ginger steps and...you know what.

When I entered Global Fusion—little surprise, this—but I saw I was late. Mehek was seated with her parents at a booth strategically located in a far corner diagonally opposite to the loo. As I inched closer towards her parents with each step, I saw more distinct versions of them. The mother was reasonably pretty and well kept, which explained Mehek's attractive features too, because the father was anything but charming. And this was despite him not having that flowery moustache I had been imagining him with. But there was something very unhappy and fidgety about his countenance. His hair had grayed, but his upright posture and his taut shoulders clearly suggested he was crazy about fitness, which was not good news for me. I breathed in a large puff of air, sucked my jelly-belly in and tucked my shirt out just enough to convey that any sign of lack of fitness was only coincidental with a loosely kept shirt. Of course his sharp eyes saw through the farce and fell instantly on my girth before I even got a chance to introduce myself. I was so embarrassed about it I wanted to lay myself on the plate of sizzler lying on the table and melt into a puddle right then. Mehek introduced me as her boss, which was not technically true but it salvaged my pride to some extent nonetheless.

I shook hands with Police Papa the way two normal human beings would. But he clasped my hand so hard I felt my blood go running back into my head. I heard the bones of my palm crunch like someone had stomped on an empty plastic bag.

'A firm handshake speaks a bloody lot about a real man,' he said, nodding at me with a terse smile. 'Yes, young man?'

I nodded politely in response and massaged my palms while he looked the other way. He went a little easy on the hard stares thereon and began making small talk about my family and other safe questions that were difficult for me to falter on. And then, unable to keep himself from passing a sly remark, he looked at his watch and told Mehek they should begin eating because they had been waiting for A LONG TIME ALREADY. I apologetically mentioned I had been held up on account of a conference call which needed my assistance on a make-or-break deal for the company. As if only to put me in a fix, Mehek started asking me a hundred questions about the deal all at once. I calmly smiled and remarked that she was breaching company protocol by discussing confidential information outside the company premises. Mummy Gupta looked awkwardly at Papa Gupta for a second. I led them all towards the buffet in order that we could digress from the subject. I handed them their plates and told them to eat to their hearts' content because the lunch was on me. I know this sounded rude and inappropriate at various levels, but I really only meant to be hospitable. The father grimaced a little and said he ate to his heart's content even when he footed the bill himself. I laughed and shook his hand fiercely—like a real man—and said I liked voracious eaters. This was all going wrong. I stepped back and took a deep breath before thinking of something different and safe to talk about. We scattered in different directions round the buffet with our plates. Mummy Gupta led Mehek to one side, giggling excitedly. All that I managed to hear of that conversation out of earshot was 'quite a friendly boss'. I blushed uncomfortably and turned away. By God, Mummy liked me already. Meanwhile, Police Papa was marching along the lunch spread continually, frowning at the food labels through his thinly rimmed glasses and prodding the assorted dumplings with his fork as though they were some prison inmates. I, for my part, strode along to the sushi counter and laded my plate with as much sushi, pita bread and hummus as I could.

When I returned to the table ten minutes later, I saw the entire family had symmetrically selected exactly *one* dumpling each from that gigantic buffet. My own plate, in comparison, looked like it had been served at a relief camp. Sushi had been arranged in large concentric circles in one corner, and there was a stack of pita bread in another. In whatever space remained, there were large mounds of hummus and ketchup. By the time I considered returning to the counter and offloading some food, the parents had already noticed I treated the concept of unlimited food very seriously.

I sat down and commenced eating anyway, once again as a normal hungry human being would. While they, together—as though at the strike of a gong—picked up their cutlery and began dissecting those microscopic dumplings which were too small for one bite. Each time his fork would dig into his dumpling, Mr Gupta would covertly glance at my plate until he could take no more. Refusing to take his eyes off me, he asked Mehek if he had told her the anecdote of the caustic chief of the mess at the police training academy.

'When he'd see some of 'em bloody recruits serve themselves scoops of butter on their plates,' said he, laughing, 'he would say, "Gentlemen, I see some of you are mistaking butter to be the main dish!"' We all laughed. Mehek told him that was probably the fortieth time he had narrated that anecdote.

'Just got reminded of it,' he said, smiling at me in particular.

I quickly spooned the entire hummus and stuffed it into my mouth. As I began chewing on my food, the nightmarish debacle of the morning returned with its little threats of a churn and a roar in the stomach. Right then, Mummy Gupta asked me to give an account of my entire life and what I thought my life ahead held for me. This was the only polite question posed to me that far in our meeting, hence cutting her short and heading to the loo was kind of ruled out. So I stood my ground—I mean, I sat, whatever—and started talking as calmly as I could, putting the partly useful mind game theory to play. To my relief, the mother seemed pretty comfortable with my presence at the table. She even marvelled when I told her I had almost made it to the International Mathematics Olympiad when I was fourteen but had missed out finally because in the application form I had accidentally interchanged my answers to the questions on whether I had been convicted in the past and whether I enjoyed an image of clean repute. It was only the father now whose grouchiness I had to comprehend and overcome. *A pinch of patriotism and a dollop of discipline*, I recalled Mehek's advice on what got her father rolling. So when Mehek kindly added to my credibility by mentioning that Bytesphere had awarded me with the Young Achievers' Award a year ago,

I smiled modestly and said it was all thanks to the early seeds of discipline and rigour that had been sown in me.

'Quoting Hemingway, Sir,' I said, looking the father in the eye, 'talent simply sets you in motion, but it is your discipline that shows you where you got to go.'

To my credit, that quote was an original gem, and I created it right on the spot. But I didn't want to overwhelm the family with my profoundness in our very first meeting, so I passed on some undue credit to Hemingway. There was also no harm in letting them know I was into reading Hemingway and stuff, I thought. Thank God they didn't ask me Hemingway's first name—I didn't know it. Whatever the means, my plan was beginning to work. For the first time, he pursed his lips slightly and nodded purposefully in response to my quote.

'Bloody true!' he exclaimed, shaking hands with me in that same brutal manner. 'I like a man who knows his ways with discipline.'

I felt a gush of positive energy run through me. I felt like I could conquer the world now. I also thought I saw a glint of joy in Mehek's eyes when her father acknowledged me. I suddenly forgot all about my medical condition.

'So, Nakul, what does your old man do?' He asked.

I looked up at him, startled.

'Your father,' clarified Mummy Gupta a little shamefacedly.

A major feeling of WHAT THE FUCK happened. Mehek probably sensed my emotions (now that's what I call a caring woman) and sent me a text clarifying 'old man' was just a friendly reference in the army to people's fathers and her father had picked it up during those thousands of joint social gatherings at their clubs. I smiled back at her, thankful for the useful tip which I thought I could make use of in good time.

If this appallingly casual army lingo could help thaw the ice between us, I was all for it.

'The old man is among the board of directors at a bank,' I told him.

'Oh, a money man!' he exclaimed.

That was a dicey one. My old man was not exactly a money man, but considering the way the cop's eyes lit up excitedly at the thought, I nodded and said my family kind of sat on a pile of gold back home. Suddenly, he did a volte-face and cringed. He abruptly said something about rich people's offspring being unable to make a good life of their own accord. He stated his opinion with so much conviction you might think it is mentioned somewhere in our constitution. Mummy Gupta realized her husband was getting overly sadistic and cynical, and so she suggested we disband from the table to get ourselves another serving of food. I seized the opportunity and looked at my watch in exclamation.

'Oh God!' I said worriedly. 'I have another conference call I must get into. Ten minutes is all it should take. I hope you don't mind?'

Mehek looked at me a little like they minded it. Daddy Dearest didn't seem mighty pleased either. They drew out of the dining booth quietly towards the buffet while I dialled my own number and began talking loudly and very passionately about Bytesphere's strategic margin expansion model, the cost drivers versus gross profit matrix, and a three hundred and sixty degree view of the customer—to no one really, of course.

'No, no, you don't understand, Customer is God,' I shouted into the phone as I sauntered away from my audience and towards the loo.

Once the loo handle came within an arm's distance of

me, I shed all inhibitions and lunged inside. I ran into the first available toilet and locked myself in there for a good measure of time. I felt like a Jewish prisoner who had managed to escape from Sobibor. All at once, a volley of noises ricocheted across the four walls of the cramped toilet, revolting the suppression they had faced for most part of the noon. It was times like these I regretted not gunning for Architecture as my choice of discipline. The need of the hour from a fine architect was to build sound proof walls where they really mattered. Maybe I'd blog about this suggestion some day. This was most embarrassing. Fortunately I had the loo all to myself then, and if at all a patron were to walk in, I had no intention of bringing my face out of the closet for a long time. So I went about my business, utilizing the time on hand to think of a brilliant conversation I could resume at the lunch table that would eventually lead to the subject of patriotism and national sentiments. That would have Police Papa floored, if he was not already.

A few minutes later, I emerged, sweaty and thoroughly dehydrated, and what do I find! Police Papa is in the loo, zipping up his trousers after having taken a quick leak. He turned around and froze in his path on seeing my dishevelled face. For all the alacrity, wit and presence of mind I am celebrated amongst my peers for, I was at a total loss of words as the man whose good books I was desperately trying to get into just couldn't keep a straight face as he stared at me.

'It is hot, isn't it?' I ran a finger through my dampened collar, my defense completely busted.

He rinsed his hands and said as he reached for the door, 'We are waiting for you. Whenever you are done with the call.'

A part of me wanted to ask him how long had he been standing in there listening to the proceedings. But I thought wiser and decided otherwise. It wouldn't have helped anyway, except that it might have eased my anxiety and embarrassment one notch. When I got back to the table, the Gupta family had finished lunching already and was now conducting surgeries on the few grams of dessert that lay distributed between three plates. Their meticulousness was almost appalling.

'Ah, Nakul,' Police Papa grinned broadly. 'Bloody nice desserts! Get yourself some, won't you?'

Just when I thought he had had the decency to forget about the bathroom episode, he added. 'Oh, avoid the cheesecake though. Or you are going to have some serious conference calls lined up for the rest of the day!'

Absolutely useless sense of humour. He was the only one who laughed at his own joke even as his wife and daughter gave him a befuddled look.

'What's the joke?' Mehek nudged him playfully.

'Some other time, maybe,' he laughed harder. He was shaking so violently his cheesecake must have turned into curd the moment it slipped into his big mouth. 'Say what, Nakul?'

I gave him the cold shoulder and brought myself some dessert anyway, cheesecake included. I was footing the bloody bill, for God's sake. I could eat what I wanted, right? As it is, I didn't think much of men who couldn't keep a man-to-man conversation to themselves. He ought to have felt ashamed of himself, flouting the 'What happens in the men's room stays in the men's room' code of conduct so blatantly. I ignored him for whatever was left of our meeting and focused instead on the much pleasant and acceptable Mummy Gupta, who was now quizzing me on what had kept me so happy at Bytesphere to have me stick around for three years and more.

'Oh, I appeared for a lot of interviews at regular intervals.

Just that I got rejected by half of them and the other half never responded with what they thought of me after the interviews,' is what I should have really said. Instead, I said that a farmer was more likely to dig a water trench by slogging his axe over one spot of barren land than swing it blindly over a million barren spots. And a thoroughbred, diligent professional played by the same rule. I thought I saw a twinkle of nervous but unpretentious attraction in Mehek's eyes on hearing my answer. I reciprocated with a light, playful wink which I guess her father came to notice with disdain. Not that I cared.

'Mehek, why didn't you ask Sameer to join us for lunch?' He suddenly brought up the dreaded topic, surely only to make me feel miserable and uncomfortable. Why, I dare say that was most inappropriate, boorish and asocial of him, singing Sameer Kashyap's paeans right in front of me—their host for the day! Is this the kind of etiquette they were taught at the academy?

'What a remarkable young man!' he spoke of Sameer as though the latter had made headlines by discovering some life-saving drug off the bark of the trees in the Savannas. Fine, he was an MBA and he liked to tom-tom about it whenever he got a chance. Big shit, man.

'He is just twenty-six, Mehek!' chuckled Mummy Gupta this time, inviting a plain nod from the daughter. 'And my, has he travelled the world already!'

'A true statesman,' nodded Police Papa appreciatively.

Seriously? A true statesman because he had travelled the world? Why, our office runner once won a free trip to Italy on answering some questions about the FIFA World Cup. When would the older Indian generation get over this entire aura of their children travelling abroad, and that too on Daddy-sponsored extravagant holidays?

'I hear he has worked with Audi in Germany for two years?' Mehek looked at her father, who nodded heartily, thus sealing the case in favour of the brat.

Fine. So he was a statesman of his own accord. Whatever. I still had the invaluable patriotism card to play. I sat quietly and absorbed the entire conversation, waiting for my turn to cast an indelible impact on their minds with few words and much substance. Sure enough, in no time the parents, awestruck by the wonders of the West, asked me if my work ever took me to foreign shores.

'Yeah, there was this one time I almost got to go to London after licking my manager's ass for eternity. But then I was sent back from the airport with reasons of budget constraints being cited to me. The truth was my manager discovered I had been badmouthing him and he got vindictive. The entire episode only went to prove I had trouble keeping my foot out of my mouth. I was someone who even now continues to remain desperate to get onto an international assignment. But either I have run out of luck or my company really thinks I am not worth it,' is what I should have said.

Instead, I spoke about the need for qualified and determined youngsters to stay put in India and liberate their own country from the stigma of being a nation riddled with corruption, underdevelopment and poverty. I felt encouraged when I saw through a quick sideward glance the old man's approving nod. So I further ranted about our insensitivity towards our fellowmen's socio-economic progress and our own internal battles even as our uniformed brethren stood guarding our borders against external demons at the peril of our lives. A hundred bugles and a ten-rifle salute were playing somewhere in my mind now. I was so overcome by emotions I was almost ready to cry. Also, in my mind somewhere, I was regretting the day I *almost* boarded a flight to London and then never made it. I still had to get even with Chirayu for that trauma.

I swiftly brought my emotions in check and my attention back to this monologue that was reaching a fine crescendo. I had my audience in binds. Heartfelt applause was in the offing. Totally pepped by the glint in Mehek's eyes as I spoke, I let my tongue completely loose and went on to speak about how Gandhi became a Mahatma not for practicing at the bar in South Africa but for sporting a loin cloth and campaigning for his own people across the length and breadth of India.

'There is a Mahatma in each one of us!' I slammed my palm on the table so hard a gulab jamun jumped out of Mummy Gupta's spoon placed mid-air and dived straight into Papa Gupta's glass of water.

Unable to speak any more out of a combined effect of excitement and embarrassment, I sealed my opinion by saying that while escapists flee this country to seek better pastures aplenty, there are few patriots like me who will stay grounded right here and take the challenges we all face to task.

'And this was not quoted by Hemingway!' I winked to bring some composure back into the tense atmosphere.

A few minutes passed, partly because the Guptas were supremely stunned by my oratory skills and my patriotism, and partly because the steward took a good deal of time to comprehend how that gulab jamun had managed to stay afloat on water.

'Humbug,' was the first word that escaped Papa Gupta's mouth in response to my heartfelt speech. He said it was ludicrous to equate leveraging lucrative opportunities with escapism, and propounded his own long theory of the need to imbibe the pros of foreign cultures and to migrate them to our own.

'And what patriotism are you talking about?' he added bitterly. 'Patriotism in India has been reduced to a bloody fable. We'd rather each be on our own and fend for whatever best we can.'

He proceeded to vociferously state that illustrious, educated and ambitious young men like Sameer had learnt such invaluable lessons in life by exploring the world that no textbook could otherwise offer to a run-of-the-mill, ordinary business school graduate (read me, obviously).

What was this man's problem in life? Like his only purpose was to counter every damn thing I said. I had so had it with him.

The bill arrived after half an hour, by which time this man had nearly killed me with his scathing and distasteful speech about the appalling rise in mediocrity of thinking on part of the country's youngsters. When the steward presented the bill to me, which I need not mention was of an astronomical amount, Papa Gupta did not so much as *offer* to pay. Instead, when Mummy Gupta gestured to him to snatch the bill from my hands, he simply offered a vacant stare at me and at the bill alternately.

'Not at all,' I insisted, smiling at Mummy Gupta. 'This is on me.'

I slipped in the corporate credit card offered by Bytesphere, which was returned to me within seconds, claiming that the transaction had been declined. I instantly hid my discomfiture by laughing heartily and telling Mehek our settlements team at Bytesphere really needed to learn a lesson or two in managing our corporate card accounts. Papaji who was getting impatient by the minute began fumbling for a wad of cash in his pocket, but I brushed him aside with a slight gesture.

'Won't take more than a minute to get resolved,' I assured

them and dialled the corporate card helpline which took nearly five minutes to finally get answered.

After struggling with the customer service representative forever in getting my details on to his system, he regretfully informed me that my corporate card had been placed under suspension for non-payment of six hundred and thirty rupees by the company's settlements team. A fusion of anger, frustration and shame flowed through my veins and arteries. I peeped into my half-open wallet and saw I did not have sufficient cash to even tip the valet outside. Meanwhile, the steward, shuffling impatiently across his feet, had asked me, 'May I help you, Sir?' so many times I almost felt tempted to ask him to help me by forgoing the bill altogether and letting me run away.

I looked helplessly at Mehek and her parents in turn. 'I... could get some cash from a nearby ATM,' I muttered.

Mehek looked at me blankly. I felt sorely guilty for having disappointed her. This was most unacceptable, and I made a note to take this reimbursement menace up on the company's bulletin board whenever time permitted.

'Don't worry about it,' Police Papa muttered, slamming some cash onto the bill and passing it to the steward. 'Shit happens—figuratively and literally!'

Saying so, he burst into another bout of laughter. I don't know where he had imbibed this old-fashioned and unfunny sense of humour from, but it was past my tolerance now. I smiled back nonetheless and whispered to a bemused Mehek that was a very funny joke her father and I had shared and laughed over in the men's room. Once out of the restaurant, I offered to drop them back home, but her father said they had a car and would manage fine. I thought he was still upset about having paid that bill. Or maybe it was just him. But his sullen red face looked like he brought the summers to Bombay.

I thought of something friendly and rather informal as a parting note, because bowing down and touching their feet would sort of make my intentions a little more than obvious.

'Thanks for the lunch, old man,' is what I finally managed to say with a pat on the old man's back.

He started a little on hearing the unexpected remark. Mummy Gupta cast me a horrified look, like a holocaust was drawing close. Mehek simply stared at the traffic passing by and pretended she hadn't heard a word.

'Mehek, what are we waiting for?' he demanded irritably when he had no repartee to spare in my honour. 'Call the driver so we can get going, won't you?'

I opened the rear door of the car to let Mummy Gupta in. 'Hope to meet you again soon,' I smiled.

'Oh wow, buddy!' Police Papa grumbled softly with the weirdest smile I have ever seen, as the car roared to a start.

As a cloud of dust kicked up by the car smothered me, I wondered what that cryptic, anti-climactic comment by Mr Eccentric Gupta really meant. *Oh wow, buddy!* Weird. Very weird. As weird as the man himself.

Months later, Mehek confessed what he had actually said was, 'Over my dead body.'

# 7.

# Cascaded Knowledge Percolation

Two expensive suitcases and a Benetton airbag lay unattended in my cubicle the following week. Somewhere in the passage, I heard a loud Punjabi voice complain to some relative about a prominent taste of salt in the drinking water provided in the office. As the voice drew closer, I saw a slightly stocky, somewhat handsome and a definitely loud fellow yelling his lungs out over the phone.

'How many times must you repeat yourself?' he spoke with evident irritation. 'Now stop crying foul over it...no, I won't... yes, I will...no, I am not being a kid, you are being a kid...now get back to work, ok...yes, love you too, Dad.'

He hung up and walked over to me with a broad smile. His hair looked like he had been held by the ankles and dipped in a puddle of Brylcreem.

'Dude, you must be Nakul?' he extended his hand. 'Akshat Mehra. Nice to meet you.'

I couldn't help but wince a little on being called 'dude'. I had two good reasons. One, this Akshat Mehra guy was supposed to be my subordinate. And while as a future senior consultant and eventually as a business partner with Bytesphere, I would always deploy a friendly, open-door policy with my resources, I expected a basic deal of formality here. Backslapping buddies in no way could give me the feeling of self-importance I expected to get out of the coveted position of a project manager, which would be disastrous for my motivation as an employee aspiring to move up the corporate ladder. Secondly, he pronounced 'dude' as 'dyood'. If words could kill, this was what the phrase would really mean.

'Did you just drive down from the airport?' I looked enquiringly at his luggage.

'No, I went to the guest house first,' he said. 'But I got there and saw the HR has fucked up big time.'

His voice was too loud already. On top of it, he was swearing. And on top of it, he was swearing at the HR. He had no idea what he could land himself into. I pulled him to a corner and asked him to calm the fuck down, not in as many words. He said he was promised a room in the company's Mumbai guesthouse, but the administrators at the guest house told him they had received no notification from the HR and that the rooms were fully booked in any case. I told him it was unfair to have undue expectations from the HR; I would try investigating this matter myself.

'I am going to be out most of the day,' I told him. 'So let me have my colleagues familiarize you with the office as well as with the project, and I will be with you once again in the evening.'

I took him to the conference room that had been booked for our project. Apparently, the morning call with the client had just ended, seemingly on a good note—because I saw Radha smiling broadly like never before. Mehek told me later they were smiling because the call for the day had actually got cancelled because the team at Lex had run into another emergency meeting, and Jerry had only called in to apologize and reschedule to the next day.

I introduced Akshat to Radha, who nodded at him with a faint smile and whispered to Mehek with a giggle. 'So white!'

Thankfully Akshat did not hear any of it as he had already launched into a hefty introduction of himself, followed by how he proposed to personally tackle the requirements of the project. Every time I thought he was done and I would be about to excuse myself, he would pop up a question: 'Say what?' and proceed with further gusto. It was only when the monthly alarm for the fire evacuation drill went off thirty minutes later that we got a recess. Down in the drill area, I told Mehek we were running late to get to the institute where we hoped to pick at least one of our final candidates for the team from. Radha, who was still not friendly with me, turned to Mehek and asked her if she could consider herself free for the day. Considering it was high time I won her faith, I intervened on behalf of Mehek and said that was hardly an option because she was the pillar the success of our project hinged on, and that she should not even think of going home without scripting the tests allocated to her for the day. Diplomacy works like magic. In less than a second, Radha transformed from a state of boredom to unfettered enthusiasm, and assured me she would attend not only to her own allocation for the day but would also go the extra mile and try scripting some tests allocated to me. I smiled and assured her that her teamwork skills were to take her a long way ahead, just as they had taken me.

'You sounded a little like Chirayu back there,' said Mehek when we got into our company's cab to the institute.

'As garrulous?' I cocked a brow.

'As pompous and slimy,' she retorted. 'To ask your juniors to do your work!'

'This is work too!' I gestured towards the road, indicating I wasn't taking her for a picnic. 'And isn't this how we all grow? Take up work from our seniors and walk the rope upwards.'

She laughed and looked out of the window. 'You would know. You are the senior guy here.'

'Oh come on,' I prodded her. 'It's not like I am taking advantage of my position. I will reward her for the extra work.'

'And how exactly will you do that?' she tested me.

I paused for a minute, and then said, 'I don't know!'

We laughed. I can't stop raving about how gorgeous this girl looked when she laughed. It felt like a one-stop solution to all my problems ranging from my car loan to my pending payments lying with the settlements team. Oh drat, I had almost forgotten about that. My recurring woes with the settlements team...but before that, there was also this guest house issue I had promised Akshat I would sort out.

I called someone from HR—not Parul this time, for I didn't want to let Mehek know there was someone else I went weak in the knees while speaking to—and quizzed her about this entire guest house fiasco. She said her team was only responsible for recruitments but not for relocation formalities of the new recruit. She asked me to contact someone from the relocation department. I gasped and asked in disbelief if there was indeed a separate department for every policy that a normally behaving company would include in a single function.

'Yes, almost,' she said matter-of-factly, and hung up. Must have been busy selecting a Baisakhi greeting card to send to the entire organization the coming Friday, I grunted to myself. I called her back and asked her to at least give me some contact in the relocation department I could speak to on the issue. She gave me the number and in the same breath added that I could always look up numbers by departments on the company portal as the portal had been planned by the HR keeping in mind a very employee-friendly interface. So much footage for a simple number I had asked for. HR will be HR.

I called the contact at the relocation department and asked her what had really gone wrong with Akshat's stay arrangement. She checked her system and said nothing was wrong at all, and that Akshat's guest house had already been booked in Koramangala a week earlier. Koramangala Bengaluru. Bytesphere. Akshat Mehra was to join the Mumbai office, and they booked his guest house in Bengaluru. I was at a loss for words. I explained to her the guy needed a room in Mumbai and he needed it immediately because he had landed in the city with bag and baggage expecting basic level of efficiency in the company's processes to help him settle in. She insisted I should have specified earlier the room was needed in Mumbai and that all rooms in the Mumbai guest house were now booked. I gave up and asked her to put him in a company approved hotel in that case. She said a hotel arrangement would require an exception approval from the finance head of Bytesphere.

'Fine, so can you please talk to the finance head?' I requested her.

'Akshat will have to write to him,' she said.

'He doesn't have a laptop yet,' I explained. 'Not so much as an email account either.'

'Ask his resource manager to send an email to the finance head,' she suggested.

'It's his first day in the company,' I said. 'His resource manager gets assigned only in a week.'

'Tricky situation,' she pondered. 'Let me check with my senior and call you back.'

I agreed and slumped back in the car, tired for the day already. The company's rigid policies and processes were a good reason for me to try out my society secretary's Ayurvedic potions some day.

I looked out of the window. 'How far are we? I feel we haven't left office yet.'

These drives across the city almost always made me feel I was lost in a time warp. The driver came up with his standard response which could never be of much help.

'Depends on the traffic,' he replied.

'We might have to return empty handed in that case,' I grumbled.

'What does that mean?' asked Mehek.

'We are picking up the leftovers from the institute,' I explained wryly. 'It's their last day of placements, and from what Parul told me, there are all of eighteen students still waiting to get placed.'

Three more students had got placed by the time we reached the institute. But we were accorded a grand welcome nonetheless by a representative of the students' council, who kept telling us through various expressions that it was a privilege for the institute to have a prestigious company as ours visit them to pick one of the last few students of their batch. He led us to an executive cabin next to the staff room and asked us if we'd like any refreshments. I asked him if I could get a chicken sandwich and lemonade, while Mehek made do with whatever they had to offer. They regrettably informed me they did not have chicken sandwiches with them, but enthusiastically added they would arrange for one at any cost. I first thought of going with whatever they had in the cafeteria, but then I decided having someone—after all—scout for something for *me* would do my ego a world of wonders. So I told them I was very much in a mood to dig my fangs into a chicken sandwich, specifically.

'Only if it isn't too much trouble,' I added casually, to which they said it would only be a pleasure. Three boys ran down the stairs to arrange for a chicken sandwich.

I winked at Mehek. 'It's fun to make a statement sometimes!'

'Like I said,' replied Mehek, 'you are beginning to turn into a Chirayu.'

Before we could plunge into another round of argument on the matter, the core members of the council began prancing all around us, pleading with us to participate more actively in their placement processes henceforth because the Bytesphere brand had major aspiration value in the minds of all students. I asked them if they were serious when they said that. No, I mean, what abysmally low aspirations students were setting for themselves! This was shocking. I subtly told them they all needed to expand their horizons if they really wanted to make good of their lives, but they were free to invite me for friendly, inspirational interactions whenever they liked.

Mehek handed out copies of a short test we had prepared for the interested candidates, which would act as a qualifier. I had let Mehek prepare these technical questions the other day, and when she had sent them to me for review, I found, to my dismay, that I knew the answer to only one of those questions. But I anyway told her that was a brilliant effort on her part and those questions would work just right for those poor unsuspecting students. Personally, I did not expect any of those fifteen fledglings to be able to take a shot at most of those questions. I had anyway carefully Googled the answers to those questions the other day itself, so I was waddling in very safe waters.

'A fairly easy test,' I explained to the girl who was to carry the test papers to the candidates holed up in the adjacent room. 'Just make sure they don't have access to the internet in there.'

Meanwhile, Professor Basu from the IT department was ushered into our cabin because he had been looking forward to meeting us and making small talk about the future of software consulting in Asia. I got chatty with this extremely well-informed and incredibly talkative professor even as Mehek walked over to the adjacent hall to oversee the examination being taken by the candidates. I much liked talking to Professor Basu. I liked people who knew their subject as well as I did. Basu told me that the IT sector was still in its sunrise phase with new platforms changing the way clients looked at their ERP solutions.

'The propensity of clients seeking open source software as their solutions has increased from a cumulative aggregate growth rate of seven per cent in the first half of the decade to a staggering twelve per cent growth rate in the second half of the decade,' he said passionately.

I nodded with equal passion and said I had indeed read that piece of information in the cover story of the latest edition of the *Geek Peek* magazine. He thought for a minute and then said he had not read any such article; these statistics were only a result of his educated guess resulting from his years of experience in the industry. I chuckled and complimented him for his precision in analysis. Buoyed by this sudden discovery of his surreal abilities, he went on to opine that with increased budgets for e-governance across verticals, he saw Open ERP as the new vista for software companies that would redefine the way vendors conducted businesses with their clients.

By now, this man had begun to give me a very severe headache. His words hit me like a tornado. I reconstructed them into a smaller sentence in my head, assimilated whatever he said each time, and simply replied, 'I completely agree.'

After every few minutes, I reciprocated with some of my unique gems of knowledge—such that new platforms like Open ERP and Cloud were inevitable for businesses of all sizes, and that embracing new technology was all about doing the right thing at the right place at the right time. The students from the council overhearing our conversation in the cabin nodded at me appreciatively. One of the more determined students pulled out a notepad and scribbled whatever I had said before smiling warmly at me.

Basu's hunger for exchanging information hadn't subsided, though. He looked like he was about to ask me to elaborate on my last sentence when Mehek walked in mercifully with the answer papers of the candidates. I told Basu that it was an incredible experience talking to him but we would need a recess to evaluate the candidates' performances.

'You remind me of my younger days,' Basu shook hands while taking leave of me. 'I have also always been just as passionate about IT as a subject. I saw that depth and zeal in you.'

He asked for my number which I provided reluctantly. My worst fears came true much later when he started flooding my phone with messages alternating between inspirational quotes in the morning and blonde jokes every night.

Mehek brought our attention to the interview process once Basu had left the cabin. The students were eager to know how we wanted to proceed with the interviews.

'Fifteen students took the test,' said Mehek, holding up the papers. 'Most of them haven't got more than three answers right. But there is this one guy—Dharmesh Desai, I think is the name—yes, it is—this guy has delivered an incredible performance.'

She handed me his paper. The students of the council peered over our shoulders inquisitively. Dharmesh had scored an ace! Not only were all his twenty answers correct, he had had the time to write the logical rationale beneath each of his answers. It was guys like him who gave me a complex. Despite all the truth Basu had just spoken about my charisma and my passion for the field, I would only be forthright in admitting I did not know peanuts about how this Aryabhatta type of student had managed to crack this test. I handed the paper back to Mehek, nervousness all inside me and contentment with the boy's brilliance on the outside.

'Look, Nakul!' exclaimed Mehek excitedly, thrusting the paper up my nose once again. 'Look how he has applied the Laplace equation to this caselet on digital communication!'

I wanted to ask her what a caselet on digital communication was doing in an assessment of a potential software tester in the first place. But Mehek had designed the test, and she was always right.

'Groovy!' I nodded tersely but added that theoretical proficiency was only one aspect of an individual's professional abilities. What I intended to judge through my experience as a team leader was how skilled the candidate was likely to be on the job.

'We will go with just this one interview,' Mehek told the council, glancing dismally at the remaining answer sheets.

As we proceeded to leave the cabin for the interview room, one of the students from the council came scurrying behind me. He said he was super impressed with my view on the right time for companies to embrace Cloud Computing as a technology, and asked me if I maintained a blog on such scintillating subjects. I said I didn't have a blog but I talked a lot about such things whenever I got a chance because it all ran in my blood. He asked me if he could get my number or an email address where he could send me a few queries he had on design principles in service oriented architecture. I assured him that would not be needed and that he should instead just watch out for my blog, as I would write something interesting about it very soon. And then I quickly darted out of the room.

Mehek and I waited a quarter of an hour for Dharmesh to grace the interview room with his presence. Our food was brought in during that time. The chicken sandwich tasted a little like cotton balls stuffed between two slices of stale bread. But I obviously appreciated the gesture of the students rather than crib about the quality of food like a self-indulgent black suited ass.

'We'd very much like to see the candidate now,' I reminded the council impatiently when we were done with lunch. The council apologized for the delay and looked at one another perplexed.

'He will be right with you, Sir,' they assured me repeatedly, but they were clearly trying to cover something up.

I excused myself and walked towards the loo, which smelled exactly like a loo in a government engineering college is supposed to smell. You don't need directions to a loo in a government engineering college. You just need to walk through a random alley and follow your nose to the nearest loo. You can hardly ever go wrong. Outside the loo, I saw a student sporting soda glasses. He seemed to be hyperventilating even as a smartly suited colleague, arguably from the council, patted his back to comfort him. The boy's thick glasses were now coated with translucent deposits of dried tears or sweat beads. The suited council chap was telling him to breathe deeply and chant the inspirational college anthem. When I returned to the interview room, I saw the same boy waiting outside, pacing up and down the alley.

'Dharmesh Desai?' I enquired of him.

He nodded with a faint, 'Yes'.

He tiptoed into the room and took his seat, avoiding Mehek's gaze even as he stuttered uncomfortably in his formal introduction to both of us. We complimented him on his incredible performance in the written test, which he acknowledged with a very subdued smile.

'Are you aware of the role you are being interviewed for?' I asked him.

He replied he didn't know anything about the role, but he knew a great deal about the company.

'Tell us about the company then,' I asked of him.

He spoke about the company like he was a Wikipedia bot. He knew *everything* about the company we had never bothered to know, such as why the company's founder Dayanand Lalwani decided to forgo his lucrative business in textiles and venture into software. He went on to discuss the company's latest annual report and told us the six per cent increase in the company's administrative costs was the main reason for the annual decline of two per cent in our net profit margin. At this stage of his quantitative analysis of Bytesphere's balance sheet, I was nearly convinced he was trying to fudge these figures. I quietly downloaded the company's annual report on my phone even as I pretended to listen to him further. To my utmost surprise, he was absolutely right. I should have trusted a Gujarati with his knack at spotting cost overheads and margin shrinkages. I quietly gestured to Mehek to change the question before he realized we were the ones who really needed to be asked how much we knew about Bytesphere.

She tested him on his ability to work in a team as new and unorganized as ours with a few hypothetical cases of client conflicts and how he would try resolving them. We didn't manage to find a single snag in his responses, except there was this constant nervousness and restraint we observed in his body language.

'That should hardly worry us I must think,' said Mehek as he waited outside the room following a conveniently short interview. 'He is a bright guy.'

'Yes, but he is not very communicative,' I mused. 'I am not sure he'll be the best fit in a client-facing role.'

'He is the genius we need in saving our skin when we encounter problems with the application,' insisted Mehek. 'I can trust the rest of us to fumble a little with bugs and codes.'

After a brief debate, we made up our minds and summoned Dharmesh inside.

'Congratulations,' I shook his trembling hand. 'We are pleased to hire you.'

Once again, like a true blooded Gujarati, he asked me how much money he would be making. I told him a highly efficient and timely HR team would provide him with a very lucid dissection of the salary structure as soon as they got the time. I also added euphemistically that working at Bytesphere was all about making a fine professional out of yourself and about committing yourself to the service of your clients, and not so much about making money. A stream of tears flowed down the boy's face. He was now crying freely. For a moment I thought that was his way of expressing outrage at my idea of placing his salary expectations down there on the priority ladder. In fact, he began thanking us profusely—alternating between his words and his whimpers—for giving him the chance of his lifetime. Money was only circumstantial, he said. I told him he was on the right track because once in Bytesphere, money became circumstantial to everyone.

On our way out, we asked the council what was with Dharmesh's nervous disposition. They told us they didn't really know for sure because he was the most reticent and withdrawn colleague they had ever come across—the kind who abstained from attending all college festivals and was mostly seen in the college canteen eating his lunch alone in a corner, with a book or two in his hand.

'Group dynamics, group dynamics!' I hissed anxiously when we sat in the car. 'I hope we are making a fine team here.'

'As long as you lead from the front,' Mehek teased me with a pinch in my arm.

The woman from the relocation department called back with an apparent solution to Akshat's accommodation screw-up. She asked me to ask Akshat to write a letter of motivation to the finance head in order to get an approval to stay in a company-approved hotel. I asked her what on earth a letter of motivation was supposed to mean.

'A logical, convincing explanation on why he must get to stay in a hotel,' she explained coolly.

'Well, you guys messed up his guest house accommodation!' I yelled. 'That is motivation enough, isn't it?'

'Not good enough,' she went on in the same calm, flat tone. 'There is a template he needs to follow for the motivation letter. And it needs to be appended with a generic expense approval mail from his resource manager.'

'I already told you he doesn't have a resource manager!' I couldn't believe this conversation was taking place.

A long period of silence followed. She muted her phone

and consulted her colleagues before getting back on the line. 'Is he a new employee?'

'For the third time, I confirm—yes, he is,' I said, exasperated.

'In that case,' she said, 'he can mail us a scanned copy of his dated offer letter and a proof of his residence being in another city.'

'Won't that take awfully long?' I asked her. 'Moreover, I already told you he doesn't have his mail account set up yet. How do you expect him to send you all these details today? It is four in the evening already.'

'I can't help him there,' she replied bluntly.

'Alright, I'll have him book a hotel tonight,' I relented. 'He will mail everything across once he has his mail set up.'

She said she was afraid that wasn't possible because all approvals were required pre-accommodation and not post accommodation.

'Approvals post accommodation will get classified under exception approvals,' she explained. 'And those can take long to get resolved.'

'So what should he do now?' I asked her.

'Maybe he should just choose to stay in that guest house,' she suggested.

'The one booked in Bengaluru?' I mocked.

'Has he been booked a room in Bengaluru?' she asked, surprised.

I pretended I could not hear her any more and disconnected the call. I thought I had aged by about a year during this entire conversation.

When we returned to office, Radha had finished scripting her own tests as well as the ones allocated to Mehek and me. I checked her work—perfectly mechanical but accurate. Fancying my chances, I went overboard in my feedback on her work, saying I couldn't in a thousand lives have perfected the art of scripting test cases in such little time. She gloated with satisfaction and offered me a forgiving smile. She said she strongly believed in fostering team spirit and would only be glad to shoulder more responsibilities on the project as long as she could complete her daily work within respectable work hours—which meant six o' clock in the evening. I first waited for Mehek to walk out of the conference room towards the restroom. Then I turned to Radha and told her I was very happy to hear that and was willing to offer her fifty per cent of my daily allocations, because, as she would surely know, as a project manager, I had various other responsibilities to address—such as building client relationships and sustaining healthy team dynamics.

'Time is a project manager's biggest enemy,' I clucked my tongue.

Radha nodded sympathetically.

'Where is Akshat?' I asked her, looking around.

'Strange boy,' suggested Radha, frowning hard.

'Why?' I asked, surprised. 'What did he do?'

'Rude also,' she added. 'He speaks too loudly.'

I laughed. 'Oh come on, that's alright. We are all strange in our own ways!'

Her expression turned hostile once again.

I changed tack. 'Not all of us, of course. Where is he anyway?'

'Sleeping in the dormitory,' she replied before walking out of the room with her bag slung over her shoulders.

That was not the neatest start to his new job, I thought. Tucking into the dormitory bed without a believable explanation for the need to sleep was, really, living life on the Bytesphere edge. I stormed into the dormitory and woke him up as gently as I could. He sat up straight and had the audacity to offer me a seat on the same bed.

'I just got a little tired,' he smiled widely.

'Of what?' I asked him. 'You haven't begun anything yet.'

'I got a little tired of that Radha chick, dyood,' he said. 'She doesn't look like she wants a lot of fun in life.'

'I know she's a little quirky, but she works hard,' I told him. 'And that's what we are supposed to do here. I know, of course, you've had a lot of fun in the previous company.'

'Excuse me? Dyood?'

I winked at him. 'Don't get startled. You don't think I wouldn't really find out why you left your previous company, do you?'

He turned red. He picked up his blanket and cowered underneath. 'You didn't...'

'Yes, I did,' I laughed. 'I made a few enquiries. It turns out you had taken a liking to a certain website after work hours which your company didn't really appreciate. What was the name again—blue nights dot com? Now that is some fun alright.'

He clutched at my feet all of a sudden. 'Dyood, can we please keep this under wraps? I am a changed man now. I swear!'

'I will try to,' I promised him. 'But I am not very good at keeping secrets. Let's just say you are safe as long as you put your two hundred per cent at work.'

I also reminded him the use of the dormitory was monitored very strictly and that the management did not take kindly to employees who used it to while away working hours. 'I couldn't help much with your guest house issue,' I apologized a little later. 'I guess you can go ahead and book...'

'Oh never mind,' he interrupted me. 'I have got Daddy to book me a room at the Hilton till the time this mess gets cleared.'

'The Hilton?' I looked at him shocked. 'That is not a

company approved hotel.'

'No worries,' he said. 'Daddy will pay for it if the company doesn't.'

I looked at him in awe as he told me he had got an automatic upgrade to an executive suite as he was a long standing member of Hilton Honors, which would include a twenty-four hour pass to the hotel's spa and a fifty per cent discount on alcohol after nine in the evening. Smelling an opportunity, I told him I was hoping for a one-on-one mentorship discussion with him that very evening so that I could apprise him of everything about the project. I jumped out of my skin in excitement when he offered I could come over to his hotel and that we could discuss everything over a nice refreshing swim and dinner. After a few obligatory moments where I politely declined the offer saying it wouldn't be right for me to ruin his evening, he clarified we would split the bill for dinner and that the swimming pool was anyway free for use for him and his guests. I agreed and also added we could lounge around a bit at the bar later if our discussion went on a little longer than expected. He looked happy with the offer and said he really could use some interesting company for the evening.

'I will be there in a couple of hours,' I told him as I walked back towards my work station.

I scanned through my mails for the day and found to my pleasant surprise a rather encouraging mail from Jerry on the unexpected rate of progress we had shown so far in the test development phase of the project. He also added a postscript asking if I had managed to get in touch with Marlon Pacino yet. I deleted the last line and forwarded the rest of the mail to Chirayu expecting him to take note of the client's appreciation of my work. Instead, the self-centered scumbag sent a one-liner asking for the daily status report so he could decorate it and forward it to Anand. He also added I still needed to watch out for Lex Technologies—while we hadn't had to deal with them directly so far, it wouldn't be long before they would raise their hoods and start their dirty games of one-upmanship in some form or the other. Frankly, I felt Chirayu and Anand made a rather big deal of the Lex threat. I didn't think there was any trouble; they were going about their business, we were going about ours. These people in the senior management had a tendency to get their underwear in a bunch sometimes.

I joined Akshat at the Hilton's lavish swimming pool a couple of hours later. Once in that lustrous blue water, I forgot all about the one-on-one mentorship programme. We picked a basketball from the poolside and played a few spontaneously created water games which I am a little ill at ease to describe now. After we had waded around in the pool like two jolly buffaloes, Akshat surprised me by flashing a free extra pass to the spa, where we were spoilt silly by a gorgeous Chinese-looking masseuse with an incomprehensible name. For the sixty minutes that she went about poking my body with her masterful Reiki therapy, I swear I was transported from this mucky, scheming world to marshmallow candy land. In a purely platonic gesture, I suggested to Akshat he could ask her if she would like to join us for a drink later. Akshat replied he had already checked with her. She said she'd need to take a rain check that night but she promised to join him the next evening. Rich boys. Hmmpf.

Over dinner, Akshat suggested we get going with the mentorship discussion. I told him about the project, the client contacts, and everything else except the Marlon Pacino fiasco. He asked me if we'd get to travel to Melbourne, which I thought was very unlikely given the budget stinginess this account was prone to displaying. I also alerted him he would be spending a few good hours every day for the next week with Radha and Mehek as part of the *Cascaded Knowledge Percolation* approach I had planned for our entire team to get comfortable with its targets for the project.

'And for any problem whatsoever,' I added, crunching my teeth into a delicious piece of prawn, 'I am always there to help.'

We pigged on the buffet till we nearly dropped dead. Akshat outplayed me on the appetite scene clearly, though I could have done much better were it not for that uninspiring chicken sandwich I had at the institute earlier that afternoon. Akshat was so overwhelmed by my willingness to keep him company for dinner in this unfamiliar city that he insisted to foot the dinner bill all by himself. I had no chance against his doggedness, hence I quietly agreed.

We transgressed to discussing spiritualism at the bar. Akshat was an engaging talker. He even had a few European tourists at the bar in rapt attention as he explained to me how the zero sum game dates back to the time the Pandavas and Kauravas fought a futile battle to ultimately leave the kingdom they were fighting for ravaged and in tatters. He said it was high time multinational corporations began prioritizing social and environmental progress over competition with their rivals, or else every society was only going to find itself a part of a zero sum game.

The last thing I remember of that night was the bartender asking us very unenthusiastically if we'd like yet another round of scotch. The next morning, I woke up feeling like I was sleeping on a large, white cloud as opposed to the hard, thin mattress I had at my apartment. The room smelt uncharacteristically fragrant too. I faintly heard the sound of a shower being turned off somewhere beyond. I opened my eyes wide in shock to find myself in an unfamiliar room. Before I could gather my senses, Akshat walked out of the bath with a towel wrapped around his waist, his dense wet chest hair left mangled along his midriff.

'Morning, dyood,' he greeted me merrily. 'Would you like some juice?'

I flinched awkwardly. The bed was as soft as a cake and it took me like forever to clumsily crawl out of it. I can hardly explain my state of mind at that moment. Nothing of this sort had ever happened to me before and I had no idea how to face a near naked man in a hotel room, and more so if he were supposed to be my subordinate at work. He told me I had passed out after guzzling six glasses of alcohol and I was woken up by the hotel staff with some difficulty so I could be placed in a taxi. But apparently I revolted and demanded I be given the presidential suite of the hotel for the night. They tried using my corporate credit card, the transaction of which got thankfully declined. And I didn't have sufficient cash either.

'So I had to carry you up to my room,' explained Akshat. 'And boy, you slept like a baby!'

I crossed my arms over my knees and was about to bury my head in them, when Akshat sensed my discomfort and walked up to me.

'Relax, dyood,' he patted me on the shoulder. Presently he took off his towel to expose the tiniest trunks I may have seen on an adult male's body and began wiping the streamlets of water running down his face. 'There is nothing to feel shy about.'

I was not shy, I told him. I just wanted to get out of there so I could get to work and bring my life back to its predictable and boring normalcy. I also casually mentioned that while nothing that had happened the previous night was really worth feeling ashamed of, it would be utterly fantastic if he would keep his mouth shut about the entire episode. He assured me that what happened in the Hilton would stay in the Hilton as long as I erased his voyeuristic travails of the past from my memory. I asked him if he was blackmailing me. He replied blackmailing was a very subjective term and I could well think of it as part of his persuasive skills. I struck a deal reluctantly for the sake of harmony and positivism at the workplace.

He escorted me in his bathrobe to the hotel gates. As we crossed the reception, a young lady at the reception shot a long stare at me. I waved at her with a smile, but all I got in return was a tired grimace. Akshat told me I had vomited a little on her shoulder as she was trying to assist me towards the elevators the previous night.

I was disgusted with myself. I had hit a new low in life. I picked up pace and left the hotel, swearing never to come back again. In every sense of the phrase, there was no looking back now. I needed to find my purpose in life, that one inspiration. My raison d'etre.

# 8.

# In the Thick of Things

Hola, Australia!

Less than three weeks after that harrowing drunken episode at the Hilton, I discovered the key to my long lost happiness, lying hidden in a long, unending monologue by Jerry White. We were going to Australia!

It was Dharmesh's first week at work. We were all holed up in the conference room. Jerry's anxious voice boomed through the speakerphone as we listened on in rapt attention. Basically, the management at Oz-Mobil had been giving him some stick as the project was lagging behind schedule. After detailed analysis, it was concluded that both the Bytesphere and Lex teams needed to work in close conjunction, from the same location, to deliver quicker and better results. Which meant we would need to travel to Melbourne with immediate effect. We did not complain at all.

Of course, we understood very little of Jerry's angst. But deny as we might, the very prospect of travelling on an international assignment is like every IT chap's aphrodisiac. We were too excited to read any deeper into the insinuations of such a move, until Chirayu played spoilsport later that evening and told us to be very careful, as this was very likely a move suggested by those insecure Lex fellows in an effort to start exerting control over our activities once we got there. Personally, I thought he was being just plain paranoid. Or to some extent, even insanely jealous of the fact that I had led the team to some fabulously executed work that far and was now getting us deputed in Australia. I told him to take it easy, but he maintained we needed to be cautious. Despite all my resistance, he insisted he would send us a revised project strategy over a couple of emails, which we would need to adopt going forward to counter 'unforeseen circumstances' in the new work environment.

After keeping us guessing through the day on what this so-called revised strategy could possibly be, the lunatic emailed us a brand new status report titled SLUT: Strategic Labour Utilization Tracker, asking it to be refreshed and sent to him every four hours so he could keep a tab on what progress we made with every passing day thereon. I was tired of this man and his obsession with status reports. I shot back an email, asking him how in God's name was this report supposed to help us combat any likely hostility from Lex Technologies anyway. He took that entire evening to come up with an appropriate reply to my question, and the next morning he sent in a totally unrelated answer. He said the SLUT would be directed at a 'well driven rise in our utilization meter' and 'a cognizable upgrade on the client satisfaction index'.

The sudden dynamics in the project apart, the team was feeling completely overwhelmed by the look and size of the SLUT.

'Have you filled the SLUT today?' he would send us a one-liner every morning and ruin our peace of mind.

I calmed them down by narrating untrue but inspiring anecdotes from my past experience where the teams I worked with were faced with higher pressure situations, and I told them there was no need to freak out.

Later that afternoon, I freaked out myself when I was placed on a call with Pat and Mike, the design leads from Lex Technologies, for the first time. Apparently, they had called only to break ice and to tell us they looked forward to having us join them soon. But my sharp sense of observation saw through their shallowness when, during seemingly harmless banter, they started asking me to share all our documentation and test results with them. Like they were my fucking bosses! Chirayu was right after all. These guys didn't look like they were up to any good. I politely excused myself from the subject, stating Bytesphere confidentiality for almost everything they demanded. They weren't even exactly polite; they sounded the way my landlord did when his rents were overdue. I managed to end the call without acceding to any of their stated requests. But this was an ominous sign, which became more evident when they signed off saying they would talk to Jerry about a certain basic level of co-operation the two teams needed to expect of each other while working towards a common goal.

'With pleasure,' I said, making no effort to hide my sarcasm. Inwardly, of course, I was freaking out at the very thought of reporting to two separate teams in time to come. As if handling Jerry's eccentricities wasn't painful enough.

Or maybe, just maybe, I was overreacting. Barking dogs seldom bite, after all.

Once again, Chirayu reinforced my fear instead of trying to pacify me, by warning me that these two dogs were more likely to bite first and then bark in delight later. But as always, he added, he had the solution to all possible problems, and that I should go meet him in his cabin that afternoon.

An unknown visitor was seated with Chirayu when I went to visit the latter that afternoon. The guy was roughly my age, but enviably handsomer and better carved. I nodded at him briefly before turning to Chirayu.

'Be warned,' Chirayu said, once again. 'Those guys always get a little jumpy with us around. If they want you to share your documents and results with them, they are going to get them.'

I cribbed about these unexpected developments, saying it was plain ridiculous to expect us to share the progress of our work with Lex, when we already had Jerry and an entire management at Bytesphere breathing down our necks. On top of it all, we had Chirayu's SLUT to fill everyday.

'Calm down,' he said, motioning me to take a seat.

The visitor watched us in rapt attention as Chirayu asked me to sit back and first tell him my problem statement.

'We have little time to deliver,' I said. 'And so we can't have multiple teams to report to. It will only end up wasting our time.'

'That's not your problem statement,' he clucked his tongue in disgust. 'That is a consequence of the problem. What's the problem statement?'

I looked at him blankly, and then stood up. 'I think you want me to leave. I get the point.'

'No, no,' he pinned me back to the chair. 'I only want you to learn to tackle problems piece by piece, in a structured manner—like a consultant.'

The visitor in the room cast a sheepish smile at me. He looked for a second like he was going to prompt me with the problem statement, then he just reclined in his seat once again and enjoyed the proceedings.

Chirayu banged his palm on the table, almost knocking the visitor over. 'Your problem statement is that your resource to effort ratio is very poor!'

I looked at him irritably and asked him how this was any

different from what I had just said. He widened his hands beyond his girth indicatively. And then he gave me the most nonsensical solution to the problem statement. 'Start putting in extra hours.'

'That was very helpful,' I smirked, beginning to get up.

'You are welcome,' he said with the wave of a hand. 'And listen up, Nakul. I don't care how you manage the show. But the last thing we are going to want is Lex running its authority over us. It is the documents they are asking for today; tomorrow they might try and wrest control of the entire assignment. That's how they roll.'

'These warnings don't help my cause,' I complained. 'I need a solution.'

'Consultants provide solutions,' he said dismissively. 'Don't they?' he turned to the visitor, who nodded admiringly.

Then, he turned to me again. 'Do what it takes to ward them away. All I can tell you is if we lose control over this project at any stage, it's the management's axe and your neck, and whatever else.'

And what was he here for? Doling out motivational speeches on demand? Fucker. As though he had read my mind, he instantly added he was always around to provide lip service on suitable strategies worth considering at various stages of the project.

'And may I also add,' he continued, 'that I am well aware of the burden you are laden with. Which is why I went ahead and recruited the final member who will join your team. So much for complaining about resource shortages!'

He gestured towards the visitor, who had now stood up to shake hands with me. That was when I truly observed how sharp the man looked. He was hardly older than me, but I looked like the 'before' part of a Sandhi Sudha advertisement standing next to him. He wore the crispest business suit (which was kind of wannabe to be honest) that made no effort to conceal a perfectly carved body, and a jaw line so taut it could be used to cut stone.

'Sameer Kashyap,' he introduced himself with a sunshine smile.

A thunderbolt struck the conference room as we shook hands. A sharp streak of lighting cut right through the space between our pumped up bodies. A wild storm developed outside; we could hear the rustling of leaves and dust in the yonder. The gush of the wind caused the window panes and the door of the conference room to clang loudly against the walls. Our hair blew violently (not Chirayu's—he was nearly bald) as we contracted our eyes and examined each other sharply.

'Sameer Kashyap?' I asked after the storm had subsided and a deathly silence engulfed the room.

'A highly qualified and sharp consultant, I must say,' chimed Chirayu smugly in his seat. His heaviness had kept him unaffected by the tempest that had nearly brought the room down with all its fury.

Chirayu was lucky I didn't have a gun in my hand. Or a knife. Or a club. Or anything with which I could bonk him on his fat, mindless head and cause him to bleed to slow, torturous death. How dare he appoint some random guy to the project without my consent or approval? I was supposed to make my own team, right?

I looked at both of them, red with rage. I tried concealing my outrage but did ask Chirayu anyway what made him take this crucial step without batting an eyelid, especially when he wasn't involved directly in the project and had no fucking business to recruit the guy whose very existence on the face of this earth threatened to ruin my personal life? (Of course, the last few words of my question did not escape my parched mouth). Chirayu explained he had called for the profiles lying idle in our database and decided to informally speak to some of them, before he came across Sameer's profile that had been referred by Mehek barely a fortnight ago. He concluded Sameer was the ideal fitment that was missing in the team thus far.

Furthermore, as though this were all a part of a larger conspiracy to destroy me word by word, Chirayu began raving about Sameer's gamut of experience that began as an automotive engineer with Audi in Germany and continued in his excellent academic run at the Indian School of Business. Sameer immodestly looked at me and asked me if I was an MBA too.

'Which institute?' he asked me when I replied in the positive.

I smiled wryly and told him I would discuss unimportant trivia with him at leisure soon after I was done talking to Chirayu. Much rather than hearing out my reservation against this unannounced addition to the team, Chirayu went on to tell me Sameer would be the ideal balm to my woes of inability to manage my team, because he had the traits of a remarkable leader as well as a problem solver. I angrily clarified I was not 'unable' to manage a team and my managerial capabilities were all in the right place.

'All I meant is Sameer can share your responsibilities going forward,' said Chirayu. 'It only lessens your burden, doesn't it?'

Sameer stepped forward and shook hands with me again. 'Don't worry. I am here to help now.'

WHAT THE FUCK? I don't remember saying I needed help! And what made him think I was going to ask HIM for help even if I needed it? I WAS THE PROJECT MANAGER!

Chirayu disrupted the volley of rage that was ready to burst through the top of my head by suggesting I show Sameer around the office and introduce him to the rest of the team. Sameer agreed and said he hated staying out of work for long because he was intrinsically a very zealous, passionate professional always eager to get into the thick of things.

On my way out, I reminded Chirayu I was not done talking to him on this subject yet and would come back and meet him soon.

I showed Sameer around the office blocks, the apathetic cafeteria, and a library that had not been used by anyone other than the librarian and four enthu-cutlet employees who also always liked to stay in 'the thick of things'. He ran through the library like an excited child and picked a gigantic book titled *Progressive Statistical Analysis and Related Tools*. By the time I could finish reading the title, he had commented at least three times on what a wonderful book it was. He reckoned I surely must have read it during my MBA. I skirted the topic once, but he seemed keen to get an answer. So I told him our B-school did not believe in learning by rote from textbooks and almost all our MBA knowledge was imbibed through on-the-ground assignments (and also café soirees, bunked lectures, drunken dreams on the hostel terrace under starry skies—but I did not include these). Before he could get into a deeper comparison of our B-schools, I looked at my watch and said I had lost a good deal of time in unproductive banter. I walked him back towards our working bay, which must have been the longest and the most awkward walk of my life.

I was playing on slippery turf here. One opportunity for him to show everyone he was the boss here, and I would be more than likely to lose Mehek forever.

On our way up, I subtly reiterated my position in this

team by informing him of the vast and diverse experience I had earned in my career of over three years. He admired my body of work and then added in the same breath his experience spanned nearly five years and was studded with a black belt in the Six Sigma certification and a gazillion other certifications I had heard little of.

This guy meant business. He was here to destroy me.

My worst fears came true when I guided him into our working bay. As though she had smelt him from a distance, Mehek turned as we approached them. She saw Sameer and sprang out of her chair excitedly, landing directly in his unnecessarily muscular, almost artificial-looking arms. Whatever happened to the office code of conduct? I had last heard a handshake was the only way colleagues could greet each other. I could have exerted some muscle (of my position, not of my arms) and asked them to go easy on their display of excitement. It turned out Mehek was aware of Sameer's recruitment, but she did not know he was to join our team. I whispered to Mehek it was interesting to note she did not bother to tell me about the development, but I don't think she heard me because Sameer had caught her attention with details on how much love his parents had sent her. Their friendly chat continued for a good ten minutes even as the rest of the team looked on curiously. When I realized I couldn't take it anymore, I disrupted their reverie and summoned everyone to the conference room.

'We need someone to help Sameer get on speed with what we have done so far,' I began, and before I could finish speaking, Mehek had raised her hand, offering to volunteer. I immediately turned to Dharmesh and put him on the task of training Mr Kashyap.

'And for everyone in general,' I continued. 'Get your visas

ready on priority. We need to fly soon.'

I sat at my desk later that evening, moping over this unpleasant Sameer development, when Radha walked up to me and hurled another grenade at me.

'Cannot come to Australia,' she said, somewhat sadly. 'Cannot cross shores.'

'Why not?'

She explained through a lengthy dialogue it was in keeping with some religious tradition they followed back home, the essence of which was there was no way on earth her authoritarian father would allow her to travel out of India. I asked her if reasoning with him by way of a healthy debate was an option.

'Maybe, in the capacity of my manager,' she said hesitantly. 'But you never know with my father.'

Most unique situation, I mused. It would take a glib persuader to work his way around a circumstance of this accord. I told her I'd handle her father, and that she should initiate her visa request anyway. She said she didn't even have a passport. I sighed.

'Alright, I'll help you get one,' I sighed, horrified at the very thought of the time a passport application could take.

I returned home and slumped straight into bed. I just couldn't get my mind off Sameer. What sort of a dumbass graduates from the Indian School of Business and joins a company like Bytesphere, seriously? This had to be a ploy. There was no other explanation...

Suresh Shah arrived at my doorstep unannounced, telling me he had heard a lot about this internet page called Wikipedia. He wanted to know if he could have a page for himself built on the site. I told him I was too disoriented to entertain him, and would respond to his questions on a better day.

# 9.

# Brainwave

'Dharmesh, you are a divorcee????!!!!!' Akshat's voice boomed across the entire floor of the office. Everyone in the building stood up and took notice, eager to get a glimpse of a person called Dharmesh.

'But you are so young, dyood!' continued Akshat, blissfully unaware of the attention this discussion was getting, besides the obvious Surf whiteness on Dharmesh's hapless face. 'I wouldn't think a person your age was even married!'

The equation between Dharmesh and Akshat thereon would never be the same. All thanks to those visa application forms I had requested Akshat to collect from everyone so he could submit them to the travel desk. Unable to contain his curiosity, he began reading everyone's application forms before stumbling upon Dharmesh's secret. And then he began discussing it publicly despite prohibitive stares from all of us.

'It was just a harmless question!' defended Akshat, when he finally sensed this was not going to end up being a memorable discussion. Dharmesh took off his translucent soda glasses for the first time since we had seen him. We got to see his eyes for the first time—well, almost. His eyes were shut tight, and streams of tears escaped them and rolled down his face. He was shaking violently in his seat.

Akshat walked up to him and held him by the shoulder, 'It's alright, Dharmesh Bhai. Just let it out.'

Dharmesh let out a lengthy series of words none of us understood before storming off to the bathroom. Some Gujarati slander, I was sure. Overcome by guilt, Akshat tried to follow him to the bathroom but Sameer and I held him back and pinned him down to his seat.

'Get back to work, for heaven's sake,' I told them all before accompanying Sameer to attend to Dharmesh.

When we entered the bathroom, we saw Dharmesh talking to himself in the mirror. He had calmed down; his manner was somewhat composed now. His fists were tightly clenched and he refused to look at us until he had finished his ritual. Two minutes later, he turned to us and said he was in no mood to discuss his marital status any further. We comforted him and told him he didn't need to if he didn't want to. Then, after some time, when we had pacified him with some bit of effort, we prodded him to tell us more about his divorce.

Reluctantly, he told us his saga that started with the day he was born. We asked him to jump straight to the moment we were curious to know about. It turned out that since the day Dharmesh sprouted his first facial hair, his family had begun worrying sick about his future—his marital future, the profession was anyway decided; he was to be the heir to his father's business of selling pickles across Saurashtra. But he rebelled and decided to become an engineer instead. The day he entered his twenty-first year, his family and his extended family informed him they had started looking for decent, cultured girls for him. They would choose the girl themselves and let him know. When he tried to put forth an argument, he was told that children in the family were allowed to rebel only *once* in their lifetime, and he had had his chance already when he chose examining industrial valves over selling pickles. On his twenty-first birthday, while still struggling with switching circuits and control valves in college, Dharmesh was married off to a decent, cultured girl who never got enough of nagging him for his capacity to bore the living hell out of her. He pleaded with her to appreciate the fact that he was pursuing a degree that had carved ultimate bores out of even the finest youth in the country.

'"It is just a phase!," I kept telling her, but she wouldn't listen,' he rued.

Then, one day he came running home excitedly to tell her that despite all her seductive and shrewish efforts to distract him all along, he had topped his university exams once again with a staggering eighty five per cent. But all he found lying in his room was a note of farewell from his wife. It said she was never into the marriage, but had had to comply. And then, she had started dying a slow death thanks to his never-ending rendezvous with his academics and his weird robotic projects he used to work on behind the closed doors of his study.

'I always loved her,' he said coldly. Thankfully, he was not crying any more. 'But sometimes it is just not enough.'

'I know what you mean,' I said sympathetically, glancing slyly at Sameer. If I didn't set this man right soon, I would be turning into a Dharmesh Desai very soon.

I urged Dharmesh to ignore Akshat's loud mannerisms for behind that boisterous and uncouth boy was a compassionate person (who never minded inviting you to his hotel to indulge in excesses like free buffets and spa sessions). We swore to secrecy and promised Dharmesh his story would not leave the doors of that bathroom. But later that very afternoon, Akshat went back to Dharmesh and sympathized with him, saying that bitch of his wife was probably not worth him anyway. Needless to say, Dharmesh offered him another service of the choicest swear words in his collection and asked him never to speak to him again.

It leaves little to one's imagination as to how a team with such dynamics was likely to function. It would suffice to say we were like a hub that had its spokes all pointing in different directions. Akshat hated Radha, not only because they had had an exchange of words earlier but also because she spelt his name as *Akshath*. Dharmesh and Akshat had locked horns over the divorce episode. And I hadn't particularly taken a liking to Sameer. Also, the positive vibes between Sameer and Mehek never failed to distract me when I was at work. But more importantly, I felt concerned every time the fissures within the team would show during our interactions with the client and the Lex morons, as well as in the decreased efficiency our work output had begun to show. The pressure on the team had increased, and everyone was being forced to put in late hours. Before we knew it, we had started looking like the Indian cricket team during the 2007 World Cup in West Indies.

And then, later that week, Sameer chose to take matters in his own hands. For once, I was running late to work. And the rat chose that very day to run the rest of the team through a suggestion that could help ease our miserable lives. Not that there was anything wrong with the idea—it had stemmed from an ISB brain after all—but I would have very much liked to give my approval to him in person before he went and created a hero out of himself before the team.

There was nothing fantastic about his proposed approach, if you ask me. It could have occurred to me, for all you know, had I not been keeping insanely busy managing all these junior fellows. It struck his idle mind first, that's all. He suggested through a boring, indulgent presentation that going forward, we align our responsibilities with our respective core competencies in order to derive optimum results. At some point, someone in the team requested him to translate that suggestion into a language that normal human beings could understand. He said, for example, not all of us needed to attend those daily calls with the client, for they wasted a whole lot of time that could otherwise be used in working on our allocated tests. He recommended only the senior folk be present on the calls—in which he shrewdly included his own name apart from Mehek and mine. While Radha and Dharmesh could take up the bulk of the test allocation between themselves, Akshat would be left to manage the multitude of status reports that would need to be sent to various stakeholders every evening.

I had just walked into the room when I found Mehek marvelling at Sameer's brainwave, saying she could always trust him to come up with such an ingenious idea. I interrupted the discussion and immediately asked Sameer to send me an email with his proposed approach, so that I could conduct a due diligence on its feasibility before granting my approval—in the capacity of his manager—I subtly added.

Later at lunch, I told Mehek I thought it was pretty lame of someone to resort to a PowerPoint presentation in order to explain a solution as simplistic as what Sameer had run us through. The Indian School of Business hangover, maybe, I giggled to her. The joke did not go down well with her. Clearly, she was being drawn towards Sameer's suave but shallow charms. I told her I had noticed she had been drifting off focus at work ever since Sameer had joined us, and that we needed to talk offline about revisiting her professional goals for the year, maybe over a candlelight dinner or such. I don't know what ticked her off, but she got up abruptly and stormed off, muttering something about how I first needed to get my act together.

I needed to leave her alone for a while, I figured. Until she realized how wrong she had been.

Meanwhile, I decided to tackle Radha's unique problem by reasoning with her father through a mature, well thought out conversation. Through a brief introduction provided by Radha, I learnt Mr Murthy, an illustrious jeweller in Tamil Nadu, was a no-nonsense man who didn't like people who talked too much. I wondered why she needed to tell me so. Was there no end to slyness in this world?

'Just leave it to me, will you?' I motioned her to leave me alone.

I called Mr Murthy and gave a crisp, clear introduction of myself and the purpose of my call. I told him this embargo on Radha was very likely to jeopardize my very future in the company, and that I would be grateful if he could bend the rules this once—after all, this opportunity would also give his daughter an experience of her lifetime. I don't know what he made of my introductory pitch, but he started lashing out at me all of a sudden, demanding who I thought I was, offering to give his daughter an experience of her lifetime. It took me some time to convince him this was a strictly professional request, but he wouldn't relent. Finally, I resorted to the most trusted weapon in my arsenal: a tear-jerking discourse. I reminded Mr Murthy he had arrived in life as a reputed jeweller only because he chose to digress from his family's occupation of agriculture, and had dared to defy protocol.

'Wouldn't you grant your daughter that one chance?' I asked

him, my voice reaching an impactful upsurge.

Stunned silence followed. I thought he was overcome by emotion. Two minutes later, he quietly concluded the call with a simple, heartfelt approval. 'Fine, she can go.'

Say what!

I was convinced I had reached a stage in my career where convincing people about a certain point of view was hardly a challenge any more. Radha told me later her father had confessed he had agreed simply because he was fed up of listening to me go on and on over the phone in that melodramatic voice. Fine, I think the accomplishment of the goal was more important than the means of attaining it.

When Mehek got time off discussing her Delhi Public School memories with Sameer, she came to me to make good for her irresponsible behaviour. She admitted she had not made time lately for me, and that she would like to make it up to me very soon. Then she asked me why I had not initiated my own visa application already. I told her as team leader I felt obliged to first ensure everyone else was through with the formalities; as it is, I was well aware of the rigmarole and would need little time in getting my application approved.

# 10.

# Benetton

Horror of horrors! I was so ashamed, afraid and frustrated all at once.

After more than a week of actively leading the team's visa application efforts and other project management drives like fetching and relaying updates on the SLUT and other trackers, negotiating the budget for the project party, and calling various hotels to haggle over proposed costs of a team dinner, I finally got down to applying for my own visa. A day after I sent my passport to the travel desk with all requisite documents, I got a mail informing me that my passport had expired.

Fuck!

On one hand, I was very embarrassed, because everyone else in the team—barring Radha—already had their visas stamped and ready. What would they make of my carelessness? This was most shameful and unacceptable, given my reputation that usually suggested otherwise. On the other hand, Jerry White had been driving me nuts every morning with his calls to check if we were all on course in terms of our travel preparedness. I really thought he needed to learn to start taking life a little easy. The moron didn't even seem to understand the concept of time zone differences. I would wake up at six every morning and see a missed call from him, with a follow up message using a standard template:

Hey mate! We must talk. Call me please.

And so I would make calls to him from my personal mobile number every morning, none of which would ever last any less than thirty minutes. I was not even surprised I was never reimbursed for those personal calls—the reimbursement team would send a rejection note each time claiming these calls were made on weekdays and I could always have been present in the office to use my desk phone. Now you wouldn't expect them to delve into important details such as the odd times at which I made those calls, would you? The reimbursement team was never equipped to use logic.

But what upset me more were Jerry's burgeoning expectations (I once told him I was just short of donning Superman's cape and wearing my briefs over my trousers after all that I was doing for him—very uncharacteristic of an Aussie, but he didn't laugh at the joke) as well as his daily questions on how early we could get on a flight and get to Melbourne.

And now, this entire passport mess. I'd have to think of a solution quickly. Without letting the others know about the mess, of course.

So I went to office that morning and suggested we plan a phased mode of travel to Melbourne so as to ensure a twenty-four hour support system to the client even as we settled in there. That did not make the slightest sense, but I had no better explanation.

'Radha and I will stay back an extra week,' I explained. 'While the rest of you get there and begin working from the client's office. In the time you take to settle in, I will continue to spearhead the project off-site so there is no loss of time.'

As if I wasn't stressed out enough already, Chirayu announced

Sameer would serve as the stand-in project manager in Melbourne until I got there and took over from him. Which also meant that all team decisions would rest with Sameer during that time. I thought this was most inane a suggestion, but Chirayu could not get enough of Sameer's obsession with pretending to know it all, riding on the back of random graphs and reports no one except him usually understood.

Unable to contain his excitement, like a typical newbie straight out of B-school, Sameer got carried away with the announcement and summoned an immediate meeting with the entire team. He ordered me to attend it too! The cheek!

As expected, he had nothing to tell us in the meeting that we did not already know. Desperate effort to reinforce his position before all of us, clearly. I cut short his meeting, took him to a corner, and reminded him as politely as I could, that his glory was short-lived and I would be there soon to regain what was rightfully mine. And thus, he could go a little easy on all this self-created footage. What upset me more than him replacing me in the role was the calmness with which he always smiled at me. Like he was the good boy who would never care about why I was always so mad at him!

'Of course, buddy,' he comforted me with a light pat. 'Don't worry, I will have things in my control.'

In what better words was I supposed to tell him that was exactly what I did not want? Smug moron.

Anyway, I had a lot more to worry about before I worried about his smugness. Anand called on me that week, telling me for not the first time what the successful completion of this project meant to the company. He also subtly added, again, not for the first time, that my performance on the project would be monitored closely. I told him I would live up to the expectations of the management, just as I had during the project at Dhokli two years earlier.

'What project at Dhokli?' he asked, and then rolled his eyes. 'Was that you?'

I excused myself from his presence with utmost disappointment. Sometimes I thought he pretended not to recognize me only to show me down.

Getting the passport renewed was not as cumbersome as I had imagined it to be. And because Radha had her passport ready by then as well as her visa application filed, I simply picked up the template she had used and replaced it with my personal information. Hopefully, the wait would not be long.

Mr Murthy called me again to enquire about the travel and stay arrangements made for his daughter. I assured him of the best efforts being made to ensure his daughter stayed safe and snug. He sounded a little, or maybe a lot, concerned when he learnt his daughter would be flying alone with me while the rest of the group travelled a week earlier. He threw another volley of questions at me with a tone that reeked of suspicion about my intention. I promised him he had nothing to worry about and that Radha would stay safe with me. I don't know if I should have framed that sentence better, but he didn't sound happy at all. He told Radha he'd come meet her before she left.

ᔕ

We finally had a project party! I had never seen my team half as excited in all this time as they were when they heard the management had shown some mercy by allotting us some spare money to entertain ourselves for an evening.

Unfortunately, planning this evening had ended up taking slightly longer than the time it had taken me to understand the plot of *Inception*. I'd have been better off working on the SLUT and letting Akshat take over all the planning instead. I first booked us a bay in a pub at a thousand bucks a head, but Radha had her eyes popping out at the prospect of paying a thousand bucks for the alcohol she would not touch. I then got a reservation at Barbeques, but Dharmesh vetoed the idea of even stepping near a counter that served meat hanging by iron rods. And then, just to prove a flimsy point, Akshat rejected the idea of a banquet dinner because he was not willing to pay a penny extra for the Jain counter he wouldn't venture close to. Dharmesh and Akshat exchanged a few unfriendly words, after which I delegated the task to them with a specified budget so they could get their minds off their brewing hatred for each other. Akshat won the contest finally when he came up with the most unlikely group booking at a discotheque where every member would pay in line with what he consumed, with no cover charges involved.

'I have my contacts!' he beamed proudly. 'No one else could have worked out such a fancy deal.'

We scheduled the party for the evening before the team boarded its flight to Melbourne. We took the day off by mutual consent so we could unwind after having had our brains virtually chewed out by those oversmart Lex creeps who had been shamelessly pushing their proposed testing methodology to us so that both teams could 'stay on the same page' by the time we reached Melbourne.

The week before the project had hardly seen any real work done. Most of our time had been spent on inconsequential phone calls with Pat and Mike, who had also apparently taken charge of mentoring us with the systems and infrastructure at the client's office. Their strategy of gaining brownie points through such cheap tactics seemed to be working, because Jerry was clearly beginning to trust the Lex duo a bit too much for my comfort. Something told me they were up to some mischief which we didn't have a whiff of just yet.

The news of the party seemed to offer everyone some respite. In fact, that day could have turned out to be one of the best days I had seen in recent times. Mehek had called early that morning, insisting she wanted to spend some quality time with me before leaving for Melbourne. I loved this typical feminine trait of leading the guy on, then blowing his brains out by getting friendly with another guy who gave you an inferiority complex for every valid reason, and then squaring it all up with a tender smile and a beautiful promise. Total below-the-line seduction, I say.

As I didn't want to sound desperate right at the outset, I told her I'd check my schedule and get back to her in half an hour. In less than twenty minutes, she called me and said she had completely forgotten she needed to go shop for some urgent things to pack before her flight the next morning. Me and my tantrums. Fuck.

But, but! She added she would be free by that afternoon at the very latest, and asked me if I would fancy coming over to her place for a cup of coffee in the evening.

'We could leave for the party together later,' she offered.

Eat that, Sameer Kashyap! Oh alright, I'll admit I also felt just a tad bit sorry for Sameer, scoring over him like this, behind his back. But certain sacrifices were inevitable in the hot pursuit of love. So I chose to sacrifice my conscience and go ahead and accept the offer. To be honest, and you might believe me if you know what a drab youth I've had so far, I had never been invited by a girl for coffee at her place. I had heard coffee invitations usually opened up a world of possibilities. The very thought sent ripples across my large body. I could not wait until evening. Maybe some day in the future, I would meet Sameer somewhere and let him know there was nothing personal...

Super pumped after having talked to her early in the morning, I made my debut on the nearby jogging track and ran so much I swear I thought I had felt my abs soon after. By the time I returned home, I realized I had overworked myself. I felt like someone had folded me and thrown me into a washing machine. I felt dizzy, broken and almost certainly dead. Just then, I came across a newspaper advertisement of a killer discount in a suburban spa.

FROM FEELING LOW TO RAPID GLOW IN TWO HOURS! CALL NOW, read the advert.

Suitably impressed, I called them to sign up for a booking that noon. All I wanted was a basic massage to make me feel alive again. But they read out an entire array of therapies in their directory, none of which I understood. I explained I had a big evening coming up and I was looking and smelling like a wet, sick cat as I spoke to them. So it would be great if they could narrow down the options and give me a wholesome package that worked for me in the most basic form. They narrowed down to three options: The Midas Glow Therapy, The Ivory Touch, and Pearl Purity. The Ivory Touch sounded like the safest option, but only until I woke up later after the massage and stared at a shockingly white version of me in the mirror. They first said my skin would now glow like shining ivory for eternity. When I angrily demanded my old skin colour back, they said it would come back the moment I went home and took a shower. I found to my dismay I was also positively smelling of papaya for some reason. The loud-mouthed receptionist said it was part of The Ivory Touch therapy and I smelt and looked much greater than what I did before I had walked into their spa. I felt cheated, but the thought of spending a quiet, romantic evening with Mehek (finally!) kind of made up for it. When I returned home I saw the bastards had also made the hair on my forearms and eyebrows disappear, for all practical purposes. All that was left of them were a few random strands of bleached, golden hair here and there. Bloody cheats. The only positive outcome of this disastrous trip to the spa was probably that I looked a little like Shane Watson because of this complexion change.

I took a long nap during the day to recuperate from this recuperative therapy gone wrong. And then I spent more time in the shower than I had collectively spent all my life to try and get rid of that whiteness. I scrubbed the living hell out of the helpless soap bar on to my face. But when I stepped out, I saw I was maybe a little whiter than before, save for a few thin strips of whiteness that had peeled off my neck to reveal my contrastingly brown skin. It was like I had worn the Benetton poster on myself. I researched this queerest condition of a white face and a brown body on the internet. A forum recommended a cream, which I bought and applied all over me. I don't know what it was supposed to do, but that wretched fluid only stuck to my skin like fucking superfine Plaster of Paris. I scampered back into the shower and stepped out almost an hour later. Nothing much had changed, but I at least felt a little less itchy. The eyebrows looked like they had nearly gone missing, but I was too tired to do anything about it any more. I dressed to cover up as much of the mess as I could, and was just about to leave my house when I heard some extremely loud, angry voices from the floor above.

I went up to Suresh Shah's apartment and rang the bell. He opened the door and looked at me, confused.

'Yes?' He peered through his reading glasses.

I sighed and gave him my identity. He looked closely and then asked me if I had contracted jaundice or something.

'Just eating a lot of aloe these days,' I said. 'Is everything alright? I could hear you right down at my apartment, and you sounded a little...troubled?'

And then, he placed me in one of those thousand awkward moments I experience all the time—when I don't know how to react. He removed his glasses and began crying like a little baby.

'No one cares for me,' he bawled. 'Why must you? And what's wrong with your face by the way? That can't happen even if you eat an entire plant of aloe.'

I skipped the irrelevant details and asked him to settle down in a chair comfortably and tell me if there was anything I could help him with other than being made fun of.

'No, no, go away,' he kept repeating. 'Why must you bother?'

Presently I heard a loud, imploring voice emanating from the room inside. Suresh Shah refused to budge. He was now sobbing into his cushion. Curious, I gingerly walked into the other room and saw a woman's visibly disturbed face on his computer. His webcam was left on, and the woman at the other end hadn't tired of trying to call him back. I hesitated for a moment, and then presented myself before the camera.

The startled woman stopped calling out for Suresh and spoke to me. 'Who are you?'

'I am Suresh's neighbour,' I said. 'I just stopped by. I am sorry if...'

'IT boy!' she smiled for the first time. 'My father speaks often about you. I am Nandy.'

'Yes, IT boy,' I nodded unhappily. 'Is everything alright?'

'Come back!' shouted Suresh Shah from the other room. 'Shut that damned computer off and come back.'

'Wait,' Nandy stopped me. 'We must talk.'

'Your father is crying.'

'Oh, you see he is a little upset with me,' she said, and then paused for a second. 'Are you Caucasian, IT boy?'

'No, I am just a very uncharacteristically fair Indian,' I said, hoping to get to the crux of the matter. I looked at my watch. I was running late already. Mehek must have been waiting for me.

'I had promised Dad I'd visit him this spring,' she said. 'But you know, things are always difficult here, with my husband touring around and this little kid dancing on my head...'

Just then, a young boy of about three sprang into his mother's lap from nowhere and made a very monkey like face before the camera. I waved at him. He looked much like Suresh, only more beautiful thankfully. Nandy explained this was the third time in succession she had had to cancel her plan of visiting her father after having promised him otherwise. And ever since her mother passed away, her father was getting crankier on schedule, and very obstinate at that. I nodded in agreement and told her I had seen mild traits of his behaviour earlier, but he was a nice man otherwise.

'He tells me you care a lot,' she surprised me with her words. I hadn't seen that coming. 'I have a favour to ask of you. I know he won't talk to me right now. But please see to it he doesn't feel too lonely, won't you?'

'Give it up, IT boy!' cried Suresh once again from the living room. 'Let her go bake her pancakes or go barbequing with her American friends or whatever. I have nothing to say to her!'

By now, Nandy had also begun crying just as systematically

and violently. Here I was, with the daunting task of consoling two strangers I had nothing to do with even by the widest stretch of imagination. Poor Mehek. She must be so disappointed in me. And all those coffee plans and the exciting possibility of what could have followed... Why did I get into this muck? I should never have come to check on Suresh Shah. Now that I was here, though, I would have been a total villain to walk out on him in his moment of anguish.

'I think you must go spend time with him,' Nandy instructed me, holding back her tears.

This was brilliant. First cancel your own visit, and then ask your neighbour to do some damage control. She asked me to note her number, so I could keep her posted on the progress her father's mood made over the next week or so. As if this was all I was left to do!

I signed off the chat anyway and returned to the living room, where Suresh Shah was now slouched in his sofa, staring vacantly out of the window. He had stopped crying, but his face still looked turbulent enough to erupt into another outburst.

'Leave me alone,' he muttered, refusing to look at me.

In that case, maybe I could still make it to Mehek's, I reckoned. And just then, he called me back.

'Or wait,' he raised his hand. 'Sit. I can talk now.'

B-L-O-O-D-Y. He had given me hope. And then he ran over it himself.

'You must be hungry,' he considered my face. 'You can get yourself some food from the kitchen. Nothing fancy—I just made some basic dal and chapattis.'

I told him that sounded exciting, but I'd pass. I also told him very firmly I had a social do to attend in almost no time, but he paid no heed to it.

'You youngsters,' he launched a vitriol. There, that was enough indication that coffee with Mehek would have to wait. By then, I had also got a message from Mehek telling me she had waited for me awhile and would now need to get ready for the party. She said Sameer would be coming to pick her up, and that they would leave for the venue after 'a quick cup of coffee'.

WHY DIDN'T THIS BLOODY BUILDING HAVE SOUNDPROOF CEILINGS? WHY DID SURESH SHAH HAVE TO SOB SO LOUDLY?

I comforted Suresh Shah anyway, telling him material problems spared no one—such as the one I had just been inflicted with over an SMS. Damn. He cried a little more and said it was easy for me to give a discourse because I did not know what loneliness meant. I advised him not to challenge an IT executive with vast experience in slogging his butt off on round-the-clock support projects on the loneliness quotient. We endorsed loneliness in its purest form. He fetched two thick, dust-coated albums from his attic and ran me through around one thousand old pictures of him with his once complete family, by which time some really terrifying visuals of Sameer drinking coffee in Mehek's living room had started haunting me. I tried humouring him for a while by telling him why I had actually turned so white. He felt a little better after getting a chance to laugh at me, but then he pushed it too far by asking if he could sweep a little white off my face to cover the seepage on his walls. After he had had his share of fun, I told him I really needed to reach the party or else I would be left with no food that night.

'There is always food at my place,' he grinned hospitably.

I said I hoped that need wouldn't arise, for I would not want to bother him late in the night for those chapattis. He thanked me for coming over and keeping him company yet again. I looked at his plain, honest face and almost felt sorry for him. I was just about to tell him I had a week before I flew out of the country and that we must dine together once before that—preferably somewhere out. Just then, he got totally emotional about me and said he was grateful at least I was around him whenever he needed someone to talk to or share his life, and his food with.

'Thanks for being there,' he came forward and hugged me. 'I know I can always count on you. Hopefully, I won't let you go.'

Once again, I was in that same awkward position of not knowing what to say in response. Hence I just smiled and took leave of him.

Skimming through Suresh's albums made me realize what a drastic change in sense of fashion the average Indian household had undergone over the last two decades. But more importantly, they gave me a snapshot of Suresh's current life: broken and desolate—the kind that should have made me feel remorseful about being remorseful about the more than decent state of affairs in my life. I had a job that kept me occupied, and I had my family and friends too, even if the friends only called when they needed to send me their CV for a job opening. In fact, age was on my side too—if I looked at it relative to Suresh Shah, that is. I should have felt ashamed of being such a wimp and should instead have had the courage to hold fate by its horns and turn it in my favour. Various 'Eye Of The Tiger'-ish songs began playing in my head as I confidently strode towards my car and drove to the party. I meditatively recalled the self-confidence building measures I had imbibed from various self-help books I used to read ahead of every engineering exam. All they ever asked us to do was to *think and believe* everything in our lives was nice and dandy. That's exactly what I did then. Sadly, the effect lasted only till I reached the discotheque and found Mehek and Sameer dancing merrily to the *Dirty Dancing* theme, oblivious to my arrival.

All those *You Can Achieve* books can go take a walk. How do you solve a problem of that kind? I plunged right back into depression in lesser than the running time of the *Rocky* soundtrack. Here I was in all my shining splendour with a face bright enough to light up the dark discotheque, and she didn't even notice me. I walked over sulkily to the bay where the rest of the team was seated, looking very disgruntled. They all sat a good distance from each other, looking in opposite directions and refusing to make eye contact.

Akshat came running to me as he saw me approach them from a distance.

'Dyood, I am upgrading my ticket to business class,' he said agitatedly. 'I don't think Dharmesh Bhai and I can pull along well over sixteen hours next to each other.'

'What's the matter?' I asked.

'He is the matter,' he said, loud enough for Dharmesh to hear him and come charging towards him.

'What is he saying about me?' demanded Dharmesh, pacing rapidly towards Akshat.

'I was just telling him we share excellent chemistry,' Akshat smirked even as he distanced himself a little from his adversary in anticipation of a fit of violence.

'Nakul, I can't work with Akshat,' complained Dharmesh. 'He has been poking fun at me for very long now. And he gets very personal each time.'

'I just asked him how it felt to be single again!' Akshat rolled his eyes like an innocent baby. 'I swear! How does that amount to poking fun? I was just trying to break some ice!'

'I will break your head if you talk about my wife again!' cried Dharmesh, lunging for Akshat's throat.

I threw myself between the two warring, mentally teenaged men to pull them away from each other, but only got knocked over a little myself.

'Easy, Einstein,' Akshat sputtered, holding his reddened throat. 'That is my throat, not a gyroscope in your fucking engineering lab! Nakul, I can't work with this lunatic either.'

Meanwhile, Sameer and Mehek had noticed the commotion and had come running to us while Radha continued to sit on the couch and watch the proceedings like an observant referee.

'What's the matter?' Mehek asked.

'Nothing at all,' I hissed bitterly. 'You guys carry on dancing. You were doing just great.'

I took Dharmesh and Akshat to a corner and asked them what their goddamn problem was and what had really inspired them to come to hate each other so much right when we were knee deep in a pile of shit with a lot left to do on the project. It turned out that there was nothing much apart from the two guys being like chalk and cheese in every possible respect. I attempted a motivational speech on team spirit and tried explaining Tuckman's Teamwork Model by nicely drawing the 'Team Relationship' versus 'Focus on Work' graph on a tissue I picked up from the bartender, but they ran down all my peacemaking efforts with systematic, well defined arguments against each other's ineptness. Dharmesh said Akshat was no good a team player anyway and he freeloaded on the rest of the team all the time. He said he was very unhappy about being allocated the chunk of the tests while Akshat got away by claiming to spend most of his time preparing various status reports which were actually automatically downloadable from the testing tool using appropriate filters. Akshat sarcastically offered to trade places with Dharmesh but was very confident Dharmesh would not know how to draft a sensible, coherently worded email to the stakeholders while sending out the status reports and would have to seek external help only to get his semantics right.

'You should probably stick to working on those colourful reports,' snarled Dharmesh. 'As it is, you don't know shit about code and testing.'

'Maybe,' bellowed Akshat. 'But I am awesome at the way I handle all the programme management and I don't need to know shit about code to do that. Do you know why? Because a programme manager needs to be a classy, smooth talker, and not some robot sitting and debugging repetitive code.'

I pulled Akshat closer and whispered, 'Dude, you are not exactly a programme manager.'

Akshat looked at me crestfallen. 'Dyood, I thought you and I were a team?'

I sighed. 'Alright you guys! Ease up now. Dharmesh, get on the dance floor.'

Akshat sniggered. 'I will just go check with the DJ if he has some *Banaskantha On Rap* kind of number.'

Dharmesh scowled. 'I don't dance. I am just going to go sit and get some food.'

I stared hard at Akshat.

'Good riddance,' he said, once Dharmesh had left. 'Come dyood, let us dance.'

'I don't feel like it,' I said, sulking as I watched Sameer hold Mehek by the waist and guide her on to a suave dance move I could not even imagine myself emulating. Bloody perfect acrobat in a corporate high-flier's garb.

'Why not?' asked Akshat.

'Because it is awfully hot,' I replied, dabbing my forehead with my handkerchief. The summer humidity was getting to me indeed.

Akshat frowned intensely, staring at my forehead. 'You are sweating,' he said. 'And why does your sweat look so white?'

I flicked a sweat bead on to my finger and examined it in dismay. 'Oh darn. It's a long story.'

Akshat swayed lightly along with the music in his position, staring intently at the dance floor. 'Dyood, Cinderella is being pursued by Prince Charming. Are you going to be content being the guy who drives the pumpkin coach?'

I pretended to not understand what he was arriving at, but Akshat was too smart to miss out on what people around him were up to—truly programme manager material. I said I did not want to disrupt the two minutes of ecstasy Prince Charming had claimed right to while making a futile attempt to woo Cinderella.

'Because she will ultimately go back home in the same pumpkin coach,' I winked.

'Don't be too sure,' he warned me. 'He's got a lead time over you in Melbourne. He will have a go at her.'

'A lead time of only a week,' I added assertively, or maybe self-reassuringly.

'That's more than enough for an early starter,' he quipped. 'Ask me about it, dyood. Your girl's going to go running into his trap.'

I was beginning to incline towards Dharmesh's view of Akshat's loud-mouthedness. I voted we talked about something else or even better—didn't talk at all for some time. Akshat shrugged and started trudging back slowly towards the couch, when I reconsidered his self-claimed facility with charms and called him back.

'So what do you reckon I do?' I asked.

He grinned widely on being given so much importance. 'Make her curious about your behaviour. Do something drastic— like get into a fight with the bartender, or something like that.'

I looked at the bartender, who looked like a harmless, docile Nepali migrant. I refuted that option as very lame and stupid.

'Maybe you should ignore her then,' he suggested. 'Or drive her crazy by showing her she isn't the only one you can drool over. She will come following you herself.'

Now, this idea, I did like. I had tested it earlier and I knew it worked, except of course my charms never lasted long enough for me to propound such theories so coolly, holding a margarita in my hand.

'I think I can pull that off,' I said, and then added, 'What do I do to show her there are others I can drool over?'

'Pick a girl who can dance with you here,' he said matter-of-factly. 'And then pretend to be totally into her. Simple!'

I looked around the room. 'Surely you are not suggesting I approach a stranger for a dance?'

'Maybe not,' he said, craning his neck. 'But then…'

Our sights collectively fell on Radha, still sitting in a corner of the bay, evidently bored out of her wits.

'Sorry,' grinned Akshat. 'Limited choices! But a man's got to do what a man's got to do.'

I glared at him.

'For Mehek!' he shrugged, but refused to stop grinning.

I saw some merit in his suggestion. Unfortunately, that is. Because a disaster of epic proportions was to follow soon after. We waited patiently by the bar for Mehek to finish her never-ending dance jig with Sameer. Akshat pushed me towards Radha when we saw Mehek approach us finally.

'Shall we dance?' Mehek asked me what I wished she had done earlier so I would not have had to do what I was going to do.

'Uh, probably not,' I shrugged dismissively and ambled over to Radha with a soft whistle.

I drew closer, looked Radha in the eye and softly whispered if she would like to join me for a dance. She looked completely stunned. And floored. I admit she hadn't seen this natural charmer in me before. Maybe she wasn't expecting it. She began trembling nervously even as I held her hand and guided her towards the dance floor. Shit, she was heavier than I had imagined. I thought I heard a snap in my shoulder when I tried tugging at her hand.

'No, no,' she shook her head and stuck her tongue out in futile protest. 'I can't dance.'

But I dragged her towards the dance floor nonetheless.

'I thought you didn't want to dance?' Mehek intercepted me, engulfed by a wave of fury. Score one for Akshatisms!

'I changed my mind,' I cooed softly into her ears.

'And where are your eyebrows?' she demanded, staring over my eyes.

'Humph!' I stepped aside and whisked Radha on to the dance floor.

I hollered to the DJ. 'Oye DJ! Play *Dirty Dancing*, no?'

Radha looked highly uninterested and was moving around in a manner that looked more like aggressive resistance than dance. It did not matter; Mehek looked crestfallen alright. A frustrated DJ played *Dirty Dancing* for probably the third time that evening. I held Radha's hands and initiated a standard set of dance moves I had learnt circa 1997 when our class had participated in a dance competition and had faced a humiliating defeat in the points table.

'No, no,' she kept repeating, but my attention was totally fixed on Mehek's face which was rapidly turning red. With each growing shade of red, I raised the tempo of the dance. Radha was a slow and reluctant learner, but was learning to at least tap her feet in tandem with my swift, sharp moves. I tugged at her hands one more time and pulled her closer to me, swirling her rapidly around her ample axes as the song reached a crescendo. I almost forgot about Mehek at one point of time; this dancing thing actually felt like fun. Radha was beginning to show some semblance of nervous excitement as well. We were just getting comfortable with our dance moves when we gyrated around the dance floor so hard we almost went off the stage, sending my head crashing into a very tall, dark, robust and very angry-looking object. The impact of collision was so severe I think I may have passed out for a few seconds. When I opened my eyes, Radha had left my side and was cowering behind a pillar, frightened. I looked up hazily at the body I had rammed into, and saw a dark, well-built elderly man with a thick, curved moustache towering over me angrily. I first thought he was a bouncer at the disc. Then I heard Radha nervously yell 'Appa! Appa!' and realized my reputation, and possibly my life, were in danger.

A series of outbursts followed. The DJ had changed the track to *Character Dheela* and was grinning very widely. I could not understand most of what the father-daughter duo were discussing. Also, I was feeling very faint.

'So this is your important project, ah?' was the only line from the father's mouth that I latched on to, apart from *Baadu* and *Thotti* which I think were directed at me.

After sufficiently gathering the attention of the entire club, the raging father led Radha out without giving up on the constant mumble. He didn't even offer to haul me up from the floor.

Akshat and Sameer came running to help me up on my feet. I was so dazed I could see a total of four of them.

'Are you alright, buddy?' asked Sameer with apparent concern. Bastard. If it weren't for him I wouldn't have gotten into the entire drama in the first place.

'What do I look like?' I asked, holding my head.

I got up and strained my eyes to look at Mehek. She was standing shocked, a few feet away. The jealousy had turned to disdain. But the disappointment still showed on her face. I opened my mouth to say something to her, and then passed out again.

# 11.

## Correct Rate, Boss!

All was well after all. The debauchery at the club the previous week had milder repercussions than I had imagined. There was a small hiccup when Mr Murthy arrived at the airport the following week, minutes before Radha and I were to check in with our bags. As rightly advised by Radha, I scurried into the airport premises, out of his sight. After briefly doing an Amrish Puri by threatening to take her back to Chennai, Mr Murthy finally let go when Radha assured him she would not come in measurable radius of me ever again.

Earlier that evening, Suresh Shah had dropped by and had thrown a major tantrum on seeing three giant suitcases lying packed in the foyer.

'You too,' he said sullenly. 'Very well. Maybe I should leave.'

He ran up the stairs into his apartment and then returned an hour later. He said it was all his fault that he had begun to think of me as his son and that he had no business trying to stop me with all that emotional blackmailing business. And then he continued to emotionally blackmail me for the rest of the evening. I told him it was just a matter of three months, and moreover, it was work after all.

'It always is, IT boy,' he grumbled, getting up to leave. 'It always is. Have a good time.'

He didn't see me again until I left. But I left him a note nonetheless, and I don't know why, but I also left a suggestion that he could always get in touch with me over email. I thought that was the least I could do to give him some comfort.

The flight was very painful and awkward. Radha refused to speak to me through the journey, sending currents of awkwardness by fidgeting uncomfortably in her seat next to me all the time. I tried telling her it was all a harmless dance and she didn't need to take her father that seriously, but she pretended I didn't exist. The first time I heard her speak was to a rather polite gentleman at the taxi counter at the Melbourne airport.

'Hey, you guys havin' a great day?' the guy at the counter asked us.

Radha ignored the pleasantries and jumped straight to the point. 'We want a cab.'

The heartbroken chap looked almost apologetically at Radha. I jostled Radha to the side and made some room for myself.

'We'd like to go to Little Bourke, please,' I smiled at him. My poker face wasn't good enough to make up for Radha's abruptness, but it helped some deal.

'Eighty dollars it will be,' the guy tried hard to continue to smile.

'No,' snapped Radha, knocking me aside with her elbow emphatically. 'Fifty.'

'Sorry?' asked the flabbergasted man. 'Eighty it will be, ma'am.'

'Fifty,' Radha repeated assertively. 'Eighty is too much. I know Little Bourke. Not so far also.'

'Radha, stop,' I pleaded, but she wasn't listening.

'Give it for fifty,' she continued to demand till the man nervously picked up a phone and quietly dialled a number.

Two minutes later, two hefty cops arrived from nowhere and whisked us away to a small but airy room and started talking to us very rudely. So much for Australian hospitality. I nervously explained to the officers this was all a minor cultural misunderstanding, but Radha screwed it all by demanding the guy at the taxi counter submit his rate card for proper scrutiny. Like proper chivalrous men, they asked Radha to just sit comfortably in a corner of the room while they let out all their homily on me for trying to impose taxi fares on an authorized car rental agency with prefixed, valid fares. Half an hour later, they let me off with a stern warning not to mess around with government rules, and offered a hat tip to Radha for the inconvenience they had to put her through. We went back to the taxi counter. This time, I asked him for the cab coupon at whatever rate he wanted to so we could just get the hell out of there.

We were driven to the budget hotel allotted to us by the company, located in the heart of Melbourne's central business district. We were greeted by Geoff and Marla, a very happy-looking couple at the reception who thought it funny that I should think of that building as a hotel. They said it was only a very old condominium owned by them, and they had recently started renting out some of its rooms to hippie travellers and backpackers when the occupancy in the building began to fall.

'Your company tied up with us last year and asked for a nice deal,' said Geoff, grinning. 'But this is lovely. We've got to be the first condominium in town to strike a deal for corporate bookings.'

'And we've got the cheapest rooms in town too!' added Marla in delight.

I said that perfectly explained how they had got Bytesphere to sign up for that deal. All those painfully tedious processes to gain approval for two tiny rooms in a condo. How petty. We picked up our keys and headed for our respective rooms. I asked Radha if she'd like to join me later in the evening for an exploration of the town, but she seemed determined to sleep right into the next morning. Moreover, she was still upset about the eighty dollars. Clearly, she thought little of the trouble she had put me through with the officers.

I tried opening the door to my room, but it went straight into an object placed right behind it, forcing me to squeeze my fleshy body and three giant suitcases through. I got in after a brief struggle and saw a small television set placed on a stand right next to the door. A square bed was placed in the centre of the room, occupying nearly three-fourths of the bonsai enclosure. There was no closet, but the bed had a handful of drawers at its base, and some thin blankets therein which hardly looked comfortable by any standard. In the meager space that yielded was a kitchenette with a microwave and a small frying pan.

The room also smelt horrible. I tried opening a window so I could try breathing in some real air, but it was jammed, thanks to a generous coat of rust that had formed on its hinges. I called Geoff for help. He said I would need to first pull it a little towards myself and then give it a firm swing outward. I did as instructed, but all I got was a painful groan from the hinges.

I tried calling Mehek a number of times, but I could not get through. Also, I was too tired to admire the aesthetics of the room any further. Exhausted, I threw myself on to the miniature bed, only to be woken barely three hours later by a phone call.

'You have a visitor,' said Marla.

Akshat was waiting for me downstairs. Like the nice guy

he sometimes turns out to be, he had offered to show me around town.

I wasn't particularly sold on the idea of staying put in my luxury suite that entire evening, and sleep had turned quite circumstantial anyway. So I accepted the offer gladly.

We walked down to Transport, a noisy but rather lively bar at the city's Federation Square. We got ourselves a table overlooking the Yarra river, ordered our mugs of beer and got talking about mostly depressing things that had transpired in the week gone by at work.

My fears had turned true. Pat and Mike had turned out to be complete assholes. Akshat told me that since the time the Bytesphere team had landed on Australian turf, the Lex leeches had begun throwing their weight around and were dictating terms on everything ranging from daily allocations to assigning workstations. Early that week, they also secretly conducted a meeting with Jerry where they expressed their suspicion about Bytesphere offering rather redundant and irrelevant information in the test results on the application design. Further, they had prepared a detailed report with some boring mathematical calculations on how much money Oz-Mobil could save by doing away with at least forty per cent of the tests created by Bytesphere, and better still, by slashing half the team at Bytesphere and having a specialized team from Lex Technologies merge to provide more desirable results. Jerry got so excited on reading that ridiculously long and complicated report he immediately called Sameer for an explanation.

'And what did Sameer do about it?' I asked, my legs trembling with nervousness already. This was not sounding good at all.

I was right about Sameer, as it was to turn out.

Akshat told me Sameer first spent the entire afternoon

following that meeting in his cubicle, cowering around like a scared pussy (Akshat did not add that last bit about Sameer, but I trusted that wuss to do no better). Then, Sameer prepared a just as ridiculously long and complicated report with equally boring mathematical equations on how we could cover our ass before Oz-Mobil bade us goodbye. He then called everyone over to the expensive penthouse with an in-built jacuzzi and a large water bed that he had rented on the Saint Kilda beachfront to run everyone through the report, pompous MBA style. Two hours into midnight, no one had understood jackshit about the report. Sameer summarized it simply by saying they would propose a 'prioritization by business perspective' initiative on the tests to confuse Jerry out of his wits, and somehow manage to retain their position in the project.

'What is the prioritization by whatever?' I asked. My head was spinning now, and it was not only because of the third mug of beer in my hands.

The prioritization by whatever, I was told, was Sameer's grand idea of cutting down on the humongous number of tests we had written that far, by weeding out whatever the client thought was irrelevant. Just like that wimp to play into Lex's hands like that. I hated these spineless kinds who aspired to become leaders when they didn't have the basic gall to push back random demands made by the client. They were the kinds who gave consultants a bad name. If a consultant were to pay heed to everything a dimwitted client asked for, why would he be appointed a consultant in the first place. And all this, when Sameer well knew we were charging the client our bills in direct proportion with the number of tests we wrote them. I had made it pretty clear right at the outset we needed to align our goals with Bytesphere's values of fleecing the client of all its money, even if it were at the peril of corporate scruples. And yet, Sameer had to go all ethical before Jerry and offer Bytesphere's ass on a platter.

Now who would explain this sudden reduction of tests to the Bytesphere management? I was the only person they were looking up to with a ray of hope to get us some serious business from Oz-Mobil, right? How would I explain this drop in anticipated revenue? Sameer was such an ass. I wanted to kill him already.

'And that is not all,' Akshat continued. 'Lex further complained a large number of defects we had been raising in their system design were meaningless, and reeked of pure vendetta rather than contributing anything meaningful to the client's business processes.'

'I will give them a fitting reply to that allegation,' I fumed.

'I am afraid Sameer has already taken care of that too,' grinned Akshat.

Apparently, Sameer got crazily emotional about the allegation by Lex, and he stormed into Jerry's cabin and challenged him to hire a set of independent testers to revalidate the defects we had raised in Lex's design, and hence shut Pat and Mike up forever. To everyone's horror, Jerry took an instant fancy for this implausible idea and decided to hire two independent testers—some kind of contractors—who would retest *everything* we had *already* tested.

What the fuck was wrong with this Sameer fellow?! Is this what he had learnt in his ivy league B-school? Nonsense! So now, apart from whatever burden we were already bogged down under, we had this additional threat of two independent testers sprouting from nowhere, potentially to challenge whatever results we had furnished to the client all along. I don't know what this strategy was called back at the Indian School of Business, but to me it looked like plain stupidity.

Akshat asked me what I had in mind to tackle the problem. I told him my short-term approach would be to run back to my condominium, lock myself in the room, howl my heart out and then spend the rest of the night desperately browsing job sites. If that did not provide immediate results, my longer-term strategy would be to abduct Sameer, dump him into the deep blue Pacific, then run back to India, take voluntary retirement and settle somewhere in the hills and pray for salvation. Akshat thought I needed to calm my nerves first, and for that, I first needed to move out of that decrepit condominium before its depressing environment gave me salvation ahead of my time. He offered I could move into his townhouse—a not too distant suburb from our office—for he could do with some company too.

'Dharmesh moved in with Sameer,' he said. 'And they just don't socialize after work. They just sit at home and do depressing things like watching National Geographic.'

I told him I would consider his offer but would like to search for an independent unit in the city centre. Then he cleverly incentivized me by adding that Mehek lived in the building right adjacent to his. I told him I'd keep my bags ready and move in the next evening after work.

'Which reminds me,' I said, 'Why can't I get through Mehek's number? Do you know where she might be?'

'She is at Phillip Island with Sameer,' he shrugged. 'Your wealthy adversary hired a convertible and drove her down early this morning to show her the march of the little penguins. Look, she has posted a picture too.'

I did not want to look, but because he thrust his phone into my face, I happened to see Mehek's picture with Sameer, holding a disinterested koala bear between them. Sameer held the koala from the other side, not as tenderly—his arm looked like it was trying to strangulate the poor creature. The picture was tagged and captioned: MY LITTLE CUDDLY BABY!—with SAMEER KASHYAP. Now, I am not paranoid or anything, and I perfectly understand it must have been a harmless road trip for want of anything more productive to do on a chilly weekend. But what was with such immature, misleading captions? And anyway, what did this woman see in a guy who couldn't think like a man when it mattered to take important, bold decisions? I didn't even want to brood over his utter lack of conscience on Sameer's part—screwing up everyone's lives at work and then running off sightseeing over the weekend. Akshat probably sensed I was a little disturbed. So he handed me a piece of paper—something like a form—from his satchel, which he said would be the one-stop solution to all worries that plagued me.

'Fitness Freaks?' I read the form carefully.

'Less than three blocks away from home,' he said. 'And it is more than reasonable.'

I promptly declined saying gyms were hardly my thing. I was instantly reminded of that forgettable day when I took to the jogging track and felt like a pack of sodden cement soon after. He pleaded; apparently he would get free access to a personal instructor in the gym if he could get at least four friends to sign up as well. Sameer and Dharmesh had signed up already, and Mehek was to follow suit the next day. I immediately filled up the form and handed it to him, but told him this was only so he could get his personal instructor and had nothing to do with Mehek joining, because I really, really did not give a flying fuck.

'You are so going to want that personal instructor!' he showed me a picture of Eva Swenn, the instructor in question, on his

Facebook page. He proceeded to give an alluring description of the woman and then drove me crazy with envy and despair by telling me he was a fast mover and had already scored his first date with Eva three days after meeting her. And here I was, struggling to get one to fall prey to my failed charms for nearly three years. I told him I thought it was very cheap of him to objectify a woman like that and to stalk her Facebook profile like a total loony, and that he needed to grow up.

I returned to the condo late in the night and registered myself on all the job portals I could think of. Fifteen minutes later, I had started getting spammed by a thousand job alerts ranging from start-up real estate firms in Pune to open positions for a lecturer in Dimple Business School, Patiala. I took a breather and logged into Facebook to non-lustfully stalk profiles of some random women. By absolute coincidence, I stumbled upon Eva Swenn's profile again. I had to give it to Akshat, man. This Eva Swenn was quite an item.

# 12.

# Jordan

Women and the mind games they play, uff! After worrying me sick an entire night with that little junket she had planned with you-know-who, Mehek met me at the condo the next morning to show that she cared. I tried acting a little grouchy about her not having called on me the previous day. But before long, I had melted yet again, when she presented a bunch of gigantic grocery packets filled with stuff she had very thoughtfully purchased for me to ensure I got by fine during the initial days at the condo. She hurried out soon after, saying Sameer had called for an emergency meeting at nine o'clock.

I rummaged through the packets: chips, short bread, milk, shoe polish, toilet roll...

Aww!

Pancakes!

I forgave her instantly for going off unannounced to that penguin parade with Sameer (although she hadn't asked for forgiveness) and felt a resurgent gush of love for her. No one else really knew of my love affair with well made pancakes.

'Ready to cook,' she instructed me on the phone when I called her and got all emotional. 'Just toss them on a frying pan. There's some maple syrup as well.'

I shed a tear or two of intense joy and tossed myself some

pancakes on that half-broken frying pan. Gosh, did anything in the room work right? I also could not figure the stove knob very well, but it would do, I guessed. The aroma of the pancakes spread through the room as I got ready for work alongside. Just then, Marla called to know why I had decided to check out of their condo earlier than planned and if it had anything to do with their service. I was in the midst of telling her I had thoroughly indulged myself in the comfort of the room but needed to move out for personal reasons, when I felt the aroma of the pancakes turn into a pungent, repulsive smell. I turned around. Yikes! The pancakes were on fire! I slammed the phone and ran to the rescue, but they had died a gruesome death in the pan by the time I got there. Before I could react, a shrill whistle went off from God knows where, freezing the blood in my veins. I looked up at the ceiling, where an attached smoke detector had begun hooting like a wild owl. Marla called again to tell me she had been alerted of the smoke alarm going off in my room. I asked her for immediate help even as I wildly swung my office jacket at the smoke detector hoping to keep it from hooting insanely. She first asked me to calm down and asked me if I had opened the windows. I told her of the rust on the bloody archaic windows, and that they wouldn't open for the life of them. Then she took the longest possible sentence one could take to tell me that as per Australian laws, if the alarm did not stop in ninety seconds, a fire brigade would soon be on its way to rescue me from the fire, and if they discovered it was a false alarm the condo would be levied a fine of seven hundred dollars—which they would eventually fork out of me during the final settlement. By the time she had finished her sentence, ninety seconds had almost elapsed anyway. Frightened out of my wits, I tried taking a wild shot at one of the windows again. It wouldn't yield. I recalled Geoff's instruction from the previous afternoon and tried pulling it firmly towards myself before swinging it outward. In the heat of the moment, I swung it outward so hard the friggin' beast went off its hinges flying downward in a perfect parabolic projectile. It missed crashing on Geoff's bald head, who had lazily spread himself on the lawn with his morning tea, by a small whisker. He toppled off his lawn chair under the impact of the sound of a lot of glass crashing right beside him. Half of him got entangled in his overturned chair, and the other half looked up at me very angrily. Well, at least the alarm had stopped after all. But by then the fire brigade had already arrived at the scene and had slapped a fine of seven hundred dollars on Geoff who, in turn, slapped that fine on me along with a hundred-dollar reimbursement for that broken window. Frankly, that was a little unfair given that window clearly belonged to the Victorian era. But I was running late for work and was also still very upset about the burnt pancakes. So I paid up without bothering to argue. I asked him if he would be willing to consider adjusting those four hundred dollars against 'laundry and other miscellaneous items' in the final bill. He bluntly rejected the request. I informed him I would be back in the evening to check out of the room. He said he couldn't wait until evening.

∽

Sameer called twice as I made my way to the Oz-Mobil office three streets across, asking me to hurry up because I was late... Wait. I must spend some time absorbing his commanding tone each time I recall it...

Ok. So Sameer called twice, asking me to hurry up because I was late. I asked him if this was some sort of an order.

'Important meeting coming up,' he spoke urgently. 'Be there fast. Jerry might be waiting for you at the third floor to get you access.'

I rubbed my hands vigorously as I walked down the road, to provide myself some warmth and also in candid anticipation of wanting to slap Sameer so hard he'd never talk to me like that again. I reached the office and took the elevator to the third floor. Jerry was seated in the lobby, enjoying a leisurely cup of coffee. Why, he looked way younger than what he had sounded on the phone. And very stylish too. He was dressed in a dapper black shirt and cream corduroys, and also a rather fancy pair of suede leather shoes. I shook hands with the man and apologized profusely for keeping him waiting, which is when he told me he was, in fact, the janitor of the building and Jerry was probably somewhere inside. I examined his clothes once again, almost screamed in disbelief, and asked him if those shoes were an original brand. His expression suggested I should have framed the question better.

'I mean, where did you get them from?' I corrected myself.

'Footlocker on Lonsdale,' he replied curtly. 'You might get 'em for a ninety dollars if the discount's still on.'

I did a quick calculation, almost fainted, and then told him I had only enquired about them out of curiosity and just wanted to be let into the working bay. He let me in. I walked straight into the conference room.

I was late, but I had not missed enough to figure something very unpleasant was being discussed in the room. Sameer was taking everyone—my team, Jerry, and two fat Caucasians, presumably Pat and Mike—through a presentation titled 'V Are Unified'. Score one for cheesiness. A large 'V' was drawn on the introductory slide, indicating progressive reductions in cost and effort via the *Prioritization by Business Perspective* approach proposed to be used going forward. I glared hard at Sameer, who had now welcomed me into the room and was introducing me to the three men. Judging from Jerry's expressions, he was rather taken in by this nonsensical idea of cutting down on our tests. So I spared us all the lengthy pleasantries and instantly launched into action, telling Jerry I had my two pence worth of reservation against this suggested approach of streamlining our tests. Jerry laughed and said he didn't care about a reservation worth two pence if a suggested strategy proposed to save him thousands of dollars instead. Sameer smiled and nodded at Jerry like a typical sycophant. Pat and Mike smiled at each other and winked…those bastards.

'The proposed percentage cost savings in each iteration of the prioritization approach,' Sameer continued nonchalantly despite my resistance, pointing at some percentage figures that had popped up next to the 'V' on the slide.

Obviously, he hadn't felt compelled to mathematically show how he had arrived at those percentage figures correct to two decimal places. And clearly, it didn't occur to anyone to ask him either. The claims were good enough. Jerry got so turned on by the redundancy wrapped in lovely PowerPoint animation he started clapping excitedly. I quietly spent the next half hour or so responding to a couple of emails offering some relevant job opportunities even as I heard some disastrous decisions being taken around me.

I looked up only when the meeting had concluded and Jerry asked Sameer if the induction of the hired test contractors was proceeding smoothly. Wow. I had almost forgotten about those contractors.

'Maybe we should put Nakul on to them,' Sameer suggested,

much to my annoyance. 'He could train them on our adopted testing practices.'

I couldn't take it anymore. I stood up and resented this ridiculous idea of first training two testers on our testing practices and then watching them refute the results produced from our very same testing practices. Jerry walked down the pitch, gave me the glare, and positioned himself to begin sledging. I observed him carefully—white jaws, green eyes, pink ears and a red nose. His face, basically, was an oblong rangoli perched on a body that looked like a mannequin. You would think he was made in a factory, except for the strong evidence of nervousness on his face as he spoke.

'Are you trying to tell me your colleague has engaged me in this discussion for five days only for the approach to be discarded now?'

'Of course not!' Sameer nearly jumped in the air in an effort to land in Jerry's lap. 'This will happen. I will brief Nakul about what we have planned.'

Jerry nodded with satisfaction and then asked to be excused because he had to wrap up some meetings and leave early because he had to go sign some papers for the purchase of a horse he had bought the previous week.

I turned to Sameer angrily when we were left alone in the room.

'In business interests,' Sameer shrugged. 'Some tough decisions, man. I am sure you will understand.'

Fucker. I would now have to undo all the chaos he had lan...

One second. Did Jerry say he had bought a horse? Was this man for real? Or was every person on this project a perfect loon? Oh, actually. He must have meant he had bought a HOUSE. It was going to take me some time to get my head around this Australian twang.

Meanwhile, Sameer led me to the working bay that had been provided to the so-called contractors Jerry and he had collectively selected after some detailed interviews. He waited till just before we got to the bay to give me another shocking piece of information: the contractors knew nothing about software. One was a retired rugby coach who now ran a gas station in Cranbourne. The other was a Russian brunette who was trying to make the scene in the modelling industry and scoured for miscellaneous work assignments to support herself financially in the interim. I pulled Sameer to a corner and asked him what the fuck they were doing here if they did not know a thing about software. The idiot explained that after having sat through various steering committee meetings, Jerry and he had come to the shockingly stupid conclusion that because this exercise was a mere revalidation of what our team had already tested, it would suffice to hire a layman with elementary understanding of software to run through the system and provide a layman's sign-off on a product worth ninety million dollars that, apparently, was to be launched to market in three months.

'Also, they look like quick learners,' he added, with very little conviction.

Minutes into my first conversation with them, I realized that was far from the truth. Sameer had provided them with detailed documents the previous day that would guide them towards conducting the required tests. And the Russian brunette was quick to spot a glitch in the stated processes therein.

'The second step in this document tells me to launch the application from the system tray,' she said worriedly. 'I have been looking all day but I can't find a system tray on my computer.'

The gas man suggested she look for it in the hidden folders on her system. I ran out of the bay citing a highly confidential and critical business call I needed to attend to. I asked Sameer to help the brunette and the gas man out with the system tray mystery, and added I'd like to have a sensitive discussion with him offline later in the week, maybe when I had gained some composure.

I went out and drowned my miseries at a nearby bar and tried to think of the positives in all the ugly developments...

Well...

Well...at least the Russian brunette was hot. Maybe I could train her after all. I'd give the ugly gas man to Sameer, or Radha, even. At the end of the programme I could also possibly tell the brunette I knew someone who ran a modelling agency in Mumbai and that she could fly down any time and discuss interesting business prospects with me at leisure—of course, only if Mehek continued playing truant with my sincere, loyal sentiments. But all this could be deliberated upon later.

I convened another meeting with everyone after lunch and proposed a methodical segregation of all deliverables within the team, *without* using a single slide on PowerPoint. There. That's who you call the one-minute manager.

I would train the brunette and back her at all times, and would—if the need arose—stay late hours and mentor and nurture her into a professional, independent testing consultant. Sameer could have the gas station guy all to himself. I also told Sameer that since he had been so ingenious as to propose the V-shaped iterative cost saving by prioritization randomness, he'd better work on that exercise all by himself. As long as he ensured he wasn't bothering anyone else with his smartass strategy, he could also continue creating as many PowerPoint decks as he pleased. Sameer looked very upset. He looked at Mehek, seeking sympathy with his puppy-like eyes. Mehek instantly volunteered to help with the prioritization exercise. I told her she could very well help if she wished to, but I wouldn't consider it under the ambit of her deliverables during her annual appraisal. She reminded me I was not going to be rating her in the annual appraisal anyway, after which I had little left to say. Very well. At least this would ensure Sameer would never try messing with me again.

Dharmesh and Radha would continue playing anchor as far as executing the tests and pushing relevant defects up Lex's ass was concerned. There was little doubt in the fact that the rest of us knew very little about the technicalities in Lex's complicated system and that it would be best to leave all of it to the two soundest minds in the team.

'And what about me?' asked Akshat.

'You will work morning shifts,' I said to his disappointment, 'to ensure no changes to the test environment have occurred overnight. You will be the guy who will pre-empt any kind of trouble lying ahead for us.'

Akshat looked crestfallen. He said he had been very happy handling all those status reports and it would be wonderful if he could stick to the same worthless task going forward.

'Fuck the status reports,' I sneered. 'I will handle Chirayu if we need to. We are knee deep in shit. We don't need status reports.'

Dharmesh suppressed a snigger at the thought of Akshat dragging himself to work early every morning. I averted another imminent bout between them by disbanding the meeting immediately.

∽

Early that evening, I checked out of Geoff's five-star condo with the usual formalities of telling him it had been a pleasure being his guest. He didn't reciprocate. Neither did he place those eight hundred dollars under the 'laundry and other miscellaneous' section. As he organized the papers for settlement, I relentlessly quoted Porter's theory of customer retention even though there was no such theory, to drive into his head the importance of treating his customer with some basic respect and consideration. He told me his condo was sponsored by the government of Victoria and he didn't give a rat's ass about customer retention. While bringing my luggage down to the lobby, I tried getting even with him by choking the garbage chute with my burnt pancakes. I don't know what advanced systems these guys have in place, but in five minutes the janitor of the building came running to Marla and told her I had choked up the chute. Marla charged me another penalty of fifty dollars before finally letting me go.

I moved in to Akshat's townhouse in Richmond. It wasn't as plush as the deluxe suite he had at the Hilton, but it would do. It was a spacious house—a king-sized bedroom, one kitchen and ample space in the hall to lounge around. Moreover, Mehek's apartment was visible from the French window overlooking his balcony. Perfect.

He helped me settle in and later took me to the gym. Sameer and Mehek were in the workout zone already. Sameer was offering her some tips on the right way to execute abdomen crunches, it seemed. Dharmesh was with them too, but he ran into the meditation hall on seeing Akshat walk in. The lady at the front desk threw her hands up in the air excitedly on seeing a new prospect walk in.

'Your friend sure has a way of bringing us business,' she winked, referring to Akshat.

She got me to sign up with a lengthy application form which, among other things, asked me if I'd like a personal instructor at a nominal surcharge of eighty dollars a month. I instantly drew a picture of Eva stretching it out with me on the exercise floor, her smooth luscious body glistening with sweat beads, her tiny exercising outfit failing to conceal those perfect bends...eighty dollars?

Probably worth it. I chose to go with the personal instructor. The lady at the desk first charged me for three months, then told me the fees was non-refundable, and finally said she had the prerogative to choose my personal instructor.

'Jordan will be your instructor,' she said, directing me towards the workout zone. 'He will be waiting for you near the dumb-bells' rack.'

What the fuck? Was there *any* organization that believed in integrity and transparency anymore?

I was tired of the workout even before I had begun. The name Jordan itself had nearly paralyzed me mentally. I trudged along reluctantly with Akshat, when I saw Eva stride forward from a distance, waving at Akshat excitedly like they had known each other for eternity.

'Akshat, darling,' she folded her arms around him. 'I thought you weren't coming today.'

I stood still and gazed at Eva for as long and as shamelessly as I could allow myself to. She was a little older than us, maybe nearing thirty-five. But she had a raw appeal that was admittedly hard to resist. And although Mehek was in the same room, I must candidly confess Eva was totally worth the fuss Akshat created about her. And this is not because of those delightfully short exercising shorts and the barely-shall-cover sports vest, but yes, maybe they contributed a small deal. Akshat introduced me as his project manager. She looked suitably impressed, wowing at me as though that were equivalent to being the governor of Victoria. I didn't mind the attention. Eva was very uninhibited in her body language when she spoke, if you know what I mean. I haven't had such a mind-numbing experience too often, so I stood my ground and let that Jordan fellow wait for me near the dumb-bells. The moment of joy lapsed sooner than I thought though, when Akshat reminded Eva they were running out of time and that she should help him warm up. Eva laughed and whispered something, presumably wicked, in Akshat's ear and whisked him away, waving teasingly at me.

Frankly, on second thoughts, she wasn't that great after all.

Sameer got off his treadmill and accosted me as I walked over to the dumb-bell rack. He asked me what was the sensitive discussion I intended to have with him. I skirted his question saying it wasn't a good time and place, but he insisted. So I told him very curtly I was unhappy with the way he had dealt with these abrupt demands from the client and that it was very unbecoming of him as a Byte to compromise on Bytesphere's long standing principles of squeezing fat margins out of key clients and fudging data to project higher effort and cost estimates than required. He then gave me some hogwash on how he had been brought up on the three pillars of honesty, discipline and something else (not important) and that his conscience would never allow him to forgo his ideals for personal or organizational gains.

'Is this why you are bitter with me sometimes?' he asked. Either he was dumb, or he was playing dumb.

'Not a good time to talk,' I said again, trying to make my way.

He stretched his enviably muscular arm to block my

path. Mehek turned around curiously to watch our animated conversation while sweating it out on a cross trainer nearby.

'Is this why you are bitter with me?' he asked again.

'I can't begin to cite reasons,' I muttered and pushed my way through.

'I don't know if it has to do with me taking up your role here,' he shouted out from behind. 'But if that is the case, you have nothing to worry about any more. You are the project manager, and will always be. Jerry has anyway asked me to help him out with some marketing initiative. The team is all yours.'

'Whatever,' I waved my hand dismissively and walked off towards Jordan.

Jordan looked like a humanoid. He was dark, sweaty in a very unsexy way, and at least one banyan tree taller than me, with arms jutting out of his body like giant trunks. The veins in his arms were so thick they looked like they would jump out of his skin any moment. He considered the length and breadth of me and let out a short grunt before shoving me into the measurement room. He read the measurements and let out a few more grunts. Then, without speaking a word, he dragged me to a corner of the exercising floor, just short of hauling me up by my collar. He spread out an exercising mat, threw me on it and asked me to work out an unlimited number of abdomen crunches until I spread over the floor like sheepskin and begged for my life to be spared.

He didn't give me a choice. I had to oblige.

It was official. I didn't have a life…wait a minute.

What was this marketing initiative Jerry had asked Sameer to help him with?

# 13.

# Have You Felt Velvet Lately?

This is about the week my life was rocked by a series of major scandals.

No, I am not talking about the time the Russian brunette sent me the message: 'Can you meet me for a sex?' on my chat window. That message was understandable; at some abstract level, probably exciting too.

I will come back to the brunette and her message later. There were a handful of events that had unsettled me before this pleasant digression came forth in the form of her message.

It had been nearly a month at the client's office, and the experience had not been pretty. The uncomfortable equation we shared with Lex had come to the fore with an increased frequency of arguments over the alleged triviality of defects we had been raising in their system only to get the client's undue admiration and also some extra bills. I had taken major exception to this attack on my integrity and had asked Pat and Mike to stop behaving like cry babies just because we were giving them a tough time for handing the client a phony product. After a flurry of unpleasant emails, Pat had signed off with a cryptic warning that talked about a 'Bytesphere sunset'. Too much *Godfather* influence, maybe. Later that evening, Pat ambled over to my desk and winked, 'Your move, genius!' The duffer expected me to play into his scheming hands and send an irrational response to his diatribe. I knew better and decided to sleep over this disturbing thought and come up with a well-calculated response.

The next morning I woke up early, upbeat, vengeful and in reasonably good health. I breakfasted sumptuously on a three-egg omelette at Hungry Jack's and then began strolling comfortably towards office, taking in the serene beauty of the Yarra river. The clock had not yet struck eight and the roads were largely devoid of the morning traffic. It was a perfect start to the morning. All of a sudden, I thought I felt a treble in the distance. It died down in seconds, then rose again with more intensity. The treble grew stronger—a prominent sound of something very heavy drumming against the tar roads with a sense of purpose. And then I felt a dark shadow loom over me. In seconds, a shrill sound that pierced my senses.

NEIGHHHHH!

I turned around, petrified, to find a black horse rise on its rear limbs, raising its intimidating hoofs at me. I cowered. Someone's voice asked me to calm down. I looked through my trembling palms that had covered my eyes—Jerry was mounted on the beast, taming it with the kind of compassion he never showed us humans at work. I sat cowered, submissive, before my master. Jerry took in the moment with pleasure until the horse held his, well, horses.

'Meet Velvet,' he said, proudly fondling the animal's furry back that smelled of leather. 'Come, let me give you a ride to work.'

I will admit my resilience against unexpected surprises had risen considerably in recent months. But this was pushing it too far. I had never seen a suited, senior executive ride a horse to work. Hell, I had never seen ANYONE ride a horse to work.

What's more, I was never faced with the uncomfortable situation of being OFFERED a ride on a horse to work. I obviously declined the offer very politely, but Jerry began trotting Velvet alongside me as he persisted, saying it would be an experience I would never forget; what was my problem, was Velvet not good enough for me? When onlookers began sniggering at the proceedings, I finally gave up and agreed. It took me a grand total of ten minutes to be able to mount the stallion. When I had settled down, Jerry asked me to make sure I held on.

'To what?' I asked.

'DUH!' He shook his head, patting the sides of his waist.

WAS THIS MAN FUCKING KIDDING ME?

Of course he was not. So after a brief debate, I held Jerry by the waist and asked for Velvet to ride us to work in as little time as possible so the ordeal could end for all three of us. For the first few minutes, Velvet walked peacefully. This was the moment I was actually beginning to enjoy the ride. I took in the same view of the Yarra from a good elevation. I felt princely. I could even have considered doing this more often. Only, just then, Jerry shouted, 'Trot, Velvet! Trot!'

And Velvet began prancing around like a fool, trotting violently along the cobblestone walkway. To another person, this could have looked like fun—like sailing on a magic carpet, or sitting on a nice massage chair, maybe. But I bet anyone on that road a hundred bucks to have tried sitting on that bugger with his two legs apart, subjecting oneself to such violent trotting turbulence. At first I wanted to howl in pain. But gradually, the pain moved upward along my body, travelled through my gut, right into my voice box. Before I knew it, I had lost my voice to protest or to beg to be let off. Then came a reprieve. Jerry's instruction changed to, 'Gallop, Velvet! Gallop!'

The positive change brought about by the command was that Velvet had stopped trotting. The negative development was that Velvet had now gone completely cuckoo. He neighed a little at the instruction, shook his nape at a hapless cyclist right next to him, and took off like the wind, nearly toppling the cyclist over. You know how your entire life flashes before your eyes when you have a disturbing premonition? I swear, at that moment, I could even see flashes of my previous birth. I remembered I was a doe. I had had a good life then. I ate herbs and slept all my life and had died peacefully by a pond that had lent me its sweet water for yea...

Velvet was almost flying now. I was systematically crying now. Velvet rode us past the Yarra, right into the city centre where cars were now converging in healthy numbers at various traffic signals. Showing utter disregard for every colour of the traffic light, Velvet went about its purpose. Jerry's waist was not good enough for me to hold on to now. Desperate to latch on to something, I found Velvet's fat tail swinging wildly behind me.

'Faster, Velvet! Faster!' The idiot continued, tugging at Velvet's reins. I put the third Newtonian law of motion to use and pulled hard at Velvet's tail, hoping to offset the insane speed this creature had acquired. Frightened, Velvet galloped faster. Even more frightened, I tugged at his tail even harder. We must have been two hundred metres from the office car park when Velvet gave up and screeched to a grinding halt, sending its buttocks and me a few feet up in the air. I lost my balance, my body executed a perfect parabolic jump and went a few centimetres ahead of Jerry, who showed some presence of mind and held me mid-air, bringing me back down on Velvet. I settled down like a petrified hen, somewhere between Velvet's nape and Jerry's torso.

'It is alright,' Jerry tried comforting me. 'We are almost there. Ok, Velvet, WALK!'

The phase from that moment until I was woken up by Dharmesh in the office dormitory two hours later is somewhat of a blur, so I do not remember much. When I stood up from the bed, I felt no bodily sensation waist below. I regained my composure, crawled back to my working bay, and felt a little better after I resumed tutoring the Russian brunette and after sharing a little laugh over the message she had sent me.

Coming back to the brunette and her message: 'Can you meet me for a sex?'

You might think I went all crazy with ecstasy on receiving this most exciting request. I would have, but you see, I was kind of prepared for it.

I had sensed the sexual tension inside her when I first met her, when I noticed how she tried making small talk about her struggles as a model, all to attract my attention. And all that laughing at my jokes—even the ones I myself didn't find funny. I just hadn't expected her to be that direct, and that fast. Raw, raging hunger—also loneliness, maybe. I would need to deal with it a little maturely. I began typing a compassionate reply, maintaining my dignity alongside ensuring I didn't really close the door entirely on this very interesting opportunity to know her better.

Hey. Glad to receive your request...

Don't get me wrong. Of course you are super attractive and all.

But don't you think it's a little early for us to...

Maybe we should go out some time?

...And she went offline. Ah, that famous trick of dropping an obvious hint and then retreating into a corner. I quickly closed the chat window before it caught someone's attention and walked over to her bay. The gas man wasn't around. My heart started throbbing. The brunette had her head buried in her hands. After due deliberation, I compassionately placed my hand on her soft, tender shoulders. Some sort of nervous current of reciprocation was just beginning to build into me, when she broke into a short howl and began apologizing frantically for the typo.

'I am sorry I keep getting these keys mixed up,' she wailed. 'Please don't tell on me.'

If there was a mild tinge of disappointment somewhere inside me, I didn't let it show. But this was most irritating. That was no typo to make—giving someone an unexpected ray of hope and then running it down like that. I laughed heartily anyway, and told her I obviously knew she in fact meant to ask if I could meet her for a sec. When she felt a little better, I very delicately hinted she need not have hesitated even if, by some stroke of chance, that weren't a typo and she actually meant to ask what she had actually typed. She looked at me stone-faced and asked me not to push my luck too far.

Wow, figure that! *She* leads me on with a message, and when I try being nice, she makes *me* the creep. Too much attitude for an aspiring model, I thought, and instantly lost whatever little interest I was gaining in her. I quickly changed tack and pretended to be really busy. I asked her to get to the point and tell me what it was she wanted to meet me for.

She explained she was still struggling with a problem from the previous day of being able to see only partial views of the application's pages on her computer. I asked her if she had followed my instructions to delete all history from her browser before trying again. She said she had, but now all she could see on the application were blank cells with no trace of customer data in them. After driving myself mad over the problem for almost an hour, I looked at her in horror.

'What exactly have you done?' I asked her nervously.

She said she had only followed my instruction to delete all history. I helplessly explained I had asked her to delete the browser's history, and not the history of customers' data that had been loaded on to Lex's application.

'What's the difference?' she asked, confused.

∽

I called for an urgent meeting with Lex to assess the damage this stupid, insensitive, manipulative-with-her-words, snooty brunette had caused.

'Hardly anything,' said Mike coolly. 'We will have all the customer data back in the system in under four hours.'

He waited for me to heave a sigh of relief, and then sadistically added it would be a big deal for us, though, because it would only be logical we retested all tests pertinent to the lost customer data once again. I argued that wouldn't be needed because the data wasn't going to change after all.

'There could be changes in the environment when we load the data again,' he laughed.

'WE ARE NOT RETESTING ANYTHING!' I warned him sternly and asked him to keep his bloody advice to himself.

He laughed again. He kept laughing till I slammed the phone down, my body trembling with rage and frustration.

Five minutes later, in the time I had made up my mind to ask Jerry to call it quits with the contractors, I found myself reading an email from Mike to Jerry and our team, marking everyone else who probably had nothing to do with the matter.

*Jerry,*

*The contractors working under Bytesphere's directives have, well, fucked up. All customer data pertaining to our campaign lists has been deleted, which will now lead to unnecessary rework and severe loss of time and money. We are hardly surprised, given we were already afraid Bytesphere had slackened in keeping up with its efficiency. While we will recreate this data by tonight, we'd like to point out this unprofessionalism will be a major roadblock in meeting our deadlines. I'm sure everyone knows what I'm talking about. Nakul, please get your team to retest all tests connected with the lost customer data later tonight. I believe you had some reservations, but as Jerry would surely agree, there is no getting away from this.*

*Pat and I would like to propose yet another round of restructuring in the team to drive better results. We will talk to you about it soon.*

*Best,*
*Mike Green*

Son of a bitch! I would restructure every friggin' bone in his body if he proposed another restructuring routine.

Dharmesh and Radha looked like it was the end of the world. I asked them to calm the fuck down and ignore Mike's mail until I talked Jerry out of this bullshit with my well-honed communication skills of a crisp speaker and a patient listener.

Once inside Jerry's cabin, I only stayed the patient listener as a very upset Jerry lashed out at us, as though we were wholly responsible for the mess. I was not too hassled; after the misadventure with Velvet I really thought I could absorb any kind of shit. I calmly reminded Jerry I had already mentioned those dumb contractors would come to no good.

'That isn't what I am talking about,' he said, flipping a report on the table. 'Read this.'

Yet another report from Pat and Mike…sigh. I was growing out of this…what the hell was this? I read the first few lines of the report and began jumping in my seat like a headless chicken. Pat and Mike had completely lost it.

So, when the Lex chaps had begun to run out of answers to the sharp, smart defects we had been reporting against their erratic system, Pat and Mike had channelled their energies in trying to throw us out of the contest altogether. This report looked like it had been drafted by a bunch of lame teenagers— accusing Bytesphere of raising 'trivial and cosmetic' defects instead of focusing on the 'holistic purpose of the system', whatever in God's name that meant. The report further offered to take over the remainder of the testing assignment from Bytesphere at a fraction of the price we had been quoting to the client all along. This was whatthefuckness of the highest order. I told an inconsolable Jerry to disregard this trashy report because it did not make sense for the designers of an application to also test their own application—it was like the director of a film writing his own review.

'Moreover, about this lower cost proposal,' I added, 'what would you rather choose—cost efficiency or a certain level of quality assurance?'

The moron said he would choose cost efficiency. Our fate was on its way to being sealed.

I was getting nervous by the minute, and in a moment of impulse I stood up and challenged Jerry, saying that my team could bust Lex's gaping flaws in the system design in under ten days. Nothing that I had said in all those months had mattered one bit to this fellow. And he chose to take this one statement I made, in a moment of emotional outburst, so seriously that he actually gave us an ultimatum of ten days to prove our worth to him.

'Get us a report showing all defects in Lex's system so far,' he said. 'If the contractors revalidate your results as factually correct, you guys will have my continued faith.'

'And otherwise?' I wanted to ask him. But I did not.

I returned to our working bay and first told Dharmesh and Radha they would, indeed, have to retest the new customer data as per Mike's instructions because, for some obscure reason, Jerry had come to believe Lex was always right. And then, gradually, I parted with details on my latest discussion with Jerry and his subsequent ultimatum.

'Our only hope is those contractors don't refute our findings,' I said helplessly.

Mehek suggested we carry on with our usual business in the meantime; after all, we all knew we were right in the defects we had reported against Lex—all we needed was to provide Jerry with ample evidence through screenshots displaying all faults in their system.

'The solution to our problem lies in the evidence,' she said. 'Lex will be forced to go on the backfoot.'

This girl made things sound so simple. I felt a resurgent attraction towards her. Once it had ebbed, I went to the contractors and offered to buy them lunch. Very basic sandwiches we opted for, but they were thrilled nonetheless. Without making my grandiose gesture too obvious, I then carefully briefed them about our precarious situation, and that our sustenance in the project hinged completely on them. Little surprise, but they understood nothing of what I said; they just kept nodding mechanically at everything.

I went back home and muttered a prayer for myself. That was all I could cling on to.

By the end of the week, however, we were convinced we had busted Lex's ass for good. We were done testing their entire application, and were thoroughly delighted to observe that at least forty per cent of their application was riddled with defects, and overall, the system was a whole lot of shit. Buoyed by a sudden bounce back into the game, I ended the week on a high note by firing the nastiest email I could conjure, with a comprehensive report compiling our startling findings.

*Jerry,*

*Find attached our test report—complete with the set of defects, and our thesis on how severely these glaring flaws in the system can impact the business of Oz-Mobil. Nothing spectacular in here, we just did our job—but one must note the system built is nothing short of horrendous, clunky and erratic. Maybe Lex was a little too busy focusing on restructuring activities and such, but they have clearly gone off target and we are afraid they have made a mess of the system.*

*I trust your decision will weigh a well-delivered, high quality test deliverable well against mere lip service some people were desperate to offer.*

*Of course, the contractors can go ahead and validate our claims by all means. For all we know, some more skeletons might end up tumbling out of the closet.*

*Pat, Mike—there was a certain sunset you had talked about. Now what was that again?*

*Nakul Kapoor*

Mehek thought the email was a little too strongly worded, and that maybe I should have held my horses until the contractors had validated our statements. I asked her to take it easy and also not to mention horses before me ever again. I thought it was only fair I told Pat and Mike what we thought of them after all the one-upmanship they tried playing against us, and that it would be all of a week before we showed them who the boss was in the game.

We breathed easy for the next few days even as the gas man and the snobbish, typo-prone, leading-on bombshell brunette got a hold of the application and got down to validating our findings. I took the contractors into confidence and said I trusted they wouldn't deviate from the stand we had taken against Lex, especially after all the effort we had put in to ensure they learnt how to navigate the goddamn application in the first place. And after that lunch I had bought them. The gas man didn't look like he cared much about the results of the validation anyway. But the brunette, who was still very upset I had once alluded to the remote possibility of the two of us getting together for a rendezvous some day, didn't take very kindly to my request and proffered some gyan on her professional ethics.

Total snob. Whatever. I was hardly worried in any case. For all practical purposes, Pat and Mike were inching closer to a holocaust in their careers.

We called for a celebration that evening.

'Max Brenner's Chocolate Lounge at Melbourne Central—at ten,' Mehek reminded everyone before we dispersed for the day.

Akshat took a rain check, saying he had an aunt in the city who had called him over for dinner.

I spent some leisure time at the gym late in the evening. Jordan was immensely thrilled on seeing me after a long gap, and he showed me some love by giving me an exercising circuit I would never forgive him for. He let go of me shortly before the gym was to close for the day. Most of the staff had called it a day already. Only Eva had stayed back at the front desk; she told the receptionist she had a few customers' exercising cards to prepare for the next day, so she offered to stay back and turn the lights off at the gym for a change.

Akshat was still lounging around in the spa, clad in nothing but a sparse towel.

'Aren't you running late to get to your aunt's?' I asked him on my way out.

He lay still on the wooden bench with his eyes closed, merely offering a slight nod.

As I passed by the reception, Eva offered me a sheepish smile. Two minutes later, she left the front desk and tiptoed towards the ladies' room.

Something told me Eva was Akshat's, well, aunt. Of course, I had no business to pry on them. But then, I had nothing better to do. So I quietly went round the other end of the lobby and afforded myself an alternate view of the changing rooms, right behind a water fountain. Two minutes later, Eva stepped out of the ladies' room in—holy Molly!— a towel so thin I could have nearly missed it. I didn't mean to ogle at all, but I swear she was something. Every curve in her body was perfect. Her skin was smooth as ivory. Her...ok, fine. I didn't mean to ogle.

She looked around tentatively and knocked very lightly at the door of the men's room. Shortly, Akshat opened the door, leaned forward and kissed her. She pulled him towards her and kissed him passionately, her tongue scouring the dimensions of his mouth. I will honestly admit I had the graciousness to shut my eyes when I saw her towel drop. She then led him into the ladies' room and shut the door behind them.

I heard a series of giggles and short shrieks, until a shower was turned on somewhere inside. That was when I finally walked away. I could not take it anymore.

Some guys had all the luck.

By the way—what was that Russian brunette's problem in life? I probably needed to smooth-talk her out of her awkwardness. Some day, maybe.

# 14.

# Kati Patang

I walked in to resounding applause by the entire staff of Oz-Mobil. Jerry stood smiling at the far end of the queue of employees, and enveloped me in a warm hug as I approached him.

'You saviour, you!' he said, teary-eyed.

'You are our hero!' chimed the rest of the staff as I raised my hand gesturing them to take it easy and to allow me to absorb the moment.

'The CEO would like to speak to you too,' said Jerry, whisking me away from the crowd that was trying to mob me affectionately. 'But first, I need your help.'

He led me to his cabin and asked me for my invaluable inputs on the product launch plan. I nodded pensively and looked at my watch.

'Another day, maybe?' I frowned hard, struggling to cope with this unexpected limelight.

'Whenever you want,' he grinned, and then requested me to also take a decision on the final plight of the Lex team, using my business acumen and analytical skills. I mused that in a competitive business environment, such laxity by a design team was not permissible. But my humane side forced me to duly consider if they were deserving of any sort of mercy.

'Let me consider their options,' I said finally and walked out.

Outside Jerry's cabin, a hysterical Pat folded his hands and beseeched me to give his team one more chance. I tried to calm him down, but he was now sprawled on the floor, tugging pitiably at my feet...

This was probably the tenth time in the week that I had played out the above visuals in my head. This week of sitting back and quietly watching the show had kind of driven me to the edge. The wait had been long, and it was about time we saw the back of Lex on the project. Couldn't wait.

The big day arrived finally. The contractors had turned in their results of the tests to Jerry. Shivers of excitement ran down my spine. I also sent Chirayu a mail asking him to place my annual appraisal on hold until I sent him the client's feedback on my work at Oz-Mobil; there could well be some pleasant surprises in store.

I charged into the office with that extra spring in my step. That 'will take on the world' feeling, if you know what it means. I met Pat and Mike near the elevator. Their faces were impassive. Understandably so. It must have been difficult to handle the jolt. But it's not like I had not warned them or had deprived them of a fair chance. I patted Mike and asked him to hold his own; this was not the end of the road after all. Mike looked up at me, confused, and then turned to Pat. They looked at me with that same evil smile and then broke into hysterical laughter and slinked out of sight.

Poor guys. It had not been easy for them either. The stress seemed to have taken a toll on their mental health. I would consider giving them a second chance, after all—if they promised to behave themselves, that is.

When I entered our working bay, though, I saw the others

weren't half as excited as I was. In fact, they were almost distraught.

'Jerry wants to see you,' Radha said very unhappily.

I shivered a little again, this time not out of excitement.

Anxious, I stepped into Jerry's cabin, exactly the way I had in that parallel, virtual universe the entire past week. Jerry was teary eyed too, just as I had visualized him. Only, it was not out of his love for me. He was livid and upset, and he looked like he was genuinely going to go hysterical on me.

'Explain this,' he tossed the printouts of a fat report sent in by Pat and Mike.

Another report! These guys really needed to get a grip. I glanced through the report half-heartedly. Holy cow!

I broke into a sweat. This couldn't be happening. This was not how things were supposed to pan out. I smelt a dirty conspiracy.

So, we thought we had had the last laugh after sending Jerry that exhaustive report containing eight hundred defects in Lex's shoddy system. Now, Pat and Mike gave us a taste of our own medicine by sending a counter report that claimed over sixty per cent of the defects raised by us were, well, invalid, and that their system was functioning perfectly well for most parts—unlike what we had projected to Jerry. Worse, those idiotic contractors had concurred with Lex's findings.

I struggled to understand how they had managed to pull this off. We had SEEN those defects with our own eyes. Some slimy assholes, these.

I was crumbling from within. I immediately sourced Chirayu's fake vipassana smile and nodded calmly at Jerry, pretending to be unperturbed by the calamity that had befallen us. Simultaneously, my mind scurried for possible options that lay in all those useless *Guerilla Warfare* kind of books I had once trusted in my life. Those gems of advice come to no good when you really need them. When I sensed I had nothing to say in my defense, I cried foul over a possible sabotage.

'Give me a good reason to trust you over Lex,' said Jerry dispassionately.

Again, I didn't have a reason. Instead, I took him through a brief journey of Bytesphere's past client relationships and its rich professional heritage to convince him Bytesphere had never screwed up on its deliverables. He said there was always a beginning somewhere, and all it took was a bunch of dumbasses to begin a new tradition. I continued speaking for the next fifteen minutes, but I was so emotionally and mentally drained I am not sure I remember what I was speaking. I think I might have been proposing a revised, three-hundred-and-sixty degree view of customer orientation or Bytesphere's patented Rapidex Productivity Enhancement Model to make up for the losses incurred—when he told me very non-subtly that I was not making any sense. Which is when I resorted to my last option, took a quick bathroom break, and returned to him with teary eyes, lay prostate on his table and begged for a second chance. The insensitive jerk photographed me and threatened to email the image to the Bytesphere management if I didn't give up my histrionics immediately.

'I have good and bad news for you,' he said, dragging me off the table and placing me on a chair. 'What would you like to hear first?'

I said I was in the kind of state of mind where I would not be able to tell the two apart and so I really did not care. The bad news, he said, was that he had decided to ask Bytesphere to wind up its operations from the project and fly back home within the next week after handing over all documentation to Lex. Also, we needed to effect an efficient and quick handover to Lex, because Jerry was convinced Lex had done a fine job with their design and he wanted to make an interim presentation to the senior management at Oz-Mobil the following week.

The good news would not matter anymore. But he insisted on telling me, so I relented. Jerry had been promoted in the organization after he had leveraged that research report I had helped him with at the beginning of the project, to churn out some magical thesis that caught the attention of the Oz-Mobil management. He said he would like to invite us for a celebratory party he intended to host over the weekend at his humble abode—which, by the way, was a sprawling fourteen hundred square foot villa-cum-farmhouse (where, believe it or not, he reared four horses including Crazy Velvet, eighteen cows and three dogs) in Epping, somewhere on the border of Melbourne. Absurd as it was to imagine partying with the man who had just axed us, I agreed, imagining we were not likely to have anything better to do in any case, and would rather fancy some free buffet food and wine at his expense.

As I prepared to leave, imagining this was the last of the horrors in store for me on this forgettable trip, he called out excitedly and said he had managed to get hold of Marlon Pacino's email and had sent him a note requesting for his invaluable contributions on a related assignment Oz-Mobil was contemplating working on in the near future. I didn't know who it was he had written to, but he looked very happy and I didn't want to spoil the party by telling him a Marlon Pacino did not exist in Bytesphere in the first place. But then, whose email address had he got hold of? Maybe the project debacle had brought him to start hallucinating or something. Poor chap.

I thought it best to leave him alone until he recovered from the mental trauma.

'I have written to him about his sharp findings on the Bali telecom market you had quoted in the report,' he said excitedly. 'I am hopeful he will agree to help us.'

This mystery of Marlon Pacino would go down with me to my grave. As for Jerry, he could try contacting this Pacino creation of his as much as he wanted. I had stopped caring already.

Outside, I broke the news to the others with much distress. Everyone was crestfallen, except Dharmesh—who didn't in the least seem moved by the sudden change in circumstances. He seemed lost in a sea of code present on his screen.

'There is something amiss,' he insisted. 'Has anyone noticed all our defects which have been rejected as invalid are only the ones we tested after eight in the evening?'

We looked at him expectantly. That was a lovely pattern he had detected. Only, we didn't know what he was arriving at. In an absolute anti-climax, he talked about something called an error 404 due to infinite loops that he had observed in Lex's code to launch a marketing campaign.

'Yeah, like that makes perfect sense to us,' Akshat smirked.

I patted Dharmesh comfortingly and assured him while he was free to probe into the matter, we didn't stand a chance to save our skin anyway. We dispersed, leaving Dharmesh looking agape at his screen, mumbling some strange language none of us could comprehend.

Later at lunch, I overheard Sameer ask Mehek in his usual irritating, gentlemanly tone if she'd like to have dinner with him by the waterfront that evening. Personally, I didn't think that was a time to go celebrating. But then, Sameer was hardly a team player. I couldn't expect better from him. But Mehek—well, you'd think she would have seen beyond his fake demeanour after the crisis he put us all through by liaising with those cheapskates from Lex. But, no, I saw her nod in assent. She said she was considering shopping at Spencer's for her trip back home and that they could head out to dinner thereafter. Some women just learn stuff the hard way. Anyway, there was no way I was going to let Sameer go paint the town red with MY girl after all the muck he had landed us all into.

I immediately called Pat and Mike and told them I was pleased to hand over the mantle of the project to them right away and was keen to know what they needed from us during the handover. First, they spewed some sarcastic bullshit about how upset they were to see us go after all the brilliant work we had done on the project. I played out a scene in my head where I walked into their cabin, dragged them by their sparse hair, dipped them headlong into the office aquarium, and held on till the fish had feasted properly on their lumpy cheeks. There, that felt a little better. Then I told them it was all a part of the game and we didn't give a shit about who worked on the project as long as the target was met, because we always believed in customer satisfaction over our own. They laughed and said that was totally believable and equally lame, but it would be a good idea to come to the point after all. They demanded one of us, preferably the smartest of our lot—comparatively, they cheekily added—sit with them through two entire days and help them with the official handover of all the completed as well as the pending work.

'Jerry wants a presentation made to the senior management next week,' said Pat, 'and we would like to be well prepared. Because we don't like offering our client unpleasant surprises at the last minute.'

The sarcasm notwithstanding, I was thrilled by the idea and immediately told them Sameer was comparatively the smartest guy in our group, as they would have already deduced from the way he had sucked up to them by agreeing to all their demands in the earlier phase of the project.

'Great,' they chimed in agreement. 'Let Sameer be at our disposal for the next two days.'

I told them I'd have him sent to them right away, but they needed to make sure they kept him engaged at all times—so they could make proper use of his genius, of course. Then I went to Sameer, who was still chatting pretty with Mehek outside the office, and asked him to drag his sorry butt to Lex and stay put till the official handover was complete. Like the sissy he has always proven to be, he complained about having made plans for the day already. But I massaged his vulnerable ego by telling him Lex really needed the brightest chap on the block to help them with some smooth consulting and mentoring skills and we could only fall back on some brilliant, ivy-league B-school type of fellow to do the job.

'That would be me,' said the vain cheapskate.

I nodded. 'You must go now.'

'But we are not under an obligation to help them,' he argued. 'Are we? After all, we are out of the project.'

I said the handover would be a part of our final commitment to the client. And in any case, such decisions would be best taken by me, in the capacity of his senior and his project manager. I think I unsettled him a little by reminding him of our designations. Served him right.

Sameer apologized to Mehek for ruining her plans and placing his professional commitment above his personal leisurely activities and his dogged romantic pursuits. She smiled appreciatively at his mature thinking. Score one for hot blooded Kashyaperfect courtliness, it seemed. Once he was thankfully out of sight, I casually asked Mehek if she had any plans for the day—now that we were without work anyway, I didn't mind giving her another chance at discovering the charming romantic in me.

'Nothing major, really,' she replied vaguely. 'A quick shopping routine, that's it.'

Of course, I didn't tell her I had already eavesdropped on her telling Sameer she was hitting Spencer's that evening. That would have sounded cheap. Instead, I landed up at Spencer's a little early in the evening and strategically positioned myself in the central lobby of the mall so I could spot her entering the mall and then bump into her accidentally.

Meanwhile, an overexcited Chinese or Japanese or Korean girl came running out of an apparel store and literally dragged me in by the hand, insisting I try out the latest line of tees on offer. I tried explaining to her I had just had a very harrowing experience at work and also faced a good chance of losing my job very soon and that I was likely to be broke about ten meals later. But she either genuinely didn't understand English or pretended not to understand my accent, and began throwing tee after tee at my face, egging me to try them on. She finally showed me some sort of shirt that was supposed to make fat people look like Bruce Lee or such. That sounded interesting. So I simply picked it and asked her how much it would cost me. She went so delirious with joy, she pranced around the store a little and then dragged me to the counter and began billing me for it. I disrupted her reverie, snatched a notepad from her desk and wrote her a message that looked like:

SHIRT. NOT BUY. ONLY ASK. HOW MUCH? PRICE? TELL!

Her happy face suddenly turned into one of pure rage. She snatched the notepad and wrote me a curt reply.

BILL. ALREADY. PAY.

I hazarded an argument, but before I knew it three men who looked just like her emerged from different corners of the store and surrounded me. One of them pointed menacingly at the message she had written on the notepad. I fetched my wallet with a heavy heart and paid up for the shirt, after which the delighted woman wrote me another message:

ONE SHIRT ONLY? YOU PAY FORTY. YOU BUY TWO SAME-SAME, PAY SEVENTY ONLY. OR THREE SAME-SAME, HUNDRED ONLY.

Thankfully just then, I spotted Mehek sauntering into the mall. I ignored the up-selling pitch and ran out of the store, pretending to pass by Mehek like I had not seen her. Sadly, she didn't see me either and simply walked right through me, up the escalator.

What was I, The Hollow Man?

I quietly followed her up the escalator and took a table at a café in the gallery right opposite the store she had walked into. I ordered the cheapest coffee and sat patiently, sporting the saddest look I could come up with. It was an old trick I had mastered in school: hunt your girl down like a madman, wander around in her vicinity until she notices you, and then make the meeting appear like an absolute coincidence. For added measure, look upset as hell so that she goes all motherly on you and offers to spend some time with you to make you feel better. It makes a hero out of you without making you look too desperate.

Sure enough, when Mehek walked out of the store and finally saw me, she strode up to me and asked me if something was the matter (Mental high-five!). I winced maximum, Manoj Kumar style, and said I was very depressed by the way things had turned against us and I almost felt this was the end of the world, and that I felt equally responsible for the misery everyone else in the team had been put through. And then, I experienced, in physical form, what I had only dreamt of, over and over again, since the time I had first met her three years ago—the very thought of which used to send me into a state of mad, fervent, sensual tizzy.

She held my hand!

Yes! I couldn't believe my luck as she took my stubby, coarse palm studded with calluses and wrapped her delicate, petal-like fingers around it. A heavenly feeling, I must say—for me, at least—I don't know about her (my palms are a little like the ones they show in the BEFORE sections of those Vaseline advertisements). I was so overwhelmed by her touch I started crying like a little baby. She obviously thought it was the ouster from the project that had done me in, and so she began stroking my hair gently, which made me cry even more. Seeing which, she took my violently trembling head (part naturally, part dramatized) and rested it on her fragrant shoulder. I felt my world was complete. Also, right then, I pictured Sameer sitting across those fatsos Pat and Mike, discussing the handover, and my world felt even more complete. I wiped my tears and said it felt wonderful to run into her like that by sheer coincidence at the loneliest hour of my life. And that I would feel even better if she agreed to spend the evening with me over a quiet dinner by the waterfront followed by a long, leisurely walk by the Yarra. The moment she agreed, I decided that would be the day I would hold her emphatically by the arms and tell her I was so done being just a friend and I needed to define our relationship better. Score hundred for subtlety, that.

The setting was perfect. We dined at Bhoj, a fancy Indian diner by the bay, which was more about the experience than about the food, or so said the restaurant manager when I told him later the food was hardly value for the humongous bill we had been charged. But we looked happy together, Mehek and I, laughing heartily at the stupidest of jokes, made mostly by me. I also got the live orchestra to play a romantic ballad to set the tempo for the most epic proposal I was setting the stage for. I don't know why, but the violinist chose to play *Kati Patang,* of all the tens of thousands of romantic numbers that must exist on the face of this earth. Idiot. I had to tip him anyway, and by the time we left that blasted restaurant, I had figured I would be decidedly broke if we extended our stay in that godforsaken country beyond the next week.

We took a long walk by the Yarra. The chill was gnawing at me by the minute. Moreover, there was no point in delaying the inevitable moment after all, I thought. Hands had been held. My hair had been stroked. My head had found the comfort of her shoulder. I only thought the next step would be logical and acceptable. So when we stopped a while later and rested against an iron rail right on the river bank, I passionately looked her in the eye, compelling her to fix her awe-struck gaze at my face. Her lips parted, and quivered a little—or maybe I was blinking too hard. I rested against the iron rail and pulled her by the waist. A gentle breeze crossed the river and swept her hair over her face. I pushed her locks to the back of her ears and held her tight. For the briefest moment I thought she had twitched. It must have been the cold, I told myself. And then, I kissed her.

I don't know how long it lasted. For a split second, I thought she had surrendered herself to me. Her lips did not yield. In fact, when she fiercely tugged at the collar of my shirt like she wouldn't let me go, I had already scored a mental victory as I felt that nascent, burning sexual fever raging within her. But then, something unexpected happened. She twisted my collar and pushed me off her. The impact was so hard I was thrown back by God knows how many feet. I felt my back hit something very cold and metallic in the process. The last I remember of that incident was my entire body passing through a cold current of liquid, head first. Then I blacked out.

When I awoke, I saw three beefy Australians pull me out of the Yarra, asking me in awe what had prompted me to fancy a swim in the river at that time of the night. I looked around as I struggled to regain my senses. Luckily, I hadn't drifted far from the bank. Through blurry eyes, I saw Mehek standing at the bank as she looked on, disengaged and disturbed.

'This is not done, Nakul,' she seemed to say once my rescuers had left the scene. I couldn't hear her well; I felt a loud, uncomfortable drone in my ears. And my bones were crumbling to pieces because of the chill. I asked her if we could talk at length after I got some bodily heat. She shook her head disappointedly and slinked away into the darkness, muttering something I couldn't hear too well because of the cold, 'I have told you a hundred times I am not prepared, you can't be coming on so strong...' I settled uncomfortably on a park bench, moping over the disastrous date. Was this a song I had heard somewhere? *Maybe I'm wrong, won't you tell me if I'm coming on too strong...* I passed out again.

I was woken up two hours later by a call from Dharmesh. I could hardly see clearly, but it looked like it was nearing midnight. He sounded frantic, which was nothing unusual. But he insisted he had to show me something interesting and that

I must come over to the office immediately.

'This had better be good,' I said, struggling to walk in those bloody drenched clothes.

Twenty minutes later, I was seated next to Dharmesh, who was beaming with uncharacteristic positive excitement.

'You are very wet,' he remarked matter-of-factly.

'Yes, I just survived a terrible storm,' I said. 'Now, what was it?'

He pushed his laptop towards me that had a large spreadsheet containing an exhaustive list of all defects our team had reported over the months. I was still cold, and was very hopeful Dharmesh would quit his foreplay and come to the point.

He smiled as he ran me through the list of our reported defects that Lex had claimed were invalid. He explained those tests had worked perfectly well in the morning when he had tried to revalidate them. By the look of it then, Bytesphere had reported the defects in error. But when he re-attempted the same tests in the night, they failed once again.

'What does this imply?' I asked, my ears pricking up slowly.

'Simply said, it means we haven't gone wrong in our report anywhere,' he explained with a broad smile. 'All our rejected defects are the ones we reported while working on them after eight o'clock in the evening. When Lex had the contractors testing them the next morning, the defects ceased to exist.'

'Come to the point—how did they manage that?' I asked, scratching my head.

Through externally built simulators, he explained in detail. I wished I hadn't asked. He went on to read me a few heavily worded pages on simulators and their functions from the internet, none of which I understood even moderately. When I asked him to explain the crux of the matter in normal English, he said Lex's system was indeed riddled with defects, and they were trying to dupe Jerry by using external simulators to make the entire application look smooth and dandy. Unfortunately for Lex, these simulators faced a downtime from seven o'clock every evening to eight o'clock the next morning. They may or may not have known about this flaw in their master stroke, but averting such a downtime would involve a lot of costs that Lex could not have justified to their board. And Dharmesh was sharp enough to catch their bluff. Smart boy. There was something my subordinates were scaling up to under my guidance, after all.

'And such simulators are not permissible in the final product that will go to the market,' I remarked with super-intelligent flourish.

He gave me the no-shit-Sherlock look and said we needed to report this fraud to Jerry immediately and turn the tables back against Lex. I vetoed the idea, because I reckoned it would take us a lifetime to first explain to Jerry what simulators really meant. Also, as Chirayu always quoted, a consultant's job lay not in telling the client about an existing problem but in giving him a possible solution. Moreover, verbal duels were no longer an option: for every verbal attack hereon, we'd be giving Lex double the time to launch a counter attack. We needed something that would nail them once and for all and without any forewarning.

'What do you have in mind then?' he asked unsurely.

'I think I have a plan,' I said ponderously. 'Might need your help to make it work. But you know what? Let's talk tomorrow. Right now, all I can think of is a warm bath and some much needed sleep.'

I returned home to a note Akshat had left on the refrigerator that mentioned his aunt had forced him to accompany her to see the twelve apostles on The Great Ocean Road, and that he would return only the next morning. I hated Akshat.

Tired, I took a quick shower and changed into some clean clothes. I was slightly excited after what Dharmesh had just shown me, but Mehek's behaviour had been very disturbing. I would never speak to her again. Once in bed, I tried calling her one last time, but only to let her know she had overreacted to the situation and that I was disgusted with her behaviour. As expected, she didn't answer the call. So I messaged her something of a half-apology, and added expectantly that I was hopeful she wouldn't consider my sudden outburst of emotions reason enough to report me to Bytesphere's anti-sexual-harassment team. Again, she didn't answer. Now, I was not only heartbroken, but also very afraid. I had a good chance of having my bright career tainted. Fuck.

I couldn't sleep. I sat up in bed and logged into the internet to while away my time.

Hardly anything interesting, except…

Suresh Shah had sent me a friend request on Facebook. Good thing, at least he now knew my name.

# 15.

# The Ghost of Marlon Pacino

Sameer was such an insecure, conniving piglet. The vilest adjectives would not suffice to define him.

First, a brief context.

I woke up the next morning, trying to put the fiasco of the previous night behind me. Mehek had still not replied to my message, but I couldn't care less. At that time, all that mattered was that simulator stuff Dharmesh had told me about, and a kickass plan that could expose Lex and bring us back in contention. And just when I looked like I was beginning to brim with positivity the way I did in the earlier, more energetic years of my career, karma came and bit me in the ass.

Jerry had forwarded me an email with an 'FYI' enclosed. I opened the mail and scanned through it disinterestedly until I scrolled to the bottom.

It was an email sent by Marlon Pacino!

There was, indeed, a Marlon Pacino!

I read the mail chain a little more carefully this time. It had begun with Jerry mailing him about how delighted he had been to read Marlon's analysis on the Bali telecom market, and that he would be obliged to have Marlon's consulting services on a related assignment Oz-Mobil was contemplating in the near future. Whoever this Marlon Pacino fellow was, he sent a response to Jerry which looked largely positive.

Subject: Re: Exciting consulting opportunity

*Hello Mr Jerry White,*

*Pleased to interact with you. I love consulting. I don't remember what analysis and what report you are referring to, and I also can't place this Nakul Kapoor you mentioned had quoted me in your research report. But you see, I work so hard and have my feet in so many projects I tend to forget stuff I may have done in the past.*
*As I said, I love consulting. Between you and me, I hate Bali. I don't know why I am stuck here. I'd love to come to Australia some day. The only problem is I am bound to a contract here, and am obliged not to offer any consulting services to clients not currently listed in the Bali office. Let me think through my options and get back to you real soon.*

*Cheers,*
*Marlon Pacino*

I went hysterical with horror. I ran around the apartment like a madman, randomly tossing crockery out of the window and vandalizing our landlord's furniture (not really, but such was the state of mind), until I tripped over the staircase and landed straight on the front deck of the house. By the time I reached the office, I had completely forgotten about Lex's fake simulators and my supposed counter move. Instead, I went straight to Jerry and nervously started persuading him to give up on the idea of collaborating with Marlon Pacino on absolutely anything until, maybe, I quit my company, died, or at least went someplace incognito. Jerry did not relent. He insisted Marlon Pacino was a genius—yes, just because of some annoyingly long quote he had come across, which was actually NOT written by THIS Marlon Pacino. Jerry was naïve that way. As a different person in a different situation, I might have even felt sorry for him. At that time, I could only feel sorry for myself. I pleaded with Jerry to at least leave me out of this communication. He maintained he only needed me for the first introductory call with Marlon because, after all, I had interviewed him during my fucking primary research—and then, I could get the hell out of there for all he cared.

As I was leaving his room, he handed me a bag of chickpeas and asked me to go empty the packet into Velvet's feeding bowl lying next to him in the car park, because apparently, that would help me overcome my fear of riding horses. I went out and delegated this bonding-with-Velvet responsibility to Akshat. When he returned upstairs, Akshat casually quipped that it would be fun to get Velvet drunk someday. I smiled for a bit, but this was not exactly the time for silly jokes.

I was so, so screwed. Thank God Marlon Pacino had at least shown some kindness by asking for a few days to make up his mind. If any semblance of luck was to be on my side, that overenthusiastic Pacino would hold his horses till I took my flight back home. Once out of Jerry's sight, I wouldn't care much if he discovered how I had actually prepared that much hyped and extolled report.

Because Jerry looked like a relatively happier person that morning and had also shown a rare streak of hospitality by asking me if I'd care for a coffee, I gave the Bytesphere pitch one chance shot. I asked him if he would be willing to allow us to attend the presentation due to be made to the senior management the following week.

'Just in case some snags take you by surprise at the eleventh hour,' I said hopefully.

But a stubborn-as-an-ass Jerry shook his head, saying he wasn't likely to be surprised by anything half as much as he was with the quality of work we had produced in all those months. Moreover, he added, he would have liked to see us gone by the time of that presentation, because he had no intention to sponsor our stay in the country for an extra day beyond the decided date.

Finally, just as I was leaving, I casually asked Jerry how he had managed to get hold of Marlon Pacino.

'Oh, that was easy,' he answered. 'Sameer had helped me a little further with your research during his first week out here. It was he who suggested I try writing to Marlon Pacino to get more meat on the subject. In fact, he helped me dig out Marlon's email address from your company intranet. Nice guy you got there, mate!'

Now, do you see what I mean? I could so put the pieces together. Basically, this insecure, insanely jealous Sameer had his cards laid out right since the day he had barged into our lives. He couldn't stand that understated chemistry Mehek and I shared, and he had arguably been looking for a chance to nail me. Fake sense of achievement, if you please. Mehek may have inadvertently blurted out that forgettable episode where I forged a certain Marlon Pacino's comment in the report, and Sameer would have started getting itchy ever since to try getting me into trouble. I had that irrepressible urge to drag him to the Yarra, tie him to a boulder and drown him in the freezing water. I knew, after all, how that felt.

Only if I still cared, that is. For then, I would consider myself a happy man if I could just avoid this Marlon Pacino telephonic encounter and return home to safety.

Meanwhile, Dharmesh had briefed everyone else about the simulators. Hope had begun to simmer once again, only until I told them Jerry wouldn't let us into the presentation the following week anyway.

'We don't stand a chance then,' grumbled Radha later when we convened to chat further on the simulators. 'He won't listen to us.'

Akshat darted in right then, looking full of beans as he held out a bunch of bright coloured coupons.

'Eva felt terribly sorry for us when she heard we are leaving soon,' he blushed as he spoke. 'And guess what? She has invited us all to a club she is a member of—so that we can get drunk and forget about our miseries for a night. Sweet, yes?'

'Sweet indeed,' I nodded, and then leaned in and whispered to Akshat. 'That's very sweet of your aunt.'

I expected him to maybe melt with embarrassment at being caught lying through his teeth about a fake aunt. Instead, he grinned ear to ear.

'We have something going,' he whispered back.

I felt she was a little too old for him, albeit gorgeous. But he said cougars gave him a wild sense of adventure he couldn't resist.

'What if you found out she was married?' I asked him.

'I did, last night,' he laughed. 'But no, I don't think I'm going to dig her husband much!'

I advised him to be a little careful; nothing good ever came out of messing around with a married woman. Also, I thought it was a very unfair world where one average-looking fellow with a lot of money got to fool around with the cougars of the world, while a well-rounded, charmingly eligible bachelor with good looks and a slightly plump body well-covered under loose shirts—got thrown into a river for politely kissing the girl he had been politely pursuing for over three years. I didn't mention this to him, though.

'So, are we all on for the evening?' he turned to everyone else.

Everyone looked up, except Mehek—who had been sulking in a corner of the bay, her face glued to her laptop. Sameer was stuck to her like a parasite, sweet-talking her into telling him what was wrong and if he could work his syrupy conduct towards lifting her spirits.

I presumed she was still upset about the previous night—but hey, she was not the one who got pushed into the Yarra. And she wasn't the one jilted. What was she so grouchy about? I will never understand good-looking women. I would never speak to her again. Unless she got back to me with a better response than the previous night's. Or unless, at least, she held my hand again and told me there was still hope in that hopeless pursuit. Or unless, at least, she looked away from her laptop and made eye contact with me... No. I would never talk to her again.

'I am in,' Sameer looked up finally at Akshat. 'In fact, both of us are in.'

Great. So Raymond Boy was her spokesman now. This was par tolerance. I looked away.

'Dharmesh Bhai can join us if he likes,' Akshat added slyly, glancing at Dharmesh. 'We could order some Bournvita.'

Dharmesh flinched and turned to me. 'Nakul, we have something better to discuss than some random shindig being planned, yes?'

'I almost forgot,' I knocked myself on the head. 'Listen up, all. Now what do we do about these simulators?'

Our options were few, we concluded. Given that Jerry

wouldn't listen to reason, our only chance was to infect Lex's system by failing those simulators somehow. Dharmesh said that was not entirely impossible, because Radha and he had sat through that morning, carefully examining the lines of code these simulators had been built on. To our delight, they informed us they were likely to be able to tamper with those codes and upset the functioning of the simulators.

'But it will be a long haul,' Dharmesh added.

I gave them twenty-four hours; we couldn't risk waiting any longer.

'We are going to reconfigure this shit!' Dharmesh squeaked, his body trembling violently. 'Their system is going to go berserk.'

'I hope you know what you guys are doing,' is all I could say in response.

We watched Dharmesh and Radha work their way through the simulators the entire day, tottering around their screens continually to understand in vain what they were up to. When we weren't feeling over-inquisitive, we whiled our time away on the social network. I found Mehek online, and although I had no intention to talk to her, I did send in a simple, courteous 'Hi'. When I didn't get a response, I showed some much needed presence of mind and followed it up with another message: 'Sent by mistake. Not meant for you. Bye.'

Man, she was very pissed. But seriously, whatever.

By evening, Dharmesh and Radha, visibly exhausted, said they would need no less than another two days to confirm this plan was worth pursuing.

I clucked my tongue. 'Why would you need that long?'

They gave me the 'Why don't you do it yourself, Einstein?' look and then explained the codes were too complicated and they'd be lucky if they managed only to reconfigure the codes through the length of that night. Further, they would need the whole of the next day to execute some dry runs and all to ensure the simulators had gone crazy enough. If all went well, we could take Lex by surprise on the third day. Which would also be the day of the big presentation to the management.

I looked at my watch; it was nearing dinnertime. And we looked like we needed a break. Ok, Dharmesh and Radha actually looked like they needed a break, and we looked like we didn't mind an extended break. So we decided to wrap up for the evening and head out to Eva's club and drown out our anxiety. Everyone looked like they needed to get piss drunk.

Akshat left early: he'd meet us directly at the club after his workout—with Eva, naturally. Sameer left shortly with Mehek, still very restive about Mehek's gloomy countenance. I chose to stay back, thanks to those undercurrents of awkwardness Mehek was sending me.

I waited for Dharmesh and Radha to wrap up. In the meantime, I responded to a few anxious mails from Chirayu I had not bothered to read that entire week—the usual humbug about status reports and senseless spreadsheets. We had somehow managed to keep the news of our disastrous last month from reaching him thus far. I was not sure how long we'd manage that, though.

I logged on to the social network one last time before we packed for the day.

Suresh Shah had poked me on Facebook.

Wait.

Suresh Shah had poked me on Facebook!

What the fuck was happening?

I needed to get piss drunk now.

We didn't have an exciting start to Eva's party. Just as we

were about to enter the club, three completely naked men came running out of the gate, singing *Fireflies* very loudly and completely out of rhythm. She might deny it if we ask her now, but I swear Radha's eyes had popped out at the sight, and her mouth had opened so wide she looked like the Anaconda in anticipation of a delicious prey. A handful of very pretty girls, unfortunately fully clothed, stood to one side of the entrance and cheered the naked men on. Weird things happened down under.

'It is very routine,' Eva explained to us once we were seated inside. 'People get drunk and wild out here. It's a very Friday thing.'

She offered us a bottle of beer each. Dharmesh and Radha didn't touch theirs, so I happily obliged on their behalf as well. Three bottles of beer in under half an hour: this was turning out to be fun. I had not had so much alcohol in a long time. And to imagine this was all on Eva—sheer bliss. I loved Akshat, seriously.

Akshat, who already looked like he was sitting in the woman's lap, now leaned on her completely and let out a soft purr.

'Since when did getting wild become a Friday thing?' he asked seductively—seductively from Eva's perspective, that is. 'I like getting wild all the time!'

Eva giggled along with him, their hands reaching for each other's body parts in socially inappropriate manners. Dharmesh was stunned. He looked like he had just seen The Big Bang or something.

'I am not comfortable here,' he muttered under his breath. 'I am going to leave.'

He rose a little from his seat, and then stayed like that, motionless, his bums suspended mid-air.

'Dharmesh?' I looked at him, startled, wondering what he was up to.

But he didn't listen. He seemed lost in the time-space continuum. His eyes were wide open, fixed at a young lady about his age, or maybe a year younger, sitting two tables across. She looked a little pensive, and was clearly the soberest person in the otherwise loud and inebriated lounge. She was seated alone, and had been listlessly swaying a glass of red wine in her left hand.

Dharmesh had never looked happier. Or let me say, Dharmesh had never looked happy. Before he saw this girl, that is. Frankly, if I were to be asked, she wasn't all that great—not the kind you would hover around, checking her out with a slant gaze while pretending to text someone on your phone. Not even close. But fine, maybe she was attractive by Dharmesh's standards.

No, look, I am not being judgemental. All I mean is Dharmesh had had a very bad run as far as his encounter with the fairer sex was concerned. When he had his chance as a bachelor, he was trapped in an engineering course—engineering is such a bitch it doesn't give you much time to think about all the lovely women around you. In fact, if you are in an engineering college, chances are there *won't* be any lovely women around you. Then, before he could gain cognizance of his budding desire to explore his youth, his family married him off to a loud witch who made him lose all faith in the goodness of women. Poor guy. It was only fair that he felt that instant, unrestrained attraction towards that average, slightly plump and freckled blonde sitting alone at that table.

'Dharmesh, are you alright?' I looked at him, concerned.

He was still in exactly the same position, his back arched at a right angle to his half-risen posterior. I turned to the others to check if they had seen what I had seen. Radha had not; she still looked stumped after that sight of white men running around in the buff. Akshat was into Eva, figuratively and almost literally too, so he had not bothered to notice either. Until Mehek and Sameer walked in, apologizing profusely for being late.

'I was a little out of sorts,' Mehek explained as they exchanged pleasantries with Eva. 'We are sorry to keep you waiting.'

'That's alright,' Eva offered them two bottles of beer. 'Sorry we didn't wait for you.'

I looked at Mehek questioningly. My eyes met hers and tried asking her about her problem. Her eyes met mine and told me *I* was her problem. She wouldn't get over it, would she? I didn't think so much footage was warranted for a harmless, well-intended display of my love. Did one have to sign petitions to kiss a person one loved? What nonsense. Once the tension between us was confirmed as there to stay, she took a seat on the booth as far away from me as possible. Sameer got into the booth soon after and deposited himself next to her, sticking to her like a layer of termite.

Dharmesh, meanwhile, was still in limbo. I had to finally pull him back to his seat.

'Someone just got floored,' Akshat said finally, when he was done making out with Eva, full and proper. 'Do you see that, people? Our ice man has just melted in someone's presence.'

'Nonsense,' Dharmesh muttered, breaking off his reverie.

Everyone began cajoling Dharmesh for details. I silenced everyone, saying it was not right for us to prod him if he didn't want to talk about it. Then I quietly asked him if it was the freckled girl two tables across. He nodded tentatively.

'Guys, it is that girl there,' I pointed excitedly in the direction of her table.

'You must talk to her,' Eva suggested.

'I can't,' Dharmesh dismissed the advice. 'I am married.'

'Actually he is a divorcee,' Akshat explained to Eva, supposedly in a sympathetic tone.

'Aye you!' snapped Dharmesh. 'Stop calling me that!'

'That's what we usually call a guy who has separated from his wife,' argued Akshat. 'What are you getting so touchy about?'

'Now, don't get started again, you two,' Sameer raised a hand. Usual mediator attitude he could not rid himself of.

Then, Sameer spoke to Dharmesh in his own comforting, articulate way of convincing people to do all the things they should actually never do—like that collaborative approach with Lex he had put forward once. He waxed eloquent about how important it was to be a go-getter and steal an opportunity in order to leverage its real potential. No one understood peanuts about what he was blabbering. I think he had lifted it from his ISB orientation manual or something. Jerk. I told Dharmesh to use his own wisdom instead; judging from her expressions, the girl didn't look like she was going to fall for any go-getter shit.

'When it is about a woman,' Sameer argued in his preachy tone, 'you can never afford to play on the backfoot.'

I looked at Sameer and Mehek sharply, and slyly replied he had been evidently putting his theories into practice himself. Mehek gave me a quick nasty look and then started fiddling with her beer bottle again.

Presently, a steward spread out a tray with vodka shots on our table.

'With compliments from me,' Eva declared, raising her hands. 'Let's get drunk, guys! Woot!'

'I don't drink,' said Dharmesh, offering his shot back to Eva.

'Neither do I, actually,' added Radha, though I'm pretty sure she looked very enthralled by the idea of getting drunk on shots.

'Oh, come on!' Eva egged them on. 'You can't turn vodka shots down. We can't let you just sit and watch us get drunk, can we?'

'I don't mind some Coke, actually,' Dharmesh said thoughtfully.

Eva rolled her eyes in horror. 'Oh no! We don't do coke out here.'

'He is talking about Coca-Cola, Eva!' Akshat clarified before both of them burst into peals of laughter.

'Akshat, won't you ask your friends to have some fun here?' Eva suggested.

Akshat shook his head, taking another large swig of his beer. 'I gave up on them in early days.'

'Shut up!' snarled Dharmesh.

'Come on Dharmesh, prove him wrong,' Eva stoked him further. I think she was getting drunk already.

'I think she is right,' Radha said suddenly. 'What fun is it being in the midst of so much alcohol without trying a little?'

We all looked at Radha in amazement. I was a little shocked. I told her there was absolutely no need for her to succumb to social pressures and that she had rather stay away. I feared if she got drunk and passed out, no one would be particularly excited about carrying her back to her apartment. Also, who would fucking reconfigure those codes through the night if she passed out?

But before I could stop her, she had lunged forward to grab her vodka shot.

'This looks nice! Woot!' she raised her hands in the air, almost knocking Dharmesh's head off.

'To Dharmesh Bhai and his latest pursuit,' shouted Akshat

as we all raised our vodka shots in a toast.

'Dharmesh, you can't turn it down,' Eva reminded him. 'This is your host demanding you pick that thing up and join us in the toast.'

He looked at the liquid as though he were going to put it in a test tube and conduct some sort of research. He then let out a short sigh and held it in his hand. 'Cheers.'

He gulped it down distastefully. Surprisingly, it didn't hit him as bad as we had feared. He shook his head to recover from the taste and then looked at the girl at the other table once again.

'Ah, I liked it!' he exclaimed.

'Really?' Radha looked at him uncertainly, her vodka still untouched.

'Indeed, I'll have another,' he grabbed another shot and downed it instantly.

Inspired by his reaction, Radha downed her shot in a jiffy and raised her hands in the air once again. 'Woot!'

She really needed to stop using that word so often.

Two seconds later, she turned to the side of the booth, made a very weird expression, and then puked about a bucketful, just about two centimeters short of my fifty dollars worth of shoes. She was lucky I was going down myself with all that unprecedented consumption of alcohol, or else I was not going to take to that too kindly.

'I am going to ask her out,' Dharmesh declared all of a sudden, picking up his third shot.

'Maybe you should keep that down,' Mehek spoke finally, trying to snatch the vodka from his hand.

'No, lady,' Dharmesh protested. 'I am a go-getter. I am going to go get her!'

He slurped on his third shot and stood up.

The others cheered him on. I still didn't think it was a great idea, but he seemed to have made up his mind. I closed my eyes as I watched him approach the girl with something of a swagger in his gait. Luckily for him, he was nowhere close to a river.

'Go for it, Dharmesh Bhai!' Radha shouted behind him, barely able to sit straight. I had to literally push her off my shoulder. I wasn't liking where this evening was heading.

We watched with baited breath as Dharmesh had a nearly muted conversation with the girl that lasted no more than ten seconds. Twenty seconds later, he was back at our booth, demanding more vodka.

'What happened?' Sameer asked him.

'I introduced myself and asked her for her name,' said Dharmesh.

'What did she say?'

'Buzzoff,' he said dreamily. 'Her name is Buzzoff. She was so charming I don't have words.'

We didn't have the heart to shake him off his reverie. Moreover, it needed a sober, alert mind to let him know that was not really her name. But we were all drunk for good measure, except Mehek, who didn't look like she gave a damn about anything anymore.

Five minutes later, the girl walked up to our table with a sheepish smile. We couldn't see through his soda glasses very well, but we guessed from Dharmesh's passiveness to her arrival that he had fallen asleep. She knocked lightly on his hand. He was completely awake, we realized, only too stoned to react.

'I am sorry about asking you to buzz off,' she said with a faint smile.

'Oh,' Dharmesh replied. 'I thought that was your name.'

A long pause followed. Luckily, she didn't take exception

to the remark. In fact, she laughed and said her name was Gloria. She was just a little disoriented and was not particularly receptive to anyone trying to socialize with her.

'Are you receptive now?' Dharmesh asked her matter-of-factly.

She smiled a little more affirmatively this time, alongside wondering at what point of their conversation Dharmesh would consider offering her a seat. When he finally did not, Eva shoved herself inward a little and offered her some room in the booth.

'Actually,' Gloria said, turning to Dharmesh again. 'I was wondering if you could walk me home?'

'I'd love to,' Dharmesh stood up instantly. 'And then, maybe, you could walk me to my office in return? I don't think I am going to remember the way back.'

'His sense of humour!' Akshat muttered under his breath.

'You are a funny guy, Dharmesh,' Gloria laughed.

'No, I am darn serious. This guy wants me to go back to work now and finish some crappy code work,' he pointed a finger at me accusingly. 'Why doesn't he do it himself, by the way?'

I had to literally push him out of the booth finally. 'Just drop her home, won't you?'

Through fuzzy eyes, I saw them exit the lounge, and I think they were holding hands as they walked out. Wonderful.

Boys making the scene with cougars. Boys walking lonely girls home. Boys impressing girls' families by way of hollow credentials. Boys getting dunked in a cold river for a simple, honest expression of love. Was there no sense of balance and consistency this world worked on?

I drank a little more till I started smelling like a mobile tavern. And then I began speaking something about which I remember very little. It is all based on what Akshat tells me now. It may be true, but when I look back at his version of the story, it feels a little unbelievable. He said I had embarked on a long, tedious speech on unrequited love, quoting examples of 'a friend' who had been through such a journey, only to nearly get drowned by the woman he had loved. Somewhere in the middle of the speech, Akshat tells me, Mehek walked out of the club in a fit, with Sameer following her, advising her to ignore my behaviour.

Shortly after, he tells me, I called a girl called Nandy from my phone, and began a long monologue on why showing people that you care mattered a great deal. It sounded like a one-sided conversation, he says, because I spoke without any interruption. But I spoke very long. I don't know till date what I said; it didn't stay on my voicemail records.

But there was another call I made that night that stayed on records. And that, indeed, was a disturbing call. Apparently, I received a phone call from Chirayu very late that night. I refused to answer it. Instead, I threw a big fit and sent him an obscene message on his voicemail, which went something like this:

*Chirayu, fuck you and your status reports. Grow up. I don't need you dancing on my head like a ghost all the time. I don't have a life. I have sold myself to this company. And yet, nothing gives. I still have the same mediocre life I had three years ago. But you won't stop bothering me, will you? Now listen up, fathead. Stop calling me every now and then, like your pants are on fire. I don't give a crocodile's ass about your SLUT or whatever other dozen reports you have come up with for no reason whatsoever. Also, FYI, it's midnight here. Do you consider the time zone differences before picking up the phone to call people? Moron!*

I still can't believe Chirayu is still my manager. I still can't believe I got away with that message. I still can't believe we *actually* got Velvet drunk on our way home that night. If

Akshat's story is anything to go by, because I remember only some bits of it, we had taken a detour back to our office on our way home from the club. Today I feel terrible about having compromised a horse's abstinence from alcohol. But apparently that night, in a drunken state, I had been cursing a lot and must have said something silly about my experience with Velvet. Akshat convinced me to exact revenge, so we bought three cans of Victoria Bitters from the nearest convenience store and went to the office car park. As Akshat had correctly guessed, Jerry was at the Park Hyatt for his usual Friday night routine of wine-and-cheese with some equally boring friends. And poor Velvet was whiling its time away at its usual spot behind the car park. The feeding bowl was nearly empty. Akshat opened the first can of Victoria Bitters and put it to Velvet's mouth, who let out a short neigh in denial. So Akshat took a few large swigs, after which Velvet saw his happy face and changed its mind and moved closer to the can. The metallic lid of the can repelled him; we obliged by pouring the liquid into the feeding bowl. Velvet's eyes lit up with joy. But the joy was short-lived. For we heard a very angry voice boom right behind us.

'Who the hell is out there?' We saw a shadow charge towards us through the unlit parking bays—must have been the security officer of the building.

'Just feeding our friend here,' I attempted to get into a discussion, but Akshat dragged me out of the man's sight. This sudden bodily movement had us turn poor Velvet's bowl over. I let out a short cry as I saw our precious Victoria Bitters spill over the floor. But there is no point crying over spilled beer, especially when you are in serious trouble. So we ran. But the security officer was a strong-willed man. He gave us a long chase right till the nearest tram stop which must have been at least two hundred metres out of the car park. And he was gaining on us fast, because Akshat had it a little difficult trying to run with my weight on his shoulders—quite literally, because I was not quite in a position to run myself and was hanging around his arms like a polythene bag. He missed us by a whisker as we made it into a tram, which was a relief, but we were only a little scared we might have exposed ourselves in front of the security cameras. Of course this thought occurred to us only the next morning. That night, we simply sank into our beds the moment we reached home.

I was woken up from my slumber hours later by a phone call from a girl who spoke in a very shaky voice.

'Nakul, this is Gloria,' she said, her voice trembling.

I answered groggily. 'Gloria…Estefan?'

'No, Gloria from the lounge earlier tonight,' she said with a shiver. 'Nakul, Dharmesh is very hurt.'

'That happens to him all the time. He is an emotional fellow. What is he hurt about now?'

Her voice trembled. 'He is very badly hurt. I've brought him to the city hospital. Please come over immediately.'

# 16.

# Skin & Bone

Damn it. I would never touch alcohol in my life again, or at least for as long as I could help it. I woke up in steady installments after having hung up on Gloria. I looked at the watch by the bedside through bleary eyes: three in the morning. Dharmesh was hurt, Dharmesh was hurt—I repeated to keep myself from flopping back on the bed. The moment I stepped down, my feet landed in a puddle of very sticky fluid. I turned on the lights and found myself amidst a rivulet of yellow puke. Blasted luck.

I ran to the other room and woke Akshat, whom I was very pleasantly surprised to find sleeping in his own apartment for a change. If he showed any sign of waking up, it disappeared the moment I told him we needed to go meet Dharmesh in the hospital.

'Your call,' I shrugged. 'But just to let you know, there is a whole lot of puke swimming on the floor of this apartment and it might raise a stink any moment.'

In two minutes, Akshat was waiting for me outside the apartment, fully awake.

We hailed a cab and drove to the city hospital. En route, Akshat had informed everyone else about the development. Half an hour later, we were all standing by Dharmesh's bedside at the hospital. The poor chap had got a horrid facial treatment. His cheeks looked swollen and had acquired a purplish hue—not a pretty one at all. There was a huge cut on his upper lip. His mouth looked swollen too, and darkish, uneven lumps had formed below his eyes. Gloria sat by his side, her hand tenderly stroking his. He looked at us stone-faced and made some noise which we were not sure was a greeting or a whimper. The doctor came in, poured some liquid into his mouth that put him at ease, for like three minutes or so before he started moaning again.

'Two stitches on the lips, one under the chin, and a hairline fracture in the hand,' the doctor informed us as we looked on in stunned disbelief. 'We will give him a tranquilizer soon. I am afraid he needs to stay put here for the next twenty-four hours, if not more.'

We summoned Gloria outside the room and asked for the story. She looked white with fear and wasn't keen to share details, but we persisted. She said she had enjoyed a long walk with Dharmesh from the lounge back to her townhouse in Preston. And during the course of that long walk, they had formed, well, some sort of connection. When they arrived outside her house, she recalled, they spent that extra moment holding hands and looking into each other's lovelorn eyes, which did the damage. Just as he was about to take leave of her, two drunk natives accosted them unprovoked, and roughed Dharmesh up like they meant it. She asked them to back off, but they were insistent on letting Dharmesh know they weren't going to sit by the fence and applaud an Indian guy getting cozy with their girls.

'No, I don't know them,' she explained on being asked. 'I know where they stay, though. Those guys are no good; they like kicking up a storm every now and then.'

She further explained that Dharmesh, struggling to stand straight, had tried calming himself down and had said he didn't mean to cause trouble. The two men laughed as they pulled out a short baton and a metallic chain from nowhere, and asked him how would he like to receive some trouble instead. Gloria tried shoving the big men off, but failed. Exasperated, she closed her eyes to hear the sound of metal thrashing against skin and bone. Thirty seconds may have been all that it lasted, but the trauma was intense enough to last a lifetime.

'We can't let them get away,' Akshat growled.

'I know where they stay,' Gloria confirmed. 'It is the street across from where I stay. I am not sure, I think one of their names is Glenn.'

'Don't even think about it,' Mehek said, horrified. 'Those guys sound dangerous.'

'And they are an entire gang of troublemakers,' added Gloria.

Two minutes of silence passed before Sameer grandly suggested we write a petition to some authorized body asking for an apology. I congratulated him for the brilliant idea and requested him to write Tony Abbott an email right away. For my part, after all that we had been through, getting into a fight with a bunch of well-built, nasty natives didn't sound exciting. And I didn't feel like involving myself in any legality either. All I hoped for was a last effort at fixing a critical meeting with Jerry, or at least making it back to my country mentally and physically intact.

The doctor met us once again, informing us he had administered a tranquilizer to Dharmesh and that he would be put to sleep shortly. We visited him one more time for the night to assure him he didn't look too bad and that his face would get its charming features back real soon.

'I feel so terrible,' he said drowsily. 'I am sorry about having ruined our plan, Nakul. I won't be able to work on those codes any time soon.'

'I can reconfigure those codes,' said Radha.

I looked at her doubtfully. She still looked very much under the effect of alcohol. I wondered if she really meant what she said.

Shit! I had almost forgotten about the codes! What would we do now?

'But I won't be able to execute the dry runs on the programmes tomorrow all by myself,' she added ruefully. 'That process is very time consuming. I will need Dharmesh's assistance there.'

Dharmesh sulked and looked the other way, overcome by guilt, almost ready to cry. I patted him and said there was nothing to worry as long as he was going to be fine soon. Then, I very casually asked him what he thought of the idea of us getting him his laptop in the hospital room the next morning so that he could continue working on the programmes from the comfort of his bed. I withdrew the proposal the moment I got a long, disgusted stare from Mehek.

'I can't forgive myself for spoiling the party,' Dharmesh winced uncomfortably.

Akshat spoke to him finally. 'I don't know about the simulators. But I am not sure you should forgive yourself for not teaching those goons a lesson.'

We hushed Akshat out of the room. Dharmesh looked on dreamily as he gradually drifted into sleep.

သ

The timing of Radha's phone call the next evening could not have been better.

I was at home, trying on a tuxedo I had rented from a store when I realized I couldn't afford to buy one specially for Jerry's high-profile celebratory bash. The others had opted against attending the party so they could tend to Dharmesh back at his apartment instead. I thought it useful to attend it so I could bond with Jerry over a drink and try some networking—a habit I had acquired from all those MBA alumni meets. I never saw much value in these 'networking' meets, but it somehow felt good to tell people you were 'networking'. As Akshat had been strongly advised to stay away from Dharmesh during the latter's feeble mental condition, he chose to tag along with me and told me he would meet me directly at Jerry's.

Just when I was preparing to leave, Radha called with a message that had me jumping like a yoyo.

'The programmes were run successfully,' she shouted excitedly. 'All the defects we had raised are indeed valid—one hundred per cent. We can give Jerry a demo on my machine.'

Up yours, Lex Technologies! Up yours!

I rode a train to Jerry's extravagant, awe-inspiring countryside villa in Epping and waited a good thirty minutes before Akshat arrived, gasping for breath.

'Where have you been?' I asked, pointing at my watch.

'Running some errands,' he said, and ran up the steps to Jerry's porch.

An impeccably dressed butler answered the doorbell and examined our ill-fitting tuxedos a little suspiciously.

'By invitation,' I extended a hand.

'Indeed,' he grumbled and let us in after examining the list of invitees.

A huge crowd had spread over Jerry's gigantic living room. We made our way through a sea of people engaging in the kind of elitist conversations that made us feel decidedly out of place. We found Jerry by the fireplace, in conversation with a grey-haired, well titled gentleman. Pat and Mike stood alongside like sore thumbs, nodding periodically like puppets at the grey haired man. We approached them tentatively.

'Ah, so you are here!' Jerry exclaimed almost sarcastically, and then introduced us to the grey haired man as the team that was once meant to deliver the acceptance testing of the product to Oz-Mobil.

'But, well...' Jerry paused, and then looked at Pat and Mike, who started laughing like two little rotund devils.

'This is, by the way, our CEO—Vivian Seaver,' Jerry said, motioning towards the grey haired man.

Vivian looked at us rather sympathetically. 'Rather unfortunate, I heard you are leaving us. So where do you go from here?'

'Back home,' said Pat, laughing uproariously. I had a mind to toss him on to the barbeque placed next to him.

'Ah, let's not discuss work here,' protested Jerry. 'Guys, let me take you to the bar and make you a drink.'

Jerry led us away towards the bar. 'Thanks for coming, guys. Where are the others?'

'Dharmesh has taken ill,' I said, avoiding a direct mention of the attack. 'The others are looking after him.'

'I see,' he stared at us pensively, and then looked at us like an FBI agent. 'Would you have an idea, I wonder, about some miscreants who strolled into our office car park late Friday night and tried to get my horse drunk?'

'What a ghastly thing to do!' Both of us exclaimed almost simultaneously. I hoped the discussion would end right there, but Akshat went a step further and said he never did late nights and he did not even know that Jerry had a horse. At this point Jerry called his bluff and informed us that he had seen the CCTV footage of a few days ago when Akshat had gone down to feed chickpeas to the horse.

'Unfortunately, that night Velvet was not standing in a position for us to get a clear view of those bastards who tried to get funny with my poor baby. I can only hope they rot in hell, those first class dicks!'

We were trying to bring ourselves to nod in agreement when he waved at someone standing behind us.

'Oh, I must introduce you to my wife. Eva, darling—come here for a minute, won't you?'

Eva Swenn emerged from the thickness of the crowd, dressed to kill in a bottle green gown that fitted perfectly against her dangerous curves.

IN THE NAME OF CHRIST!
WE WERE DOOMED!
APOCALYPSE NOW!

The colour drained off our faces as the three of us stood facing each other. Eva skirted our gaze, looking everywhere across the hall except at us.

'The loveliest woman I've ever known,' Jerry gave her a light pat on the back. 'Eva, meet Nakul and Akshat. Make them comfortable, won't you?'

I wanted to assure him Akshat wouldn't need the slightest signal to get comfortable with Eva, and as far as I was concerned, I felt dead already. What a useless fucker, this Akshat! Did he not find any other woman on the face of the planet to fool around with? I should have known this chap would never come to any good.

We observed Jerry's expressions with mortal fear. Thankfully, he hadn't got a whiff of Akshat's antics. As yet, that is. And before he got an inkling, I had to play my cards urgently. So I nudged Jerry to a corner and told him we could swear to death about a startling revelation in Lex's application, which would force him to reconsider our dismissal from the project. What Jerry had refused to entertain while sitting in his office, he totally rebutted in his happy spirits.

'You guys try too hard,' he admonished me. 'I am not entertaining this discussion any more.'

'We only need fifteen minutes of your time,' I begged of him. This guy was more thick skinned than I had first imagined. 'If you could only drop in to office tomorrow, we could show you a demo on Radha's machine...'

He looked at me as though I had plucked his innards out by calling him to the office on a Sunday. I told him Lex had been using makeshift simulators to run their system apparently smoothly, but those simulators wouldn't work in the real environment and the system would come unstuck. He looked at me, frustrated and confused, and asked me to recap the problem statement in a layman's language. I returned the frustrated look and said what I had just explained was already in a layman's language.

He turned to Vivian, who stood a few feet away, wondering what the matter was.

'Look here, mate,' Jerry said threateningly. 'I am having none of this. Pat and Mike have run me through the application, one on one. And it works perfectly according to me.'

He said he didn't understand two pence about what simulators were and how they functioned. And he didn't want to understand them either, as long as the system worked fine when he presented it to Vivian on Tuesday.

'What if you find the system is riddled with defects?' I asked helplessly.

'Fat chance,' he smirked. 'And if at all it is, we will tackle the defects in the next release of the project. Period.'

'But...'

'That will be all, mate,' he waved me away. 'Now have a good time at the party. And I hope you have arranged for your trip back home. Oz-Mobil ain't sponsoring you guys a day beyond Monday.'

'That will be taken care of,' I replied disappointedly.

'Oh, and did I mention Marlon's response to my email?' his voice suddenly rose with excitement.

There. The final nail in my coffin. I didn't even feel like reacting to all of this any further. Jerry told me Marlon had been disallowed from officially participating in consulting engagements with Oz-Mobil, but he was more than happy to help Jerry off the record by communicating through his personal email address. A clear effort at presenting a case to get employed by Oz-Mobil for a more lucrative position in the future, I know. Not that it mattered an ounce to me. Except that Jerry still wanted me to get on to that introductory call with Marlon for some reason. Deep shit situation. He said Marlon would offer some free time the week after and that I would be expected to get on a conference call and give him a recap about that damned research report that apparently contained his findings on Bali's telecom market.

I retreated into the crowd dejectedly. There was no point being here now. I looked around for Akshat who came to me ten minutes later and said Eva wanted to give him a private tour of Jerry's stud farm in the backyard. These two had got to be kidding me, I was beginning to imagine, when a nasty idea occurred to me.

I feel continually guilty about it even today. But in retrospect, it was the only choice I had left with me then. Moreover, I made sure I didn't spell it out myself. I took Akshat to a corner, led him subtly to the idea in my mind, and got *him* to finally suggest it.

I told Akshat we had lost practically all hope of reviving ourselves on the project, but for one slim hope: that Jerry voluntarily see in the application what we managed to see—without the need for us to show it to him.

Our eyes lit up with a sense of purpose. We picked up another drink each, took a large gulp, and high-fived each other like we had read each other well.

'I will hold fort here,' my fiery eyes seemed to tell his. 'You go execute the mission.'

His eyes met Eva's in turn. I expected them to swing into action in this moment of urgency. But, no. Eva first led Akshat through a French window to the stud farm for a private tour. I stood impatiently by the window, watched her guide him into Velvet's barn, out of which they took a pretty long time to emerge. During this time I had a few hash browns and chicken teriyaki rolls and studiously examined the acreage of Jerry's animal farm, which was certainly bigger than Essel World. When they finally stepped out of the barn, Akshat grabbed Eva by the wrist. I was shitting bricks by now. I blocked the view of the guests inside by blocking the window as much as I could with my ample frame.

'I have a favour to ask of you,' he said to her.

'I just did you one,' she replied, letting go of his grip. 'And you did not even tell me you were leaving.'

'I may not have to, immediately at least,' he said, 'provided you can help us here.'

Sometime during this drama, Jerry had suddenly realized there were more guests in the room than the bosses he needed to suck up to, and some of them were really hungry. He had now frantically begun looking for his wife so she could supervise the butler serving dinner, and I was frantically hoping Akshat would not hold Eva's wrist like that again.

'Not a chance I won't agree,' Eva stepped forward and kissed Akshat again.

Three seconds. That was all that separated us from a major catastrophe. Three seconds after that unnecessary kiss, Jerry spotted Eva standing with Akshat in a seemingly harmless manner. He waved at her. She nodded and began walking inside.

Akshat trotted alongside. 'I need your husband's laptop,' he said, inviting a cold, questioning stare from her.

'I can promise you it's nothing malicious,' Akshat reasoned. 'If anything, it is in Jerry's interest too. He is just too stubborn at the moment for us to take a legitimate route at work.'

'I don't know what you are talking about,' she said placidly. 'But that guy is my husband. What are the chances I'm going to let you steal his laptop?'

'We are just borrowing it,' he tried explaining, but she had entered the living room now. She gave me a cold glance and went straight into the kitchen. Akshat stood next to me, shame-faced.

'Useless!' I sneered.

Minutes later, guests started sauntering towards the large dining area. Akshat and I stood our ground, staring vacantly at Velvet's barn. I was just thinking aloud if abducting Velvet and asking for the laptop in return would amount to much, when

Eva tapped Akshat on the shoulder.

'The middle drawer in the foyer. Now get out before someone sees you.'

'You are one remarkable woman!' I told her. She winked at us and slinked back into the crowd. We tiptoed out of the hallway. A chester stood in a corner of the foyer. We had no time to look over our shoulder. We slid open the middle drawer, pulled out the only bag lying in there, and then ran to the railway station like our pants were on fire.

'Bravo, tiger!' I congratulated him once we were safe inside the train.

He looked out of the window. I am not sure if this was his pensive look, because I had never seen it before.

'One hell of a woman,' he said. 'One hell of a woman.'

# 17.

# Cheesecake

It was nearing eleven in the night when we pressed the doorbell at Dharmesh's apartment frantically. Sameer attended to us, looking most bloody amused about the trousers of my suit reaching barely above the ankles. I didn't care to explain, but Akshat told him I had to rent a tuxedo from a cheap rental store because I could not afford one. We walked in to find Dharmesh tucked comfortably in bed. Gloria was by his side—apparently, she had barely slept a wink the previous night so she could tend to him.

Aww! So sweet, no?

Mehek and Radha were in the kitchen, cooking Dharmesh some insipid looking oats. There was a time this Mehek was sweet too. Long ago. Now she dunked unsuspecting lover boys. Sameer led me near the kitchen, and after making sure Mehek was within earshot, the bastard loudly asked me why I rented a tuxedo from a cheap store when I could have borrowed his expensive, designer Armani tuxedo he liked to carry around wherever he went. Then he chose to answer it himself when he noted the waist sizes would have differed and so that option wouldn't have worked out.

Mehek walked past me, greeted Akshat and asked him if she could fix him a quick meal. I loudly announced I was very hungry, scouting around the kitchen for food, hoping she would acknowledge my presence in some way. She did not, but Radha brought forward a bowl containing a red, slimy gravy which she said were drumsticks cooked in sumptuous coconut gravy. She said I could eat to my heart's content because everyone present in the house had collectively been unable to consume even a third of it. I took one strong whiff of the concoction and knew exactly why. I said I was suddenly not hungry anymore; in fact, we had come there with a very specific purpose for which we would need her valuable help.

We gathered around Dharmesh. We couldn't see much of his face because it was mostly wrapped in bandages, but he looked pretty happy with Gloria by his side. I told everyone of the episode at Jerry's, and his stubbornness against reason and logic, after which we stole his laptop for a night so he could see for himself on Tuesday what we had known all along—that Lex's system was, indeed, completely awry. When I saw them staring at me like I was a thief, I immediately added we took this extreme step only because Akshat had been feeling terrible at the party when he learnt of all the effort Dharmesh had put in behind this whistle-blowing business. And that he said he was willing to put everything at stake to bring Dharmesh's hard work the justice it deserved. Akshat didn't look convinced, but Dharmesh seemed totally overwhelmed by Akshat's sudden display of brotherly love.

'Really?' Dharmesh looked at Akshat, almost teary-eyed.

Akshat placed Jerry's laptop by Dharmesh's bedside. 'I don't know. But maybe, if Nakul says so.'

Of course, Sameer intervened, suggesting it was rather unethical for us to steal the client's laptop like that. But for a change, nobody paid heed to his bullshit. He and his pillars of principles could go take a hike.

Dharmesh sat up straight, suddenly re-energized by this unexpected feeling of bonhomie.

He pumped his fractured fist in the air and spoke weakly through his bandaged mouth. 'Power to us! Radha, can you stay back with me for the night?'

Radha went as red as her drumsticks in coconut gravy. 'What?'

'To copy the simulator codes on to Jerry's laptop, that is,' he clarified. Gloria looked relieved.

Radha flushed a little. 'Oh, yes, I guess I can. But this is going to be unnecessary rework.'

'That's the least we can do,' said Dharmesh, his face lighting up once again as he looked at Akshat in admiration. 'When our friends are going the distance for our sake!'

'Easy now,' Akshat twitched with embarrassment. 'It wasn't such a big deal either.'

I suggested we disperse for the night and let Dharmesh and Radha get down to business, because we would have to return the laptop to Eva early next morning, before Jerry recovered from the hangover of the previous night.

'How did you manage to reconfigure the codes all by yourself, though?' Dharmesh asked Radha, surprised, and then snobbishly added he alone would have taken no less than two days to get done with the reconfiguration.

'I didn't do it all by myself,' Radha smiled. 'Mehek and Akshat walked into office early this morning and offered to step in for you.'

Stunned silence engulfed the room. Akshat was turning out to be a hero. We were all in awe, but Akshat was nothing short of uncomfortable with Dharmesh's puppy-eyed gaze.

'So you do know shit about coding,' Dharmesh remarked with dramatic pauses. 'Eh, bro?'

That was it. Akshat couldn't take the soppiness any more. Dharmesh had just addressed him as his 'bro'. That was it.

'Good night, dyoods,' Akshat said to no one in particular, and walked off.

I called out after him to wait for me.

Hopefully this time, there would be no surprises in store. I had had it with surprises. I just wanted my boring, mediocre life back.

It was late in the night when I returned home, and I was tired as hell. But I most certainly couldn't sleep. Jerry's ghostlike face swam before my eyes through the night. I whiled away some more time on the internet to calm my nerves.

Oh no. I had almost forgotten such a thing had ever happened. Chirayu had sent me an email that looked like he had been howling his heart out while writing it. He said he was very emotionally disturbed and upset with the message I had left him on his voicemail 'after all that I have done for you'. I instantly sent him a note of apology, explaining this could quite possibly have happened when we were all drunk on Friday night and, as per my vague recall, Sameer had borrowed my phone to make an important call. And given how insanely insecure Sameer had always been of me, I strongly suspected he may have forged my voice and sent him that disgusting message. Just as I was about to send him my reply, I got this unpleasant feeling of guilt, I don't know why. And I added that although there was no doubt in my mind that Sameer lacked complete conscience and civility, it would be a good idea for Chirayu not to rake the issue with him and to forgive him this once in the larger interest of the team.

Fifteen minutes later, Chirayu sent me an ominous reply:

Fuck you, smart ass. I wasn't born yesterday. Try explaining this to the HR.

Following which, I sent him an unrelated email asking him if he could share with me the proxy links he had used to illegally download *The Dirty Picture* from the comfort of his office cabin.

At least for the time being, I didn't get any further response from him.

Suresh Shah sent me a Facebook challenge to beat his score of six hundred and twenty seven runs on Howzzat Cricket. I was just not in the mood. I was about to log off when he messaged me asking why I had been ignoring him. I remember I had begun to type a reply in the message box. But I probably dropped on the table mid-reply, and drifted into deep sleep.

I was woken early next morning. Radha called, saying the simulator codes had been successfully planted in the application hosted on Jerry's system, and his laptop had been returned to Akshat. I jumped out of my seat, punched my fist in the air a couple of times, and then threw myself on to my large, comfortable airbed. I didn't wake up even *once* more that entire day.

∽

The big day arrived. I walked in to the Oz-Mobil office, accompanied by Sameer, Mehek and Radha. We tiptoed into the office like convicts, holding out our deactivated access cards at the reception. Luckily, the receptionist that morning was Thai, and her facility with the language was rather weak. So when we told her we were once a part of Jerry's team and had been asked to leave, and only wanted to get in one last time because we had left our bags inside the working bay, she somehow got the impression we were there to deliver a bag to Jerry. Suited us fine.

She offered her most exuberant smile. 'Bag, ah? Give Jerry, ah? Two minute!'

She handed us a visitor card each and let us into the access bay. I thanked her and asked her where Jerry was conducting his meeting.

'Second or third floor, maybe first,' she scratched her head. 'No know, ah!'

We thanked her for her precise, helpful response and shot up the staircase; no one on the first two floors. We were wandering around the third floor when we heard Jerry's terrified scream sail through the closed door of a meeting room at the far end.

'That one,' we pointed to each other excitedly.

We swung the door open violently and stormed in, taking the audience by surprise. Vivian was seated at the centre of the table, his tie loosened and his hair dishevelled, his eyes droopy, like he had been through a tornado. Actually, in a way we guessed he had. Jerry's laptop was fixed to the projector, and all the projector showed was a swarm of ugly error pop-ups against the displayed application screen. Pat and Mike cowered in their seats at the opposite end of the table, like a pair of plump, petrified chickens. Jerry stared in horror at the error displays on the projector, completely at a loss of words, which was very unlike him. His face was pale with fear, and it grew a little paler on seeing us before him.

'What the hell are you guys doing here?' he stuttered.

'We are sorry for spoiling your party,' we said, taking our seats, uninvited. 'But from your faces we gather the party is spoilt already.'

Pat tried mocking us with a futile comment, but all that escaped his mouth was an inaudible squeak. We introduced ourselves to Vivian once again and proposed to unravel the mystery behind the apparently unexpected error codes appearing on Lex's design screen all so suddenly. We added we had issued warnings of such a mishap earlier, but they were not taken seriously. I shot a wicked glance at Jerry, who looked like he was going to consume me for lunch once the meeting ended. Vivian, who was already visibly tired and super pissed, shrugged disinterestedly and sank back in his seat.

Let me not mince my words. What happened over the next thirty minutes was nothing short of a revolution that was going to change Bytesphere's future forever. Or at least mine, in case you thought that was a little dramatic. I flipped a hard copy of the report we had earlier sent to Jerry, on the table before Vivian. I told him the problem, while craftily disguised by those two fat potatoes sitting opposite him, was actually so simplistic I could request my subordinate Radha to walk him through it instead of bothering myself with it. Also because I didn't personally know anything about simulator codes—but I didn't mention this to Vivian in the interest of the general impression of project managers at Bytesphere.

Radha chose to first spend some time engaging in useless histrionics like swivelling in her chair like the kingpin of some shady cartel and casting weird glances at Pat and Mike. When Vivian looked like this was going to be a long recess before she spoke, I nudged her to get done with her overacting and start talking.

'Hmm,' she stood up, cleared her throat, and began pacing up and down the length of the table. 'There are two versions to every story: one that is told, and the other that is the truth.'

Damn, this was going to take long. We all settled down in our seats.

'Except when it comes to Bytesphere, of course,' she added

hastily. 'Because our versions are always nothing but the truth.'

'The simulator codes, Radha,' Mehek whispered on noticing Vivian's face contort with utter confusion.

Radha ignored her and now ambled slowly towards Pat and Mike, who looked genuinely afraid of her as she gave them the look, dangling a whiteboard marker between her fingers.

'We knew something was wrong the moment Pat and Mike contradicted our well-documented report,' Radha said, closing in on her hapless victims. 'And that's when my colleague and I put in one sleepless night after another to unravel the truth.'

'Which is?' Vivian asked, frowning.

I hoped she would come to the point already. Jerry was leaning towards Vivian to ask us to shut up any moment.

And then, she delivered her bang.

'That these men are thieves!' She slammed a fist on the table right under the quivering faces of Pat and Mike. They were so frightened their heads nearly popped off their necks. 'Thieves! Frauds! My father was right when he said white men are not to be trusted!'

Vivian looked crestfallen at the remark. As if on cue, the colour on Jerry's face instantly turned crimson. I sprang out of my seat and pulled Radha back. Pat and Mike sat up straight; still shivering, but at least able to breathe.

'I am not done yet,' she screamed, trying to release herself from my grip. 'Who did you think you were fooling with those flimsy simulators? Did you think we wouldn't call your bluff? Also, who is going to reimburse me for all those extra hours put in behind this scandal?'

Sameer came to my rescue after some deliberation. We hoisted her off Pat and Mike and slumped her on to a chair. I gestured to Mehek to take over before we were tried by the company for racial slander.

Less than an hour later, we had made ourselves heard. Lex's simulators had been exposed. The application was unfit even for a dry run, leave alone being launched to the market any time soon. Pat and Mike had nearly melted into two blobs of white mass out of shame and embarrassment. Vivian turned to Jerry, seeking an explanation.

After stuttering helplessly for what seemed an eternity, Jerry finally stood up and started laughing like a madman. He congratulated us for a job well done and then told Vivian he always knew Lex was up to some mischief with their report that indicted us and that he had always trusted us to come out with the truth in good time. He reminded everyone it was no mere coincidence that he had handed the testing contract for the project to our team, because he knew a superstar team when he saw one. (Whatever the fuck that meant, it worked for us). He explained it had not escaped his sharp, unbeatable acumen that Lex had been possibly faking their results, but he decided to hold his observation till the day of the meeting so he could catch them red-handed before the management—with our help, he added almost as an afterthought.

He then turned to Pat and Mike and gave them a mouthful about using such low quality simulators after claiming to be the best in business when it came to designing systems. Somewhere around that stage, I had to reacquaint Jerry with the problem on hand—that the quality of the simulators didn't matter anyway, because using simulators in the first place was against the agreed protocol of the system's functioning.

'Even worse!' exclaimed Jerry, not sure what I meant.

He turned to Pat and Mike again. 'Do you know how many customers were being targeted by this lame application of yours?'

He paused as everyone hazarded a guess on the figure, and then shouted. 'MANY!'

Vivian, who had conveniently switched off from the discussion at the point Radha had tendered an unexpected outburst, woke up from his power nap and asked Jerry to give a damage assessment.

'Very severe,' came Jerry's arbitrary response even as he looked at me helplessly for more precise answers, preferably with percentages, tedious excel spreadsheets, and random bar graphs and pie charts.

I pointed towards Sameer and told Vivian I had just the right guy in my team who loved engaging in such seemingly intelligent but totally unnecessary analysis. Sameer jumped up in excitement at the mention of graphical analysis, and quite as expected, said he already had an analysis ready he would love to run everyone through. He already had a report titled *Retrospective Impact Assessment: A Bytesphere Perspective* that ran into some sixty odd pages. Because Jerry and Vivian had just been taken by a storm, they had no option but to sit through all sixty pages, although the report started to make some sort of sense only after the forty-eighth page. At the end of the walkthrough, the only element of the report that made sense to everyone present was that based on past performance trends that had shown in the project, it would take Lex no less than another forty days to undo their defects, followed by at least a fortnight of concerted effort by Bytesphere to retest the whole damn thing.

Much to our delight, Vivian announced that proposition was absolutely outrageous and that he was grateful to us for having brought to light this shoddy situation in good time.

'But we must take the product to market in no more than

three weeks,' he said morbidly.

'Which means we must finish repairing it in a week and a half,' added Jerry.

'At the most,' I concurred.

'Which means we have got no use of these guys,' snarled Radha, glaring at Pat and Mike once again.

Mike nervously suggested we get back to Sameer's nonsensical 'V R Unified' movement which had got us into this duel with Lex in the first place. Luckily, Sameer rejected the idea this time. Imagine a haughty consultant running down his own strategy as implausible! Adversity is the mother of common sense, or something like that, right? Jerry and Vivian requested a recess. I followed them to the washroom quietly and watched them engage in loud, meaningful whispers. When we reconvened, Vivian said he had vested all his faith in—hold your breath—not in Jerry, not in those Lex bastards—in ME!

Vivian had vested all his faith in me to take a call on what course we were best equipped to take thereon, and also on what fate those design buggers were in for. Tempted as I was to suggest they be tried for felony, I knew we would need Lex to help us correct the design of the system at such short notice, even if we were to take over from them on paper. So after thoroughly humiliating them by mentioning I had never witnessed a fraud of this accord in my long-spanning career, I voted Lex help us with a handover of all their design documents and a transparent, honest status of where their system really stood as of that day. Inspired by my thunderous speech, Sameer stood up too, demanding that Pat and Mike sit with him through the length of as many days and nights as it would take to effect an efficient handover.

'Bring your sleeping bags along if you must,' winked Sameer.

'But we are setting base here until you are done with your job.'

For once, his high-handedness did not upset me.

I then made an offer Vivian could not refuse. I suggested we could not only fix the system in a week but could also complete the remainder of the design that Lex had left unattended that far, well before Vivian's three-week deadline. I stopped in my tracks at this stage, wondering if I had spoken too much. But I noticed Radha nod vehemently in agreement, and so I substantiated the offer by putting forth an interesting condition.

'Anything you want, obviously,' Vivian conceded.

Until then, I had only intended to ask for a relaxation on the timeline for retesting the application. But I smartly sensed Vivian's desperation at that crucial minute, and upped the stakes by demanding a premium for retesting what we had already established in our previous report, as well as a ten per cent surcharge of our original fee for taking over the remainder of the design from Lex Technologies. I thought I saw Jerry cringe at the suggestion, but Vivian instantly acceded to the demand.

Seeing which, I went just a tad more cheeky by asking Vivian to sign a longer-term contract for at least another two years with Bytesphere, wherein all system integration and consulting opportunities would first go to Bytesphere for the first right of rejection. This time, Vivian looked like he was going to cringe, but all he could mutter was a meek affirmation.

I requested a dispersal of the meeting so my team could think on its feet and get all decided deliverables in motion. I called out after Jerry as I saw them leave.

'I will inform the Bytesphere management about our discussed conditions,' I said. 'We will send you a written memo. Please go over it carefully and send us your response by tonight.'

'Anything else?' Jerry asked, clearly not amused.

'Nothing really,' I said, turning to Pat and Mike. 'I need to speak to my friends for now.'

∽

Man, these guys had some capacity to whine! For the next week, Pat and Mike had been reduced to a pair of soppy twits who couldn't get enough of moaning over the workload imposed on them. They tried everything in the book and outside of it to keep us from continuing with this hostile takeover. One of those days, Pat also took me out to a nearby bistro, fed me the most delicious slice of cheesecake ever, and offered me a job opportunity with Lex's Melbourne office—work visa sponsorship included. I heard him patiently, but only until I was working on that awesome cheesecake. He continued his pitch after I was done, so I asked him to also buy me a nice hot latte with whipped cream while he was at it. And then, after the coffee was consumed I told him I didn't care two hoots about his proposal because I was committed to my team and more importantly, to my company. And that this proposal would not help change my mind about the takeover in any case.

I shouldn't have done that. A job in Melbourne, work visa sponsored by the company...oh, no.

Anyway, I could always consider obliging him by agreeing later, once we were done screwing their happiness during the handover.

Over the next week, Pat and Mike had lost whatever hair had collectively once existed on their heads. In fact, they were almost grateful once the handover had been completed. Mehek supervised, or rather excavated the revised application, pointed out another hundred flaws none of us had noticed in it earlier, and got Dharmesh and Radha to rebuild the faulty components in the wink of an eye. Sameer's sense of self-importance knew no bounds as he commanded major authority over our adversaries. He went through Lex's handover report and rejected it, just like that—pointing 'glaring inconsistencies' that came only to his notice. He recommended Pat and Mike not be released until Bytesphere had finished retesting the entire system and had ensured the product was good to be launched to the market. Once the system was rebuilt, Akshat and Mehek took a little under five days to retest the damn thing. No surprises there, but the defect percentage in the revised report showed under five per cent, which, Mehek informed Jerry, were but cosmetic defects with minimal impact.

Jerry was overwhelmed with emotion. He called me to his cabin, hugged me, gifted me a cricket bat and asked me if there was anything more I would like. I asked him to save the drama for someone else and first sign the conditions I had had Anand mail across to him. He said Oz-Mobil was happy to extend a consulting contract of another two years to Bytesphere, and that he would send a formal statement of proposal to Anand before I would set foot in India.

'Which reminds me,' he looked up again suddenly. 'When do you fly back?'

'Tomorrow night,' I replied without thinking. I had almost forgotten he had not gotten over that desire to speak with Marlon Pacino yet.

'Ah, because I received a mail from Marlon last evening,' he chuckled in delight. 'And he will try finding some time out for a call tomorrow, maybe in the second half of the day.'

I instantly turned into a headless chicken and told him I had almost forgotten I needed to get him to sign the closure report of the project for us. Once I had signed the report, even

Jerry's Daddy could not hold me back for any damn call with any damn Marlon Pacino without raising a formal request with an added quote. And Jerry was so stingy he wouldn't think of doing that. But the bungling bastard told me he had got an incorrectly formatted closure document prepared by his secretary, and that the revised document would be ready only the next day. So he offered to take me out for a leisurely buffet the next afternoon, by which time the revised closure document would be good and ready. And then I could also comfortably attend that call with Marlon Pacino later in the day. I told him I was likely to get an upset stomach the next day as was usually the case with me ahead of a long flight, and so the buffet option could be ruled out. Moreover, I said, I would very much like the closure document signed well in the first half of the day, because I had errands to run before heading to the airport. Just to make sure he had got the message loud and clear, I also let him know I would not make myself available for any additional calls once I had signed the closure report, and so Marlon had better adjust his schedule accordingly.

'I will try requesting him to make time in the first half,' he promised me.

My, some people just won't give up.

I left his cabin to head home, when I saw Pat and Mike staggering around in the lobby unhappily. They looked like a pair of dried twigs, poor fellows. I went up to them and said there was nothing personal in whatever had happened between us. I mean, of course it was personal, but it felt nice to part on a positive note, no? I took them to the same bistro and asked them to let themselves loose without bothering about the bill. The poor chaps were so hungry they ordered everything that lay on the display shelves and wolfed it all down in a matter of minutes. I then bought them a slice of cheesecake each. When I thought they looked a little composed after getting some food inside them, I asked Pat if he was serious about his company offering me a job with a sponsored work visa—not that I had made up my mind, I added, but I could give his request a serious thought if the offer was good enough. Pat looked at me as though I had snatched the last morsel of his cheesecake. He looked at his partner and indicated they must leave.

What the fuck! The least they could have done was to thank me for the lunch, yes?

# 18.

# Curry Boys

I reached office early the final day, and went straight in search of Maisie, Jerry's red-headed secretary. She arrived almost an hour later, excitedly waving the closure document at me. She had magically managed to get everyone in the top line of the Oz-Mobil management to sign the report the previous night.

'Only Jerry's signature remains,' she smiled triumphantly. 'And yours, of course.'

She pointed at my name printed on the report: my surname was spelt Cooper. I laughed and told her that wasn't how my surname was spelt. Goddamit. I shouldn't have said that.

She snatched the closure report from my hands, apologizing profusely for the unpardonable mistake. I told her to calm down, for it wasn't such a big deal. But the stubborn lady insisted on changing my name, taking a fresh printout and getting everyone to sign it all over again. I told her *that* was likely to offend me more than seeing my surname spelt incorrectly. But she wouldn't listen. She trashed the document and went about working on changing two bloody alphabets in my surname.

Meanwhile, Jerry came from nowhere and backslapped me in excitement, saying Marlon had promised to try calling in as early in the day as possible. Helpless and at a loss for a better idea, I clenched painfully at my hair and began screaming like a psycho. Jerry and Maisie rushed to my rescue, startled and confused. I explained I suffered from this rare version of migraine that occurred every once in a while I would be held up somewhere against my wish and if decided schedules were not met. Maisie stood stoned, trying to make sense of my syndrome, when I looked her in the eye and told her I meant to ask her to hurry up with that damned document. Jerry took me to his cabin, claiming to be in possession of a very potent herb that could cure the most gigantic headaches.

I sat before him in his cabin, watching him pour me a hot cup of water. Then he took out a brown ball-like object and threw it into the cup.

'Watch!' He said proudly, pointing at the cup.

The brown ball had begun to unfurl into a weirdly shaped flower inside the cup. Some sort of a joke, I thought. He said it was a Japanese herb that was the secret of his youthful countenance. I glanced at him disinterestedly and complimented him for his fitness, saying he did not, indeed, look a day older than forty-five, which was rather unbelievable. He suddenly stopped smiling and told me he was forty-one. I kept quiet for a good part of the remaining hour and focused on my Japanese tea, which frankly, tasted like pee. But what upset me more than the tea was Jerry's cabin phone placed between us, and Jerry's expectant gaze at it. If Marlon Pacino would make it to the call before I got the hell out of there, I had a good chance of receiving my termination letter from Bytesphere when I got back. I picked up the phone and dialled Maisie, telling her my head was about to explode like a meteor any time if she didn't get us the document.

'Very soon,' she said, yet again.

Very soon was fifty minutes, in which time Jerry had

made small talk on subjects ranging from a doctored pitch that caused an infamous Australian defeat at the recent Ashes to his latest exploits at an Ethiopian vacation. All that held my attention, though, was that phone placed between us. Each time it would ring, a part of me would die of fright. When Maisie finally arrived with the closure document, Jerry asked me if I would be willing to consider holding on until Marlon Pacino called. I started pulling at my hair wildly, and screamed so loudly I thought my lungs would jump out and fall in the Japanese tea. Jerry nervously reached for a pen and signed the document before passing it to me. I hastily signed under my name, which was now spelt Nacool Kapoor—of course, this time I kept my mouth shut.

'Here you are,' I handed the document to Maisie, and prepared to leave, when Jerry held my hand and started speaking very slowly and leisurely about what a pleasure it was to have met me. I told him the feeling was mutual but my head was pounding so hard I could hardly hear my own words.

'I hope to see you again,' he said, smiling. 'In a new assignment, maybe?'

That was the last thing I could hope for, but I nodded firmly and smiled back at him. As I walked towards the door, the blasted phone rang. I bolted out of his cabin and down the stairs, never to look back.

ഗ

Akshat and I had an appointment at Transport one last time before we bade the place goodbye.

'Keep it late, though,' he had said, explaining he had to bid Eva goodbye properly first.

Their goodbyes also occurred in installments. Sigh.

We met at the bar around seven in the evening. With at least three hours to spare and a lot of unexpected bills doled out by Jerry for the good work done, gallons of alcohol were in order. We called for our favourites and were recapitulating the months gone by, when Sameer walked into the bar, with a much fitter yet bruised Dharmesh—their heavy suitcases in tow. They walked up to our table and asked us if they could join us.

'Of course,' Akshat pulled two chairs for them without consulting me.

I spent a painful hour sitting next to Sameer even as the beer orders refused to cease.

'Drinking to success!' we repeated in chorus each time our pitchers arrived.

Sameer congratulated the team for this unexpected turnaround, and me in particular, for guiding everyone through troubled waters. Yes, yes, he was bound to say all this now, right? Now that I would be providing inputs for his appraisal back home? Anyway, I wanted to be nice and so I returned the compliment by saying we would have got nowhere were it not for his detailed analysis on the Lex issue and his path-breaking, far-from-trite 'V R Unified' strategy. He shrugged as though I had just said a plain matter of fact, before we launched into unrelated discussions on Australian tourism that we could never experience.

Gloria walked in soon after, carrying a present for—guess whom! Dharmesh blushed a deep crimson, and quietly shifted inward to make room for her. We all stopped drinking and started staring at them, much to Dharmesh's annoyance.

'Just wanted to say bye,' Gloria whispered shyly, planting a kiss on Dharmesh's ruddy red cheeks. 'You have my number.'

Tears of joy settled on the insides of Dharmesh's soda

glasses, forming a thick layer of vapour on them. He was in the middle of a tear-jerking speech on how he had learnt to live again thanks to Gloria, when Akshat stood up suddenly.

'How much time have we got?' he asked.

Sameer looked at his watch. 'Half an hour, at the most. Why?'

'I have a parcel to deliver too,' he said with urgency. 'Nakul, can you come along?'

'Where to?'

'I will let you know on the way,' he said, turning to Sameer. 'Dyood, do you mind carrying our suitcases along too? We will see you directly at the airport.'

'Are you sure?' Sameer glanced at his watch hesitantly once again.

'Dead sure,' he said, walking out with me trailing him, God knows why.

A cab pulled over right outside the bar.

'Preston, please,' Akshat said hurriedly as we plunged inside the cab.

'That doesn't sound like Eva's address,' I said, confused, as the cab zipped over an empty road.

'It is not,' Akshat said, biting his lips anxiously. 'You will know soon. Just hold your nerves, that's it.'

'Just anything is fine as long as it doesn't stop me from returning home,' I said.

'Let's hope for the best.'

The cab pulled over shortly at the said address.

'Whose place is this?' I asked, stepping out after Akshat.

'Gloria's,' he replied absently, examining the length and breadth of the empty street.

It was nearing nine in the evening, and it was decidedly

dark and chilly. He spotted a standalone row house in the street opposite Gloria's.

'Follow me,' he said.

That was when I realized what he was up to. I stopped in my tracks, suggesting this wasn't close to being a good idea. But he insisted, saying it was against his principles to step back from a well calculated decision.

'I seriously hope it is well calculated,' I said, my voice trembling.

We reached a wicker gate that guarded the row house. Akshat rapped on it very loudly. A burly tattooed man opened the door of the house and stepped towards the wicker gate.

'Whatcha want?' he asked us gruffly.

'Glenn?' Akshat asked, his fists curling into little balls.

'Mitch,' he replied, just as gruffly. 'Whatcha want?'

'I need Glenn,' he repeated. 'I have a parcel to give him.'

'Give it to me,' he stretched his hand. 'I am his roommate.'

'Excellent!' Akshat smiled. 'In that case, I need you here too. But I must have Glenn.'

Mitch examined us suspiciously and then called out to his roommate. 'Yo Glenn, over here! Some curry boys have a parcel for you or somethin'!'

Another man of nearly the same size as Mitch, but with a pointed beard, stepped out. He came forward, reeking of cocaine or such. Mitch opened the wicker gate and let us in.

'Where's the parcel?' Glenn looked at us.

'Right here, asshole!' shouted Akshat, landing the loudest slap ever on Glenn's stone-shocked face.

'Bastards!' screamed Glenn, as Mitch reached for Akshat's throat and pushed him against the wicker gate. 'Try getting outta here alive, you little fucks!'

Struggling for breath, Akshat kicked his boot into the wicker gate, breaking a nice wooden slab off it. He jerked Mitch away, picked up the wooden slab and slammed it right on Mitch's arched back, creating a blunt sound that reverberated in the winter air. By the time I had fully comprehended what was going on, Glenn had recovered from that giant of a slap, had picked up an empty bottle of liquor lying near the trash can, and was charging towards Akshat. I intercepted Glenn, tugged hard at his jacket and wrapped its free ends over his head, and knocked my kneecap in his gut. He fell to the floor, doubling in pain.

'Touch my friend again, will you?' Akshat shouted over and over again, punching Mitch and Glenn alternately in whatever body parts he could lay his hands on.

We continued socking them in their faces, looking around occasionally to ensure we didn't have an audience, until we were convinced they wouldn't come after us soon enough.

'Time to go,' I muttered to Akshat, amidst their painful moans.

We pushed open whatever was left of the wicker gate. I went back to them one last time, and landed another slap on Mitch's face this time.

'And this one was for calling us curry boys!'

We ran out on the street, shouting with joy—or nervousness, maybe. And we didn't stop until we spotted a free cab on the main road that agreed to ferry us to the airport. We didn't stop looking behind us to check for adverse movements, until we got off at the airport and tendered the said cash to the driver. The examining officer at the airport entrance considered our sweat-smeared faces with curiosity and asked us if we had just walked through an inferno.

'Something of the sort!' we waved at him as we made through the door, into the airport, and finally heaved a sigh of relief.

Sameer and Dharmesh came running to us at the check-in counter, as Mehek and Radha looked on from a distance.

'What had kept you guys?' Dharmesh asked.

'Akshat had an important parcel to deliver,' I laughed, struggling to get my breath back.

# 19.

# Happiness Index

Phew! All was well with my life finally.

Well, almost all, if you discount the fact that Mehek still wouldn't speak to me.

For one, Anand called on me in person the day I rejoined the Bombay office. He joined me in Chirayu's cabin to congratulate me on what was thought to be an impossible feat. This was a first. He still did not remember my name, but he said he remembered me by my face (presumably a compliment) and admitted he had not expected I would bring the team back with such a high score on the client happiness index (yes, there was such a term in our company). Anand asked me if I would like him to help me in any way in return for a fantastically redeveloped relationship with Oz-Mobil. I first said I was not so sure, because I had recently got some exciting job offers that were luring me to leave Bytesphere. Not really so, but I always knew the right pressure-building tactics. Anand ruefully looked at Chirayu, said that would be a total pity, and then without any sign of persuasion he directly asked me what my last working day was.

Shit.

I told him I wasn't sure yet and was still inclined towards retaining this job if certain basic demands were met.

'What basic demands?' he asked, pushing his pince-nez up his nose.

'I'd like some stock options, a company-leased apartment and a nice, high-end sedan,' I would have loved to say, but I chose not to get too cheeky. I said I would be more than happy if I'd just be considered for an already overdue promotion and a hike, and if possible, if I could start being treated a little more respectfully in the organization. He angrily looked at Chirayu and demanded to know who had kept me from these basic privileges all along. Chirayu stammered about some peer dynamics nonsense that had held my promotion the previous year, responding to which Anand warned him of some serious peer dynamics headed his way if I didn't get promoted this year. Chirayu nodded fervently and said that was exactly what had been playing on his mind too for very long. Once Anand had left, Chirayu turned to me and said he'd set my profile up for consideration of a promotion right away. He took me out to lunch, where he said he was willing to forget everything about that scandalous voicemail I had sent him. And then, he subtly mentioned he never really ended up watching *The Dirty Picture*.

The quarterly awards for outstanding performances in the company were announced later that week. I generously ignored my own contribution in terms of leading from the front, and nominated Dharmesh and Radha. They thanked each other in their speeches of gratitude without acknowledging me. I will take up the matter with them in the near future during some one-on-one mentorship discussion. Or maybe I won't, I don't know.

Akshat had finally ended up staying at the Hilton so long the hotel staff had begun to suspect his intentions. He finally rented an airy apartment on the sea face (where does his father get all this money from?), but not before collecting a million award points from the hotel he did not offer to share with me on prospective exotic bachelor vacations. But he did invite me to play pool at his apartment every Friday evening. I seldom turned down his offer.

But in the dark nights spent at Chamunda Co-operative Housing Society, I felt compelled to cry. I missed talking to Mehek. I also missed Melbourne's lovely warm French toasts and pies each time I agreed to join Suresh Shah for biting my fangs into the chapattis cooked by him.

He was very happy though, not least because I was back to share my lonesome evenings with him. But he was also ecstatic because Nandy had finally organized a trip back home, and this time it looked nearly certain. Very well, I told him—it was endearing to know people around me were getting happier while I struggled to find happiness through that one person who didn't care. He probed me for details, but I evaded the subject, lest he should start doling out free advice on sensible courtship.

He talked for hours at end about his newly operative accounts on Pinterest and Google Plus and the amazing people he had connected with therein.

'Happiness lies in networking,' he grinned even as his teeth ground into the dough of another chapatti, sounding like someone had run a sawing machine over an iron bar.

I told him I had lost all interest in networking and would much rather be on my own, to which he replied that I probably needed therapy. He forced me into his room and threw a stack of gaming discs at me.

'Gaming is the shit, dude!' he declared, promising me there was nothing better that could keep an asocial, lonesome loser happy.

I examined the exhaustive collection in awe. He confessed the internet had helped him a great deal in getting the best deals on the best games, and added there were numerous other ways to divert one's attention through the internet, such as answering vocabulary tests to donate rice in charity, photoshopping random pictures on 9gag, and so on.

It wasn't until hours later that it occurred to him to provide me with a very crucial piece of information: that a young lady had come knocking at my door the previous night only to find I wasn't home.

'Young, thin built, pretty but appeared a little disturbed,' he offered a slow build-up. 'I met her in the stairway and told her you had been drinking a lot lately and were not likely to return until late, dropping at your door like a drunk skunk.'

He said Mehek had seemed desperate to have a word with me. And in order that he could fish for interesting details of what had transpired between us, he had posed as my uncle and had asked her to confide in him. He reprimanded me for kissing her without her permission, but more for not being man enough to keep myself from being thrown into a river by her. He further said she was upset with me because after such an abominable act, I only worsened things by ignoring her and giving her the cold shoulder for the rest of our stay in Australia.

WHAT THE FUCK! Seriously! WHAT THE FUCK!

'She said she had had enough of your tantrums,' he said. 'She asked me to let you know she was giving you one last chance to mend your ways and start behaving normally once again.'

'One last chance?'

'Oh no,' he gulped. 'What time is it?'

'Nine forty-five,' I said, glancing at my watch, and then watched his face turn white. 'What?'

'She had also asked me to let you know she was leaving town at eleven thirty tonight,' he said shamefacedly. 'And if you didn't get your act together until then...'

'Leaving town?' I asked, springing out of my chair.

'Not that dramatic,' he waved his hand dismissively. 'Only for a week. She is going to Baroda or someplace, wherever her parents are.'

I heaved a sigh of relief.

'As far as you are concerned, though, it could well be forever,' he added later. 'She said if you didn't get your act together until she left town, you would be losing a friend forever.'

'That was very prompt, thanks!' I snarled at him, forking my phone out with trembling hands.

I dialled her number once. Twice, then thrice. Unreachable.

'Dude, she is pissed!' he rolled his eyes, folding his hands behind his head. I couldn't imagine how he could feel so comfortable and composed. My love life was meeting an untimely end, thanks to him! Couldn't he have parted with this sensitive information a little earlier instead of telling me how many cows he had found on Farmville that week????

'I could still make it to the airport if I drove like a maniac,' I considered my options.

'Which you always do, I know,' he said, getting up. 'Come, I will come along.'

'That won't be necessary,' I said, trying to hurry down.

But he would not relent, and he forced himself into the adjacent seat of the car. En route, he told me this was all singularly my fault that I allowed the situation to go so out of hand in the first place. I turned up the volume to keep myself from losing whatever was left of my cool. When we arrived at the airport and ran up to the enquiry counter, we were told the last flight to Baroda had left at ten in the night.

'Are you sure you heard the time right?' I turned to Suresh Shah angrily.

His face turned white again. He stuck his tongue out and smiled sheepishly.

'Are you?' I repeated.

'Of...of course I am,' he replied with a stutter. 'Bad luck, boy. We must go home.'

I felt the world had come crashing down on me. Yeah, I was still curious to know how I wound up being the bad guy in that entire dunking episode and everything thereafter. But I guess that question did not have an answer. What mattered was that it was all over and I could well go back to my days of plugging sad Linkin' Park songs at home and fantasizing about random sultry blondes on certain unmentionable websites. Not a good life at all.

We didn't talk for most of the journey back home, except when Suresh Shah picked up my phone and started meddling with it like a hyper school child.

'Just checking out your games,' he said, avoiding my gaze.

The guard at the entrance to our building told me I had a visitor waiting for me on the stairway and would not return until I permitted an audience.

So it was a mere threat after all! My heart leapt with joy. Suresh Shah looked confused, probably about to comment on the impossibility of such a situation after he had so thoroughly ensured my girl walked out on me. But, well, fortune favours the earnest, or something like that, no?

I got out of my car and ran up the staircase. Only to find Sameer at my doorstep, seated on the stairs, his face cupped in his palms.

Anti-climax max! What was this fucker doing at my house in the middle of the night? Some guys just didn't have a sense of socially appropriate times of visiting people. Maybe he was here to tell me I had been a complete asshole and that he had taken advantage of the situation sooner than possible and had popped the big question before Mehek. I promptly replaced his face with that of Glenn in my head, curled my fists and advanced towards him, when he held out a beautifully wrapped bottle of wine.

'This is for you,' he handed it to me.

I read the label. I hadn't heard of this brand before. Surely something exotic and status-defining, I presumed. But it looked awesome.

So, obviously, I had to let him in. I couldn't grab that lovely looking bottle and then ask him to fuck off, right? Tired as I was, I let him in, and even offered a seat, much in spite of myself.

'Nice house,' he looked around at the cramped one bedroom apartment appreciatively.

Basically, the twerp was only trying to show me down. I played along and told him I could have shown him around but that would have taken an entire day.

'You are funny!' he laughed, and then stopped to wonder if I was considering offering him a drink.

Reluctantly, I trudged towards the kitchen and fetched us two glasses. As I poured us a drink each, he began clearing the air between us. He said he had learnt over time why I was always so irritable while dealing with him. He said he had first believed it was his sudden takeover as an ad hoc project manager that had got my goat, because he had had to take some very tough decisions without my consent while I was away. And while I may have seen that as his high-handedness, he only did what he had thought was in everyone's interest, and that being extra smart and proactive only came to him too naturally.

'It is all over now,' I skirted the discussion and picked up a newspaper and began reading it. I had realized the paper was two days old, but it helped convey the message I wasn't interested in entertaining him too long.

That is when he added, 'It was much later I learnt the real reason for our differences was something else...or should I say, someone else?'

I threw the paper nervously on the floor and rather impolitely asked him if he was done twirling that wine in his glass, because my eyes would turn inside their sockets if I stayed up another minute. Far from getting the point, he reclined in my favourite armchair, the rat—and asked me if Mehek had anything to do with the way I had behaved with him all along. He looked me in the eye with so much conviction and intensity that I got nervous and blurted out everything about what had happened at the Yarra, and that it was very unbecoming of them to have bitched about me behind my back and discussed that sordid episode. After hearing my entire outburst, he gave me that 'I know everything because I topped the GMAT in my neighbourhood' look and smiled. He said he had known nothing about my exploits at the Yarra until I had divulged specific details. All he knew was what Mehek had told him one day—when he had compassionately and pretentiously held her in his arms and asked her what the matter was—that something had gone wrong between us because of a matter that just didn't get sorted in time.

Cryptic. Yet revealing. I was most displeased with her.

'But I made some careful deductions,' he started speaking like Hercule Poirot once he was two drinks down. 'And I wondered, maybe, just maybe, you thought I had my eyes on her just as you did?'

'How cheap,' I muttered distastefully. 'But yes, to some extent...'

He laughed. 'You went on a tangent, Nakul. Mehek is not my type.'

Ok, then. For the first time, his arrogance didn't upset me. In fact, I nodded in agreement, poured him another drink, and asked him to tell me more. He said he only shared a 'delightful rapport' with her thanks to their family connections, and that was all there was to it. Momentarily, Supercop Gupta's ominous face floated before my eyes in a dark bubble. But I burst the bubble with an imaginary needle and then smiled a little.

I shook hands with him and thanked him for letting me know what he should probably have told me long ago.

'Congratulations on your promotion,' he said, turning around.

'It is yet to be announced,' I said. 'At any rate, I am surprised I am being considered after that close shave with Lex.'

'And with Marlon too?' he chuckled.

How I wished I could forget such a person existed! And... wait. What was he laughing about? The last thing I wanted to know was he knew about the scam I had created with that name.

My worst fears turned out to be true. It so happened that while Sameer was the acting project manager in our first week at Melbourne, Jerry had told him about that senseless report I had sent him, because Oz-Mobil wanted to apparently use my findings to come up with a statement of purpose on a new venture in the Bali market, which would ultimately be presented to their board of directors. Not surprisingly at all, Sameer volunteered to help Jerry provide his assistance in preparing this statement of purpose, an idea that Jerry lapped up delightfully, especially because it wouldn't come at any cost to the company. During the week of that conversation, Jerry had chanted Marlon Pacino's name several times over, insisting that man knew shitloads about the market that could help their study a great deal. After which Sameer made a grand gesture by offering to search Marlon's contacts on the Bytesphere portal and get in touch with him for a 'holistic perspective', it seemed. It was only after he spoke to this Marlon Pacino did he realize he wasn't the person I had quoted in my report.

'Because this Marlon Pacino is only a data administrator,' he said with a throaty laugh. 'Weeks later, Mehek told me the truth about *your* Marlon Pacino. I must say, that was cheeky. You had a close shave, thanks to my timely intervention.'

He explained that the real Marlon Pacino was all gung-ho about this Australian assignment. He told Sameer he wasn't in the least concerned about the fact that he knew nothing about the subject as long as he could get the hell out of that morbid office in Bali and live a better life in Australia—for which he was even willing to learn rocket science. He wrote to Sameer, marking Jerry, that he would only be too glad to accept the offer—provided he had the approval of his management to do so. When Sameer sensed this could spell trouble, he spoke to Marlon offline and explained that the offer stood cancelled because, true to its reputation, Oz-Mobil had decided to scrap yet another assignment. Once Marlon was taken care of, Sameer wrote to Jerry from a promptly created private id that went by Marlon's initials, and requested for only offline communications thenceforth.

'Why did you need to do that in the first place?' I asked. 'The chapter could have ended there itself and we could all have breathed easy.'

'Marlon had already written to Jerry expressing his interest,' he replied. 'You know Jerry, don't you? He would have shaken up the entire management at the Bali office to get Marlon on board had I not written to him as, well, Marlon. And then, you can imagine the repercussions. All I needed to do was continue exchanging emails with Jerry and buy some time before we left that place for good.'

'So you did save me, eh?' I noted with mild displeasure. I would have to thank him now. Not a favourable situation, that.

'You are welcome,' he smiled, saving me the trouble of thanking him. 'For my part, I didn't disappoint Jerry. I wrote to him once we returned to Bombay. I sent him a dozen pages of analysis covering almost everything he could have expected from Marlon Pacino. And then I mentioned a note of regret at the end for being unable to spare time on the phone, citing management protocol and such.'

I was very tempted to ask him what happened to the three pillars of values he had been brought up on, foxing his client like that! Yes, yes, I didn't have a right to question him, maybe. But then, he wasn't perfect either, right? All this drama of being the perfect Raymond man and all…ok, fine, he helped me, I shouldn't be saying that. I told him I could have treated him a lot better had he just made me aware of his kind gesture back then.

'Mehek asked me not to let you know,' he smiled. 'She said you wouldn't fancy using my help in getting out of the mess.'

'How would she know that?'

He placed his empty glass on the table between us, wiped his mouth with a meticulously ironed handkerchief, and laughed. 'I guess she knows you a lot better than you think she does!'

Maybe there was hope! She still did care after all.

'Did she speak to you before leaving for Baroda?' I asked him.

'Not to me, she didn't,' he shook his head as he stood up to leave.

He was not such a bad guy after all. I take back all the nasty things I said about him earlier. Actually, almost all the nasty things. I think he still had that snooty ISB hangover. Only, it did not matter to me anymore. I thanked him and suggested he visit me again, maybe at a more earthly hour, so we could sit longer and get to know each other better.

'I always wanted to chat with an ISB guy,' I said, I don't know why. 'You guys are something.'

He proceeded to tell me stories about how he often had to grapple with six case studies to be presented in a span of as little as two days, when I started yawning like a python and didn't stop until he got the hint and left.

I kept dialling Mehek's number for the rest of the night. When I finally got through the number, she didn't answer the call.

She arrived at my doorstep two mornings later, waking me early with the doorbell. A trolley bag stood behind her.

'You were to be gone for a week,' I said, somewhat awkwardly, letting her in.

'Should I go back?' she asked, turning around.

'Just that I wasn't expecting you here,' I said, turning my face away.

Shit, these tear glands never worked when you needed them to. There was no glycerine at my disposal either.

'I was to be gone a week,' she explained, 'but Suresh Uncle made me feel so miserable and guilty I just had to come back.'

'He called you?' I asked, surprised.

So that's what he was fiddling with my phone for. Sweet guy, on the whole, you know.

'Yes, he did,' she said, taking a seat. 'And he told me how

you stayed an entire night at the railway station waiting for me, hours after I left. I couldn't stop feeling miserable.'

'Railway station?' my voice rose in disbelief. From what I last remembered, we had gone to the airport looking for her.

I didn't know what Suresh Shah had told her. But at least he could have kept me on the same page for the sake of consistency! Later in time, while demanding credit for bringing her back in my life, he explained it had completely slipped his mind in that rush to drive to the airport that she had, in fact, told him she would be boarding the Gujarat Express train from Mumbai Central. He couldn't bear to see me mope over her, so he called her the next morning and gave her a homily on how our generation could let go of their loved ones that easily.

There were other things he told her that he didn't need to. He didn't tell me about them, but she did, the same day.

Like how I had threatened to lay myself on the tracks if the railway authorities did not keep the train from pulling out of the city limits. Or how I had cried on his shoulder through the next day, bawling over unrequited love.

'You didn't think I would give up on you just like that, did you?' she said, placing her hand in mine.

This time, I didn't fall for the bait. Holding hands was not a green signal to pounce on a girl, apparently. I maintained a glum face and allowed her to sweet-talk me a little more before telling her I was willing to accept her apology. She let go of my hand suddenly and clarified that she was far from apologizing and if anything, she was letting *me* off for taking advantage of how nice she had always been to me. By this time I was a little tired of understanding this girl, frankly. Moreover, it did not matter who was forgiving whom as long as we could see happier times at the horizon. I told her to forget the episode at the river if she could; it would be difficult for me to, but I didn't think it would be a big deal for her anyway.

'I had forgotten about it long ago,' she said. 'It was you who kept sulking until weeks after.'

'Oh, I see,' I nodded. 'You know what? Let's just not discuss it at all, right? We have too much to look ahead to for us to mope over the past.'

'We absolutely do,' she said, and then paused. 'Like what?'

'Like, happier times together,' I smiled, trying that same artistic, passionate, sugar-coated tone Sameer used to perfection all the time.

'How do you mean that?' she asked, frowning suspiciously.

'How am I supposed to mean that?' I scratched my head. 'Listen, lady. Make up your mind. If you hold my hand like you do, I am going to speak like I do.'

She stood up suddenly, threatening to leave. 'There you go again. You never stop trying, do you? Can we not try being normal with each other, without pushing each other too much? And just take things as they come?'

I pinned her back to her chair and demanded a rational, sane explanation to this state of being annoyingly undecided—this zone between compulsively thinking about me all the time and shying away from admitting the burning desire she felt for me.

She heard me out until my throat ran dry, and all she had to say in response was, 'I am not ready yet.'

At least she could have kept an innovative answer ready that would have got me to sit up and take notice. I asked her what was holding her up; after all it wasn't like there was a swarm of men in her pursuit. Her expression suggested something about that last line was not right, so I instantly went back to telling her how deeply I loved her despite being made to wait around like that for three years.

She smiled, and then considered her watch. 'It's time to leave.'

Getting up, she added, 'I will give it a thought, Nakul. I really will.'

She stepped forward and hugged me.

Hmm, I must be honest. These moments of uncertainty are sometimes more exciting than the end result of the pursuit. After all, what would I have to look forward to once I had conquered her love? I mean, of course I would still love her as much, but that thrill does fizzle out later, no? I mean...not really, but...you know what I mean, don't you?

'I will wait,' I looked at her and smiled again.

'Alright,' she said. 'Just don't hound me with the same question.'

'I will try,' I replied, and then casually asked her if she had a ballpark estimate in mind of how much time she expected me to wait. I wasn't growing any younger.

'You have something bigger to worry about than that,' she winked as she picked up her bag to leave.

'Which is?'

'If and when I do consider your proposal,' she said with a wink, 'you will first need to get the idea past my father.'

She just HAD to take that man's name. How he still gave me the creeps!

'I don't see why that should be trouble,' I lied. 'We must organize a lunch sometime again.'

'Is that so?' she laughed.

'Of course,' I asserted. 'A man's got to do what a man's got to do. Bring on the policeman if you must.'

She laughed again as she reached for the door. 'I can hardly wait!'

# Acknowledgements

Firstly, immense love and gratitude to my parents—thank you for everything but especially for always asking, 'What's happening with your book?' You pull me up every time I slacken.

Much love to my wife, Kamini, who always laughed when I read out my manuscript to her—I promise to do the dishes for a year as a token of reciprocation. Also, you are always right.

Thank you, my wonderful sisters and your lovely families for all the love and positivity. All is forgiven for giving me a hard time in school by setting high benchmarks of excellence.

I also thank my in-laws, for being great friends and for being very understanding (did you know I am always expected to do ALL the dishes?).

Heartfelt gratitude to every colleague at Infosys—please do not take the jokes in this book seriously. They are all a figment of my imagination (appraisers please note).

Dear Gloria Jean's, Juhu, thank you for a perfect ambience, the delicious lattés and that perfect corner seat by the window.

And above all, a big shout out to everyone at Rupa—thank you Kapish, Kausalya, Ritu, Amrita, Kadambari, Maithili and the entire team—for your continued faith and guidance. I am grateful to be a part of this family!